THE MAN WITH THE IVORY EAR

THE MAN WITH THE IVORY EAR

D. S. MCDONOUGH

Matador
9 Priory Business Park,
Wistow Road, Kibworth Beauchamp,
Leicestershire. LE8 0RX
Tel: 0116 279 2299
Email: books@troubador.co.uk
Web: www.troubador.co.uk/matador
Twitter: @matadorbooks

ISBN 978 1789015 614

British Library Cataloguing in Publication Data.
A catalogue record for this book is available from the British Library.

Printed and bound in Great Britain by 4edge Limited
Typeset in 11pt Adobe Garamond Pro by Troubador Publishing Ltd, Leicester, UK

Matador is an imprint of Troubador Publishing Ltd

For those who died young.

PART ONE

CLEAR TO LIFT

His first sensation, as he begins again to be, is of intense heat. He wants to cry out but he has no mouth. He has been cast into darkness where he has no eyes. His limbs are soft and boneless, and the heat sears his soul. He is bound fast in blackness, and his re-becoming is one of searing pain…

The rain fell more heavily now, drumming on the roof of the car, and as Woodhouse gazed through the twin arcs of the labouring wipers at the queue of traffic ahead, a series of unwelcome images from the past intruded one by one on his mind's eye, like the items on the conveyor belt in *The Generation Game* but with infinitely more traumatic associations: a Swiss Army knife; a pack of Top Trumps; a used prophylactic in which a knot has been tied; a pogo stick; a marble bust of Lord Byron; an old hardback copy of *The Wind in the Willows*; a single black plimsoll; an Art Deco biscuit barrel; a grinning Mr Punch; a child's hockey stick…

'Ice duck,' prompted Bruce Forsyth malevolently. 'Un-cuddly toy.'

Woodhouse shuddered: the images were troubling enough in themselves, he felt, without the contributions of this spiteful inner-Brucie. The lights had changed, and he propelled the old Jaguar forward, shaking his head in an effort to dislodge the troublesome memories. He had another headache, he realised glumly. Worryingly, they had been troubling him a lot lately. He had been having problems concentrating at work and Greaves had threatened him with gardening leave. Gardening leave! He didn't even *have* a fucking garden… Woodhouse had to admit he could see the old boy's point though: in his rather specialised line of work a lapse in concentration could lead directly to a hospital bed or, worse, a mortuary drawer. And others were placed at risk too, of course.

He glanced in the rear-view mirror and frowned. The Citroën that had been following him ever since he left the flat was still there, three cars behind at present, its nondescript male driver impassive to a fault. Accelerating around a white Transit van – on the grimy back doors of which some humourist had sullied his finger (and his marriage vows) by writing: *I wish my wife was as dirty as this* – Woodhouse felt a welcome surge of adrenaline. No *way* was the Citroën coincidental: he had been leading it around rainy northwest London for the past twenty minutes, lengthening the odds of an innocent explanation for its presence with every unnecessary turn on an increasingly tortuous route, and now he was sure. Woodhouse grinned. He had found himself a playmate.

The late morning traffic had thinned out now and Woodhouse was able to throw caution to the wind and accelerate hard down Garden Road, the Citroën emerging smoothly from behind a scaffolders' flat-bed truck to keep pace. Approaching the junction, Woodhouse took his hand from the wheel to reach inside his jacket and thumb the safety off the Walther in its shoulder holster, comforted as always by the businesslike contours of the pistol's grip. He indicated right, slowing and positioning himself as if to make the turn on to Grove End Road, checking for the Citroën in the mirror, then speeding up again, turning sharply left instead, narrowly missing a cagoule-sporting cyclist, and powering past the Edward Onslow Ford memorial and on to Abbey Road, hoping wryly that no Beatles would be crossing this morning.

They weren't, but a bearded one-man band was, weighed down by care and the bass drum on his back (Surely he can't have been recording here? thought Woodhouse incredulously), and he was forced to leap clumsily back to avoid the onrushing Jaguar. Woodhouse glimpsed him in his mirror as he sped away, splayed backwards over the drum on the famous zebra crossing, like St Catherine on the wheel, surrounded by his instruments; and over the sound of the racing engine and the rain, Woodhouse was almost sure he heard a comedy *boo-boom tish!* drum fill, followed by an indignant *parp!*

Abandoning any pretence at subterfuge, Woodhouse proceeded at pace now, making liberal use of his lights and horn to persuade other road users to give way, while the man in the Citroën followed implacably, his face expressionless behind the windscreen. Woodhouse felt the back end of the Jag slide in the wet as he made the left turn on to Belsize Road, and the vehicle seemed to give a little exuberant shimmy as it straightened up and picked up speed. Perhaps a little music, he decided, keeping his eyes on the road as he leaned over and plucked a cassette at random from the pile in the passenger footwell, to get this party started. He inserted the tape into the machine and there was a moment of hiss as he put the car into fourth gear.

Woodhouse nodded approvingly as the bass intro to *Crazy Train* went about its business. Then the double-tracked guitars slid in and posed the eternal question.

They were on Kilburn High Road now and Woodhouse winced with mingled empathy and disgust as his offside front wheel squashed flat a tartan-clad terrier which had darted from behind a parked car. The unfortunate dog's little-old-lady owner, still clutching the animal's leash, unwisely emerged from the same blind spot to be struck by the following Citroën and sent spinning untidily through the air, the dog sailing messily after her. She landed in a heap outside a charity shop like a spiteful donation, the dog a deranged afterthought. Woodhouse glared at the Citroën in the mirror. While he abhorred both dogs and old people, considering them mutually smelly and annoying, he would fight for their right to continue to be so, regardless of his personal feelings and of their fatal disdain for (or shared ignorance of) the Green Cross Code.

'You made me kill that dog,' he muttered to the reflected occupant of the Citroën. 'And now you're going to pay.'

On the stereo, Ozzy bewailed his mental health, while Woodhouse and his pursuer weaved through the traffic at speed, causing consternation as Woodhouse awaited his moment. Finally, seeing an opportunity, he wrenched the steering wheel, applied the handbrake and braced himself. The Jaguar spun a hundred and eighty degrees, soaking an already dejected bus queue with spray, before stopping dead in a taxi rank, while the Citroën, its driver unable to react in time, collided with a bus which was pulling out of a side street, and the driver, who had unwisely neglected to wear his seat belt, burst through the windscreen and bounced off the side window of the lower deck, to the obvious dismay of the passengers.

As Ozzy lamented his woes and Randy Rhoads embarked on an intricate guitar solo that lent a strange beauty to the scene, Woodhouse got out of the car, turning his collar up against the rain, and walked over to the injured man, who lay on his back in the road, his limbs twisted and his face bloodied. A crowd was already gathering. Woodhouse dropped to one knee, feeling the rain soaking through his suit trousers.

'Who are you working for?' he enquired without preamble.

The man on the ground smiled. He was unpleasantly sallow and there was blood on his teeth but he exuded calm. On the stereo Randy Rhoads executed a series of flawless legato trills.

'Il voit avec son oreille,' said the man.

Woodhouse had had French beaten into him at school.

'He sees,' he repeated incredulously, 'with his *ear...*?'

The injured man's smile widened.

'Yes...' he whispered, 'avec son oreille.'

Sirens were approaching now and Woodhouse leant in to ask more about this unlikely employer, but the man bit down and grimaced and there was a slight but audible crack. A wisp of vapour came from the corner of his mouth and Woodhouse thought he could smell, momentarily, Bakewell tart. The man's face darkened beneath the blood and he closed his eyes, gasping yet chuckling even as he choked. Woodhouse stood up. Bakewell tart (he remembered) contains almonds, and the odour of almonds can also indicate cyanide. The guy must have had a suicide capsule in a tooth.

Emergency services were arriving at the scene; Woodhouse walked back to his car. He would have liked to have searched the soon-to-be corpse but he didn't want to waste time establishing his credentials with the wooden-tops, especially in the rain in front of a crowd of rubbernecking civilians. And in any case, he had an assignation.

When they had finished making love they lay amongst the tangled bedclothes and regarded each other seriously. Her hair was dark, her eyes cobalt blue, and she reminded Woodhouse of a girl who had broken his teenage heart in a beer garden. She pouted a little under his scrutiny then licked the end of her index finger and applied it carefully to the tip of his nose.

'My mascara has come there,' she explained in response to his puzzled frown. 'In our sexy-time.' Had she said she was Ukrainian? He couldn't remember, but he liked her accent. She tousled his blond hair affectionately. 'You are big strong handsome man,' she teased. 'I have crush on you like school-girl.'

There was a gap between her front teeth that Woodhouse found alluring.

'I'll carry your books,' he vowed. 'Any time.'

She laughed.

'My perfect English gentle-man.'

They kissed.

'I'm sorry about last time,' he murmured. 'I had too much to drink.'

She turned away from him and sat abruptly up, hugging her knees. A sheet covered her breasts and her face was concealed by her hair. Woodhouse admired the curve of her back. Outside the rain had stopped, and the sun suffused the room with sudden gold.

'There is trouble,' she suggested softly. 'In your life.'

'Perhaps,' he allowed.

'Your work is... difficult?' She peeped over her shoulder coyly, making him smile.

'My work is tiring,' he told her, yawning. 'Come and lie down with me.'

She lay down beside him, stroking his thigh as he began to fall asleep, lulled by the sound of traffic from the street three floors below. Through closing eyes he saw her reflection in the wardrobe mirror, reaching stealthily for something. He rolled on to the floor, still tangled in the sheets, and the point of the knife pierced the pillow where his neck had been. There was a brief but violent struggle and he managed to disarm her. They faced each other through a drift of feathers. Her eyes were narrowed and she was shaking with rage and frustration.

'What the fuck!' he exclaimed, adding foolishly: 'You could have killed me.'

She sneered at him and the gap between her front teeth was alluring no more.

'Beware the one who comes after me,' she hissed, 'the straps of whose ear I am not worthy to untie.'

Woodhouse no longer liked her accent, not even slightly.

'Who?' he asked helplessly. 'What?'

But she just smiled, and he could only watch as she ran to the window and hurled herself through it. Surrounded by shards of flying glass and enshrouded in muslin, she was silhouetted for an instant against the blue sky and then she was gone. There was a pause and a squeal of tyres before screams drifted up from the street below. Woodhouse got dressed, picked up the knife – a wicked looking stiletto with an elaborately carved mermaid on its hilt – wrapped it in a pillow case and put it in his jacket pocket. His phone rang.

When he becomes aware again, the heat is fading from his body and there is a sensation of movement, of being carried. He seems to hear what might be distant music, and he feels a cool breeze across his – his what? He wants to look down at himself but he cannot move and he has no eyes. He feels his limbs stiffening and he tries to scream but he has no mouth…

Woodhouse parked the Jag in the car park of the All England Club. Greaves was leaning on the boot of his immaculate open-topped MG and smoking his pipe thoughtfully. He looked trim for his age and dapper in blazer and slacks.

'You shouldn't drive a classic car,' he said disapprovingly, 'if you can't be bothered to look after it properly.'

Carefully, Woodhouse closed the door of his Jag. It was true that, whilst having been expensively bullet-proofed in the past, the bodywork was not quite what it might be aesthetically.

'I like to keep it low profile, sir,' he said, smiling. This badinage was familiar territory.

Greaves snorted.

'If its profile gets any lower you'll have to sweep the thing up.' He gestured vaguely towards centre court with his pipe stem. 'Ladies' semi-finals today,' he said. 'Of course, the biggest lesbian always wins.'

Woodhouse was shocked.

'You can't say that!'

Greaves re-lit his pipe and grinned through the smoke.

'One of the few pleasures of advancing age, dear boy, is the ease with which one is able to shock one's juniors.'

Woodhouse was incensed.

'Next you'll be telling me not to bet on the white guy in boxing!'

Greaves raised his eyebrows.

'Good God, Woodhouse! You really are the most fearful racist! I had absolutely no idea… I shall have to give you a warning about this, you know.' He appeared to be genuinely upset.

'Yes, sir,' said Woodhouse, shaking his head ruefully. The old man was impossible when he was in this mood. 'Did you want to see me about something?'

Greaves nodded.

'Apparently there's a problem out at Lakenheath airbase. Our colonial cousins are in difficulties. I wondered if you might pop over and liaise. Have a chat with a chap called O'Hara – an eccentric fellow, I'm told.'

'Any idea what the matter is?'

'It seems there's a mole.'

'Isn't that a job for a pest controller?'

'Precisely, dear boy, that's why I'm sending you. I gather you've been having one or two little complications of your own, by the way.'

Woodhouse shrugged.

'Someone's trying to have me killed – by kamikaze ear-enthusiasts.'

Greaves knocked the ash out of his pipe on the wing of Woodhouse's car and frowned.

'That does sound peculiar, even for these strange times... You'd better send me over a report when you get a chance. Oh, and leave your jalopy here, Woodhouse – the boffins want to pick it up and put some new toys in it. Don't ask me why – waste of taxpayers' money when the damn thing's about to fall to bits in any case. I'll have them drop it round when they've finished, if there's anything left of it.'

They shook hands, and Woodhouse handed over his car keys.

'Enjoy the tennis, sir. Presumably the better players will win, regardless of sexual orientation.'

'Perhaps you're right,' Greaves admitted, putting the keys in his pocket. He waited until Woodhouse had started to walk away. 'Oh, Woodhouse?' he called. 'When you get to the base, be aware that there may be people there with different ethnicities to your own. Do try and be tolerant, there's a good chap.'

High above the streets of Paris, a man of consummate evil sits making entries in a leather-bound ledger. The huge window of his opulent office gives grandly on to a stunning view of Gustave Eiffel's masterpiece and the skyline of the great city, which is lit up by the last flames of a glorious sunset. Banks of monitors displaying images of various nefarious business and political concerns fill one wall, and sometimes the man notices something of interest there and uses a remote control to enlarge a particular image: a man being ejected from a casino; a commotion in a stock exchange; a mini-riot in a sub-continental city. Once, he makes a phone call. But mostly he writes in the ledger with a fountain pen.

The man's face looks strange in the shifting light of the screens. He wears an intricately carved antique ivory ear, and the fine calfskin straps that hold it in place run across his face, half closing one eye and pulling his upper lip slightly away from his teeth. His head is shaved and the straps cross at the base of his skull and pass through a small silver buckle shaped like an inverted crucifix, which is curved to rest comfortably on the occipital bone. The ink he is using is red: it is made from a mixture of blood and semen. He writes names, lists of names, and among them there is one we might recognise. He writes names in a leather-bound ledger and as he writes he hisses quietly to himself.

He is roused from his reverie by a sharp pain that begins behind his ear and travels fumblingly over his shoulder and down the curve of his back. The sensation is of part of himself being cut away. Ach! Can this be hell? He feels himself grasped, as by a giant hand, and turned roughly around, and the pain begins afresh...

As Woodhouse drove the newly modified Jaguar through the Suffolk countryside, the sun lowered itself wearily through the evening landscape and his mind cast itself back like a cheap 1970s' fishing rod, the long line of memories becoming entangled again in the weeping willows of his childhood.

'Mother, I don't like this dinner,' he protested long ago.

'Quiet, Richard! The feet are the best part – they help you to not die when you're asleep.'

'But the claws are so scratchy... Couldn't I have a hot dog or something?'

She leaned back and folded her arms, fixing the boy with her good eye, her expression one of infinite sadness.

'Sorrow is knowledge,' she informed him gravely. 'Those that know the most must mourn the deepest.'

Woodhouse felt his eyes fill with tears: he hated it when she quoted Byron.

'I'm sorry, Mum,' he whispered. 'You know it was an accident.'

They were sitting at the long dining table, but the days of dinner parties for fashionable friends were long gone. The room was lit by guttering candles (the electricity having been cut off) and the table top was scarred and dusty. Mouldering piles of malodorous detritus loomed over the rats frolicking on the frayed Persian carpet, and cobwebs festooned the ruined chandeliers. It was what Miss Havisham's house might have become had she allowed herself to really indulge her depression.

Mother smiled and her glass eye shifted woozily in its socket, making Woodhouse feel momentarily seasick. She was rather overdressed, he felt, in a blue taffeta ball gown, and there seemed little need for the elaborate tiara she wore in her tangled black hair.

'You may push the paws to the side of your plate,' she told him magnanimously, 'if you wish. But I cannot be held responsible should you pass away in your sleep.'

Woodhouse sighed. These days, on the whole, he preferred school to the holidays. He looked down at his plate and frowned.

'Is this a gizzard, Mum?' he enquired, indicating the article in question with his fork.

His mother threw back her head and laughed gaily, dislodging her tiara, which fell to the floor, startling a rat that had been absent-mindedly gnawing her wooden leg.

'No, silly! Badgers don't have gizzards.'

Woodhouse put down the fork and pushed away his plate. Never had he imagined he could miss school food. He felt sick, and guilt overwhelmed him. Poor old Badger…

There was an ominous rattling sound and Woodhouse's first thought was that the technical boys had bollocksed up the modifications and the car was falling to bits. It wasn't until a neat line of starred chips appeared like snowflakes across the bullet-resistant windscreen that he realised he was under fire. He accelerated, instinctively ducking as he passed between two sets of intermittent muzzle flashes coming from the dark undergrowth to either side of the twilit country road. Switching the Jag's lights off he coasted for two hundred yards until a bend in the road hid him from view, before parking by a drainage ditch at the edge of some woodland and getting out of the car.

Blinking to accustom his eyes to the rapidly fading light, he moved silently round (running his hand over the fresh bullet-dings in the bodywork as he passed) to the rear of the vehicle, where he paused, listening. Silence, save for the sough of the wind and the beat of his heart. He eased open the boot and was reassured to be able to dimly discern the tools of his trade, seemingly undisturbed in their custom-built racks. Woodhouse considered the job at hand: he was outnumbered by at least two to one and, by the look of the muzzle flashes he had seen and the speed at which the windscreen had starred, as well as the pattern and spacing of the damage, his ambushers were using semi-automatic rifles at the very least. And using them with some fair degree of competence, unfortunately.

Reaching a decision, he unclipped the powerful recurve bow from its place on the underside of the boot lid and, with its upper limb in his right hand, stepped between the angled bow and its relaxed string. Bracing his left shin against the inside curve of the lower limb and, with the riser against the back of his right knee, being careful not to twist the limbs and knacker the thing, Woodhouse bent the upper limb until he was able with his left hand to slide the string up and into its groove at the top. Stepping gingerly out of the bow (like a man who has shat himself trying to escape his soiled trousers) he checked the nock point and brace height then leant it against the rear wing of the car, listening all the time for the crack of a twig or the sound of an engine starting up. He fumbled in the gloom of the boot until he found the quiver. It was too dark now to see the variously coloured fletching denoting the different arrows and Woodhouse hoped Greaves's scheme about the card suits would work.

Closing the boot, he slipped quietly into the broken woodland and worked through the rough ground until he found a point of vantage above the stretch of road where he had seen the muzzle flashes. Sensing movement below him he took the bow from his back and, reaching over his shoulder with his other hand, searched the arrow shafts with his thumb for the raised card-suit symbols below the fletching. Greaves was a bridge aficionado and was always trying to persuade the reluctant Woodhouse to play. He supposed one day he would have to accede. Feeling a

Diamond, he removed the corresponding arrow from the quiver, nocked it and sent it speeding low above the trees. As it gathered pace and illuminated the scene below (Diamond – light – tracer), he fitted another (Spade – broadhead) to the bow and sent it flying sweetly to the crouching shape revealed by the light.

There was a muffled boom as the explosive-tipped arrow (Club – Semtex) blew the erstwhile ambusher to pieces, and an unpleasant spattering as the pieces rained abundantly down on to the summer foliage. Woodhouse shook his head despairingly. He had fucking *told* Greaves that it would be difficult to differentiate between the Club and the Spade, similarly shaped as they were to the touch, but the old man had been typically obdurate.

Moving swiftly, and wheezing only a little from the roll-ups he kept meaning to give up, Woodhouse made his way stealthily down through the undergrowth and across the road in search of the surviving assailant. Pausing for a moment to listen, he could hear him blundering away through the trees, obviously panicked by his colleague's spectacular demise.

Despite the booze and fags, Woodhouse kept himself in shape, and he quartered his prey, threw down the bow he had been carrying and pounced, knocking the man to the ground and kicking away his rifle. He rolled him over and gripped him by the throat, lighting his Zippo with the other hand and glaring with disgust at the singularly unattractive countenance of the would-be assassin.

'He has heard of you by the hearing of the ear,' croaked the unlovely captive. 'But now—'

Woodhouse's grip had tightened to preclude any further speech. Putting away the lighter he removed his Bowie knife from the sheath at his thigh and laid the cold blade along the side of the man's pock-marked face, feeling him flinch at its touch.

'I'm getting a little tired,' Woodhouse told him, 'of these obscure otic utterances. Suppose you were to give me a name instead?'

He loosened his grip to admit the possibility of a reply but the man just shook his head. Woodhouse sighed. Interrogation was not a part of his work that he enjoyed but it was necessary from time to time. The attempts on his life were becoming annoying, and while, like pulling teeth, extraction of information was often bloody and unpleasant for all involved, sometimes one's finer feelings had to be set aside for the greater good – so society's smile might become all the more winning, perhaps.

On this particular occasion the patient struggled violently, so violently, in fact, that Woodhouse was forced to offer increased levels of violence in return, culminating in an unplanned colectomy performed at speed with the razor-sharp Bowie. Woodhouse wiped the blade of the knife on the man's trousers before sheathing it, then stood up and stepped back, wrinkling his nose at the stench of the individual's newly exposed entrails.

'Sorry about that,' he said. 'But you would keep struggling.'

'Lomax…' whispered the dying man. 'His name is… Lomax… He has heard of you… by the hearing of the ear… but now… his eye sees you…'

And as Woodhouse walked away through the trees, carrying the bow and his familiar burden of guilt, he could hear the ugly bastard giggling to himself, even as he died.

They laughed at him in the bakery, he knew they did. And she was so beautiful, with her blonde curls and those wistful grey eyes. He felt sure she hid a secret sadness, as did he. They were meant to be together. But she laughed at him with her friend when they thought he couldn't hear. His eyes filled with tears and he bit into an éclair. She thought he was a big fat fool. His jowls trembled with sorrow and he crammed a cream horn into his mouth.

'Say, honey, you think this get-up makes my fanny look big?' enquired the hour-glass-shaped airwoman, fluttering her eyelashes and pouting provocatively.

Woodhouse frowned. He couldn't even *see* her fanny, encased as it was in a tight skirt. What the hell was the girl talking about?

'I'm sure it's a very nice one,' he replied diplomatically. 'And I like your uniform.'

'You know what they call me around here?' she demanded aggressively, jutting her chin and blowing a pink bubble with her gum.

The words "bike" and "town pump" came immediately to mind, but Woodhouse had experienced enough pain in his life to have learned sometimes to refrain from utterance. He shrugged instead. She popped the bubble neatly. Her tongue was pink too and her hair was red, like a warning.

'They call me Sweetcakes on account of I got nice buns,' she explained proudly, half turning and presenting her rump for his approval.

She's American, Woodhouse realised belatedly: her fanny means her arse.

'Pleased to meet you; my name's Richard.'

'Maybe's I could call you Richie?' she suggested brightly.

He suppressed a shudder.

'Maybe so… I'm looking for a guy called O'Hara.'

She shrugged, crooked a finger and led him through a labyrinth of corridors, wiggling her bottom extravagantly as though worried he might lose interest and wander off. She stopped and knocked at a door that bore a nameplate reading: *Lt. Col. O'Hara.*

'See ya,' she said, giving Woodhouse a wink and undulating away.

Woodhouse opened the door in response to an indistinguishable call.

'Hi there,' said the man behind the desk, rising to his feet, 'I'm Randy – Randall O'Hara. My ancestors came from Ireland – you know, in Wales. You must be Bughouse. Good to know ya, buddy.'

He was a big man, as big as Woodhouse, but dark rather than fair, and his hair was cut short, in what Woodhouse believed was called a buzz cut. He wore a look of amused enquiry and his capped American teeth were chewing a toothpick.

'It's Woodhouse, actually,' said Woodhouse. 'Whereabouts in Ireland did your family come from?'

'County Dur-ham,' O'Hara said proudly.

Woodhouse nodded.

'I see… So, I hear you have a mole?'

'No, but I have a birthmark on my butt-ocks.'

Woodhouse sighed. He found Americans difficult.

'What I meant was that I was told you were having a problem with someone leaking confidential information.'

'Information…? Listen, buddy-boy, last week someone

stole an experimental stealth chopper – and you wanna know the worst thing? It was two days before anyone noticed it was gone. Pilot went to get in the goddamn thing and fell on his fool ass. Information, my johnson! Some asshole is fucking with us!'

'You lost a helicopter,' said Woodhouse disbelievingly. 'Christ, O'Hara, it's been a long day – I could do with a drink.'

O'Hara was willing, and in the bar they bonded with alcohol, Randy plying Woodhouse enthusiastically with boilermakers and Woodhouse introducing the American to the seemingly innocuous, yet dangerously cumulative mini-Guinness. They were deep in a conversation about the relative merits of baseball and cricket when a country-and-western song came on the jukebox. Randy jumped up, dragging Woodhouse after him, and a drunken line dance broke out. Unable to escape, Woodhouse was compelled by whooping service-folk to be complicit in a collective indignity called the *Watermelon Crawl*. When it was finally over and Randy (still in full uniform) dropped to the floor and crawled away like a startled lizard in the direction of the bar, Woodhouse discovered he was laughing so hard that there were tears in his eyes.

As the evening progressed he found he was disappointed by the absence of the girl known as Sweetcakes. He heard her name mentioned several times by leering servicemen, forming the impression that she was a recent arrival to the base and they were vying for her attentions. He was surprised to experience a pang of jealousy.

During the course of the evening, Randy addressed Woodhouse variously as Church-house, Nuthouse, Schoolhouse, Crap-house, Teahouse, Birdhouse, Crack-house, Courthouse, Flophouse, Gin-house, Grindhouse, Chophouse, Whorehouse, Lighthouse, Workhouse, Dosshouse, Jailhouse, Boathouse, Bunkhouse, Dolls' house, Doghouse, Madhouse, Cathouse and Funhouse, as well as Cider-house, Slaughterhouse, Wendy-house, Charnel-house, Reptile-house and, when they drunkenly said goodnight, Shithouse. Randy was a character.

Later, in his spartan room at the airbase, Woodhouse's mind skipped back over the years like a flat stone skimming over a dark lake, having been propelled by the spindly arm of a snotty-nosed schoolboy whose National Health glasses are taped together with Elastoplast. And Woodhouse's mind sank like that stone into an uneasy sleep and the dank, weed-strewn depths of his difficult childhood.

'Mother, please don't have any more juniper juice,' begged the infant Woodhouse. 'I don't like it when you get creative.'

His mother, who had been trying without success to balance the salt cellar on top of her gin bottle, brought her remaining eye to bear on the boy. She frowned a little and then smiled.

'All around my hat,' she sang. 'I will wear the green willow.'

'You're not wearing a hat,' objected Woodhouse.

Her head was bare apart from her hair, which was tangled and wild as had become usual these days.

'It's a meteorological hat,' she confided, stifling a hiccup. 'Prognosticating thundery showers.'

'I don't know what you mean.' Woodhouse was confused.

'It has to do,' she condescendingly explained, 'with *"weather"* I am wearing a hat. Do you see?'

He stared resentfully at the top of her head.

'You're not.'

Mother sighed and sipped from her smeared martini glass. She wore a shimmering green cocktail dress and about her upper arm was a slave bracelet in the form of a golden serpent.

'You must learn not to take everything so literally, Richard,' she told the puzzled boy. 'Now, tell me (she smiled and tilted her head artfully): what do you think of my hat? Do you like it?'

'You're not wearing a hat!' insisted Woodhouse peevishly. 'For God's sake.'

'Do not add blasphemy to your other sins,' warned Mother. 'What kind of hat am I not wearing, pray?'

He looked around wildly.

'All of them,' he cried. 'You're not wearing any of them.'

She smiled and steepled her fingers quizzically, clearly enjoying herself.

'Come, come, Richard,' she chided. 'Surely I cannot not be wearing simultaneously all *and* none of the hats…?'

Woodhouse took a deep breath: this madness was more abstruse than Latin, he felt. His young brain was supple and elusive and it tried to squirm away but he got hold of it and forced it to contemplate the matter in hand.

'I suppose,' he said reluctantly, 'you are not wearing *all* of the hats but you *are* wearing none of them.'

She nodded appreciatively, and such was the boy's confusion that he thought for a moment that she *was* wearing a hat, after all: a jaunty black pillbox with a polka-dot veil.

'Much better,' she allowed. 'But if I'm not wearing *all* of the hats then it follows that I must be wearing some – or at least one – of them, mustn't I?'

'No!' He clutched despairingly at his hair. 'You mustn't!'

'Now, come along, Richard. Humour me. (The boy reluctantly lowered his hands and clasped them on the table in front of him.) What kind of hat am I not wearing?'

Woodhouse sighed. His knuckles were white.

'I don't know.'

Mother pouted.

'You do,' she coaxed. 'Tell me.'

'No!' insisted the boy.

'Tell Mummy, like a good little soldier. What kind of hat am I not wearing?'

'A black one,' he mumbled sullenly.

'Come again?' Mother cupped her ear mischievously.

'A black one!' shouted Woodhouse. 'You're not wearing a black hat with a spotty veil-thing on! Bloody hell, Mother!'

She beamed at him.

'Good boy! I knew we'd get there in the end. It's a lovely hat, isn't it? – the one that I'm not wearing today.'

Woodhouse made no reply. He crossed his arms and jutted his lower lip as far as it would go. He was sulking. In fact it would be fair to say that he had a right monk-on.

There was a crack of thunder that rattled the windows in their frames and a voice could be heard in the distance, singing. A hoarse voice that sung *On Ilkley Moor Bah Tat*, bearing down hard on the word "tat" each time, and as it grew closer they heard also the thump and drag of heavy boots in the gravel outside.

'ON ILKLEY MOOR BAH TAAAAAAAAAT!' shouted the voice from close at hand, in some semblance of tune, and there was a crash and a thud as a pig's head flew in through the window and rolled on the Persian carpet.

'Your father is home,' exclaimed Mother delightedly. Outside the rain began to fall, hissing venomously like the mythological hydra. 'How lovely!'

A cooling sensation, as though his body, hardened now it seems, is being gently sponged. Is he then a burns victim – horribly charred and blinded in some fearful accident? He tries to reach out with his mind to the consciousness he feels nearby, but there is nothing – no sympathetic response. He has no eyes to fill with tears...

In his narrow bed at the airbase Woodhouse's sleep was troubled.

'Father, please!' he mumbled. 'Not the birds and the bees.'

Awoken by a massive explosion, for a moment he feared he was back in Ireland. Pistol in hand and suddenly sober, he ran from his room wearing only a thong. Alarms were shrilling and people scurried hither and thither like mice at a barn dance. The door of Randy's room lay in smouldering pieces in the corridor and Woodhouse ducked through what remained of the doorway.

Randy was on the floor, and the walls, and the ceiling. Woodhouse slipped, horrified, on what might have been the American's spleen and landed, aghast, on what was probably his pelvis.

'Avenge my gory death!' seemed to cry out Randy's vocal cords beneath the dado rail from which they depended.

Rising to his knees amongst the ghastly remains of his recently deceased comrade, Woodhouse raised his eyes to heaven by way of the brain and goo-bespattered ceiling, and he shuddered to feel his grip on reality loosen as someone, somewhere, pried mercilessly at the tired fingers of his sanity, and Randy's buzz-cut scalp dropped from the light fixture to which it had formerly been adhering.

A great golden moon glares balefully down on the streets and arrondissements of Paris. For every pair of lovers, eyes wide and faces slack with the joyous foolishness of their condition, there are at least as many others, less innocent, trapped in the travails of a far darker romance.

Pickpockets ply their trade up and down the Champs-Elysees. A businessman and a prostitute strike up a conversation in a bar. She intends to rob him; he intends to beat her. A heroin addict awaits a dealer on a corner in Pigalle. His withdrawal is well advanced. He shivers miserably and sneezes, and his usually pin-point pupils have opened reluctantly to admit too much of the world. His soul writhes like a salted slug. A drunken father browbeats his young daughter. He has not struck her yet and one can only hope he never will, but every harsh word forces another petal from the open bloom of her child's heart until, in time, only bitter seeds will remain to take root in hate, and so it goes on.

In his penthouse suite the man with the carved ivory ear hears these things through the ether, and while they do not bring him happiness, for he possesses no capacity for such a thing and would not wish it, they bring him strength, and his blood sings with the exhilaration of it all, and with his gold fountain pen he strikes a name from a list in his ledger. He smiles his distorted smile and gives a satisfied hiss, and outside the wind whips tattered black clouds across the mountains of the moon like a sadistic coachman.

Someone put a blanket round Woodhouse's shoulders and led him back to his room, where he sat dead-eyed on the edge of his bed, his mind a maelstrom. He had a name: Lomax, but that was all. Clearly these people were acting under instructions, which argued some kind of plan, but other than the obvious facts that they were ruthless and they feared their boss he knew nothing. A stealth helicopter... Had the Americans *really* lost one? He supposed they were probably careless enough. And now they had lost Randy, who might, given time, have become a friend. He must find his way to this Lomax and he must avenge his fallen comrade, as seemingly instructed by the American's gruesome innards. The horrible scene burst on Woodhouse's memory afresh and he began to shiver. Realising he was wearing only a thong beneath the blanket he grew angry. How could a man wear such an undignified, inconsequential scrap of nonsense at such a time as this? It had been a Christmas gift from his mother in very dubious taste. Bloody woman! Would he never be free of her tyranny? Tearing off the offending article he threw it disgustedly out of the window, where it hung sadly from the branches of a small tree in the rain. He showered numbly, washing away Randy's blood, then walked back through, towelling his hair.

Just at that moment there came a timid tapping. Discarding the damp towel, Woodhouse put on his shirt and trousers and, taking his Walther from its holster on the back of the chair, cautiously opened the door.

He didn't recognise her for a moment: her face was free of make-up and her red hair was pulled back in a ponytail. She wore a dressing gown and pyjamas that did little to conceal the pneumatic curves beneath.

'I thought maybe's you could use a little company,' she said, coming in and sitting on the edge of the bed. She placed the bottle of bourbon and tumblers she had been carrying on the floor. 'Randy was a pretty good guy. He was nice to me, you know?'

Woodhouse replaced the pistol and sat down on the chair. Watching her pour the drinks he thought she seemed very different to earlier. Without the make-up she looked younger and softer, even her movements were gentler. Maybe she was one of those girls who put the attitude on with the war paint...? He took the drink she passed him. Her freckles were sexy, he realised.

'I didn't catch your name,' he said.

'Maryanne,' she replied. 'My given name is Maryanne.'

Was she blushing? Probably just a trick of the light.

'So, what's your story, Maryanne? Or should I call you Sweetcakes?' Woodhouse asked mischievously.

She took a sip of her drink, looking suddenly vulnerable.

'I guess you can call me Maryanne if you want. I hail from Virginia,' she said, a shade defiantly. 'You know, like the Waltons?' He nodded, being vaguely aware of the show without ever having watched it. 'I guess I just outgrew it. Small towns are the same everywhere, huh, Richie?'

'I should think so,' he agreed.

'So, I moved to New York when I was fifteen and now I live in Brooklyn.' She brightened. 'That's how comes I don't talk wit' no accent no more.'

Her glance was quick and alive with humour: she was sending herself up. Maybe there was more to this girl than met the eye. There was plenty on that level too, Woodhouse couldn't help but notice again.

'So, you ran away?'

'It was complicated, I guess.'

She refreshed their drinks, avoiding his eye. He sat down next to her on the bed and put his arm round her. She stiffened momentarily then relaxed and laid her head on his shoulder. Her hair smelled like hay, comforting and disarming as a sleepy cat.

'You want I should sleep over with you maybe, in case you have a bad dream?' she asked after a while.

'That's very thoughtful of you.'

They smiled at each other. She took off her dressing gown and got into the single bed shyly in her striped pyjamas, making room for Woodhouse who removed his shirt but elected to keep his trousers on, given that his underwear was decorating the tree outside and he and the girl were still relative strangers. She settled into his arms with a satisfied sigh, and moments after he turned out the light they were both asleep. In the early hours of the morning they awoke and made love dreamily, seeming to fit together entirely naturally. She bit his shoulder with her small sharp teeth and the soft cries she made were balm to his troubled soul.

Afterwards they slept again and when he awoke she was gone. It seemed to Woodhouse that he had heard her whisper goodnight to him as he slept, and that she had called him John-boy. It pissed him off that she should have got his name wrong but he supposed that she slept with a lot of guys.

He is being held upside down – and plunged head first into cold liquid! He tries to struggle but his limbs are rigid...

Cubby lived alone in a large Georgian house, set back from the road behind high beech hedges. His grandparents had been wealthy and he had wanted for nothing growing up, except maybe friends. His grandfather had passed away first, suffering a heart attack while spit-shining his shoes, and his grandmother had followed some two years later, struck by a car whilst wandering the streets at night in thrall to dementia. Cubby had taken her death hard. The old woman had been querulous and difficult to manage in her dotage, but in the absence of his parents (his father unknown and presumed married, and his mother a teenage drug abuser who died shortly after his birth) his grandmother had become his world and when she embarked on her second childhood not long after he had completed his first, he accepted the role reversal with good grace and ministered to the old lady as best he could.

His grandfather had been a quiet man, tired after a lifetime spent amassing his fortune as a captain of industry. With an uncharacteristic flash of humour he had nicknamed the boy "Cubby" after film director Cubby Broccoli, following a particularly insistent refusal by the boy to eat his greens.

During his retirement the old man had indulged his one true passion: the creation of pottery cats. In an old coach house adjoining the property a kiln was installed, and much of Cubby's childhood had been spent watching his grandfather shape and fire his creations until the coach house brimmed with the things, all looking unwaveringly at the boy. Members of the public sometimes ventured in, usually seeming bemused or even fearful, but it was unusual to sell anything. Grandfather's cat pottery was more a seemingly harmless obsession than a viable business.

Since the traumatic death of his grandmother some nine months earlier, Cubby had become even more withdrawn than he had been previously. The garden was becoming overgrown and dust accumulated unnoticed in the house. At the age of twenty-two Cubby had inherited enough money to live comfortably for the rest of his life and was well on the way to becoming a recluse: a chubby secular hermit settling into a congenial depression. He had been bullied at school and in the end his grandmother had elected to home tutor him, with the result that he wrote in beautiful copperplate and possessed a thorough knowledge of the novels of the Brontë sisters and Jane Austen and a firm grounding in female emancipation and the suffragette movement. He was woefully ill-equipped, however, for any kind of prolonged interaction with the modern world and its inhabitants.

Starved of company, he had developed a desperate infatuation with one of the girls who worked in the local bakery. Viewed through the sepia-tinted glasses of his rather selective education, Cubby saw this pretty, probably quite ordinary young girl as a tragic heroine, forced into a life of drudgery by an accident of birth. Her often sulky demeanour, very likely caused by an argument with an immature boyfriend or too many alcopops the previous night, appeared to him as a deep unhappiness indicative of a sensitive nature and high-flown intelligence cruelly shackled by circumstance. He longed to rescue and ennoble her, Eliza Doolittle-like, thereby earning her undying gratitude and passionate devotion. Dressed in silks and furs and bedizened with jewels and trinkets, she would sit adoringly at his feet, possibly sewing a sampler or some such thing while he… well, Cubby was unsure exactly what he would be doing, aside from looking benevolent and indulgent and occasionally patting the hair of the dear sweet girl.

Sometimes he was dismayed to find his thoughts taking a distinct turn towards the carnal. He could imagine the look of bewilderment and dawning horror on her beautiful face if she should perceive the unseemly bulging of his trousers caused by her innocent proximity, her cry of disgust at such base betrayal, and his own mortification and self-loathing.

Even as he flushed with shame imagining the awful scene, the rigidity of Cubby's treacherous member gave the lie to his high-mindedness, and terrible images of only-too-imaginable depravity rose unbidden to mock his chivalry. How could he look her in the face and speak the words "cream horn", filthy beast that he was? How could he even *think* such a thing? He would have to have a danish pastry instead. His grandmother had once caught him reading *Cold Comfort Farm* and fetched him such a clump with the family bible that his ears rang for a week. Such fare was considered wildly racy, and as a result Cubby was an extremely naïve and confused young man and became so flustered in the presence of his muse in the bakery that it was small wonder the girls laughed at him.

Woodhouse's father entered the room violently and without its consent. The rats scurried away from his work boots, and his flat cap was imbued with tweedy malevolence. His moustache bristled with ill intent and the only thing great about his coat was the quantity of fear that it inspired. There was silence but for the rain outside as his eyes darted around the room like piranha fish, finally settling on the boy, who writhed in his seat as his father's gaze stripped the meat from his soul. Mother looked on impassively.

'Well, lad,' said Father at length. 'I've come home for to tell thee a story.' The boy was silent; he knew better than to speak yet. 'It's a story about t' birds and also t' bees, by 'eck. 'Appen it's his favourite, eh, missis?' This last directed to his wife who now sat contemplating her martini glass.

'I very much doubt it,' she replied frostily.

Father laughed unpleasantly and then clasped his hands and gazed soulfully up, as if to the sky.

'Aye, t' birds and t' bees,' he said dreamily. 'Birds all flyin' with they feathers and such, up in the wide blue yonder, all wheelin' an' turnin' an' callin' to they mates. Beautiful it are, just beautiful.' He sighed. 'But what about the bees, eh? WHAT ABOUT T' FOOKIN' BEES?' He was suddenly, inexplicably, shaking with rage.

Woodhouse looked down at the scarred dining table, his eyes filling with tears. Father had changed since he'd started his new job, the boy felt, and not for the better.

'Speak up, lad. Tell us about the bees.'

'The b-bees are l-letters of the alphabet, n-not insects,' stuttered the boy (Father was making him nervous).

'How many of 'em are there, lad?'

'There are t-two, Father.'

Father nodded approvingly.

'Aye, and what do they stand for, eh?'

Woodhouse appealed to his mother.

'Do I *have* to, Mum?'

She couldn't meet his eye.

'Best to get it over,' she whispered. 'You know what he's like when he's northern.'

'What do t' fookin' bees stand for, lad?' demanded Father, hands on hips.

'B-b-b-being b-b-b-buggered.' Woodhouse wanted to run away and hide under his bed.

'Aye, bein' boogered, right enough. And what 'appens if tha's not boogered, eh?'

'For goodness' sake, Lockhart. Leave the boy alone!'

'He knows I'm only joshing, dearheart. A little ribbing is character building for a boy… Now, where was I? Ah, yes… What 'appens if tha don't be boogered, eh, lad?'

'All the b-birds will die.'

A flurry of rain drove in through the broken window, extinguishing a candle.

'DOES THA WANT ALL T' FOOKIN' BIRDS TO DIE?'

'No, Father.'

'So, what must tha do?'

'B-b-b-b-b-b-bend over!'

Roaring with laughter, Father removed his coat and cap and threw them on the floor. Taking his seat at the head of the ruined dining table, he wiped the tears from his eyes, saying:

'Jolly well done, Richard, old thing. You're a thoroughly good egg. Now, then.' He rubbed his hands and beamed at his wife. 'What's for dinner, Maude?'

She glanced over at the pig's head which lay grinning evilly in the candlelight.

'We will be having pork – but it's not quite ready yet.'

Somewhere in the distance a peacock called and the rats danced a celebratory gavotte.

After breakfast Woodhouse was briefed again. By which I mean that not only was he wearing a spare pair of underpants fetched from the car to replace the garment discarded in his grief, but also that, after a breakfast of blueberry pancakes and bacon with maple syrup, he was escorted to a small room where he was informed in more detail about the problems on the base.

The grim-faced captain had an extremely monotonous voice, and as he droned on about murders and missing aircraft Woodhouse's thoughts kept turning to the girl from Virginia. Those dangerous curves needed careful handling, he reflected: a careless man could spin out and crash and be scarred for life... The captain was saying something about armaments, and Woodhouse dragged his mind reluctantly back to the business at hand.

'Are you telling me the helicopter you lost was armed?'

The captain had the good grace to look embarrassed.

'Armed and dangerous, unfortunately, Mr Woodhouse. Armed and dangerous. She was about to fly an experimental sortie with some state-of-the-art new hardware.'

Woodhouse produced a pad and pencil from the inside pocket of his jacket.

'The aircraft is a heavily modified UH-60 Black Hawk with certain classified features,' continued the captain remorselessly. 'What we would call a Stealth Hawk.'

Woodhouse began to draw a pair of generous breasts.

'Certain refinements to the wide chord composite rotors and tail boom have rendered her virtually silent, apart from unavoidable air displacement by the main blades and some slight hydraulic whine, and she is, of course, undetectable by electronic means. We were about to trial a new on-board weapons system which, I might add, was developed entirely by ourselves and not stolen from the Chinese by any means whatsoever.'

Woodhouse nodded wisely and sketched in the line of a thigh.

'The 17th Cavalry is a proud regiment with a long and distinguished history, Mr Woodhouse.'

What did Americans know about history? wondered Woodhouse uncharitably as he delicately shaded a nipple. He was drawing a 1950s'-style pin-up girl, kneeling, hands behind her head and breasts thrust proudly forward.

'This whole business is extremely embarrassing, not to mention delicate. This aircraft, Mr Woodhouse, was carrying a full payload of ordnance.'

'Call me Richard. What kind of ordnance?'

The captain sighed.

'Sixteen Hellfire thermobaric missiles, extensively modified... Richard. And a couple of Sidewinders for use in case of air-to-air combat.'

'I see.' The pin-up girl's face had gone wrong: she looked like a leering simpleton. Damn! He tore off the page and crumpled it. 'When you say thermobaric—?'

'Essentially, the term just means enhanced blast.'

'In what way is the blast enhanced, Captain –' Woodhouse checked the man's name badge – 'Short?' He was beginning to enjoy himself now.

Captain Short sighed again. He took off his cap and put it on the desk. He was impressively bald.

'On impact the missile emits a cloud of gases, not unlike aerosol gases. This becomes a fireball that causes a vacuum and a significant blast wave.'

'And these weapons are legal, are they? They don't contravene any treaties or anything?'

A vein on Captain Short's temple had begun to pulse.

'I guess it's kind of a grey area,' he said through clenched teeth.

'I'd guess it would be kind of a blackened area with pieces of bloody flesh scattered about on it, Captain.'

Captain Short stood up abruptly.

'You goddamn smartass Limey cocksucker!' he hissed. 'In point of fact this missile would crush the shit out of your stiff-upper-lipped British ass and collapse your goddamn lungs and suck your asshole eyes clean out their goddamn sockets, you lousy faggot douchebag!'

Woodhouse stood up too. He was smiling.

'And you and your *buddies* have lost sixteen of the fucking things, as well as a machine that can sneak up and deliver them just about anywhere. Sit down, Captain.'

The captain sat. He was breathing heavily and sweating visibly.

'I'm sorry,' he managed. 'I've been under a lot of pressure – my ass is on the line here.'

Woodhouse gave the man a long look and then resumed his own seat.

'Leaving aside for the moment the question of how you managed to lose this aircraft – this Stealth Hawk – in the first place—'

'It was Independence Day,' mumbled the captain miserably.

'What I want to know is who you suspect of having taken the thing.'

'Our best guess is the Chinese, or maybe Iranians.'

'Or maybe some kids who were bunking off school,' suggested Woodhouse maliciously. 'And O'Hara's death – suicide maybe?'

The captain shook his head ruefully.

'It's a helluva thing; he was a good man. We thought maybe the IRA. He was Irish, you know – his great-grandmother was from Swan-sea.'

Woodhouse smiled.

'I suppose it might be a possibility. They're a vengeful bunch, those Scandinavians. No doubt they viewed his having been born several generations removed and on a different continent as an elaborate form of betrayal... If they're sworn to kill every American who thinks he's Irish you'll have your hands full clearing up the mess, that's for sure.' Woodhouse stood up, yawning. 'In any case, Captain, it's been delightful chatting with you – you really are a most engaging fellow – but I'd better run along now and see if I can't find this helicopter of yours. I don't suppose there's anything helpful like a tracking device on the thing?'

Short shrugged helplessly.

'It hadn't been activated yet, apparently. They'd only just finished installing it.'

'Of course.' Woodhouse nodded. 'That would have been far too easy.'

Woodhouse left the captain sitting mournfully behind his desk and went out into the real world. Or so he imagined.

The bane of Cubby's otherwise comfortable life was the cats. He hated them, and this was unfortunate since Grandfather had inserted a clause into his will stipulating that, for a period of not less than five years, Cubby must open the pottery to the public for a minimum of forty hours each week and fire at least two hundred cats per month, or the properties would be sold and the proceeds divided among various charities. Grandmother had agreed to these terms on the condition that she would be allowed to remain in the house in the event of her husband's death. If the conditions had been breached during her lifetime, a sum would have been allotted for her to enter a nursing home.

Possibly Grandfather had meant well, imagining that the boy's love for ceramic cats matched his own, but in fact Cubby loathed them and every moment he spent with them was a torment. He hated cats and he hated ornaments and he hated clay, and his hatred was evident in every cat that he produced. Grandfather's cats had been sickeningly twee and a bit simple looking but Cubby's were nothing short of terrifying. Their expressions ranged from twisted malevolence to sensual sadism, encompassing hideous brutality and casual insanity along the way. It was impossible to set eyes on these monstrosities without feeling one's mind scrabble queasily for purchase as every belief was brought into question and every value callously dashed.

Cubby's cats were nasty. Row upon vicious row of glazed nightmares staring balefully into one's soul. Children who did not cry in the cat pottery were very much in the minority, and one woman had actually wet herself on beholding one of Cubby's less sympathetic creations. Cubby was not at all a bad man but his cats were seriously bad juju. The only people likely to buy them might be those who regarded Satanism as too middle-of-the-road, or someone subconsciously sentencing themselves to a karmic kicking for terrible crimes committed during a previous incarnation. These were cats symptomatic of the deep resentment inherent in their compulsory production and, consequently, each cat that pounced meanly from the kiln was more savagely unholy than the last. These cats could really fuck with your chakras, man.

Tallulah Grimes walked past Cubby's pottery every day on her way to and from her job at the bakery. She was a small girl with golden-blonde curls, a pretty face and soulful grey eyes; the kind of girl that women envy and men want to protect, and maybe defile. The youngest of three sisters, her childhood had been happy and possibly a little too sheltered and, as she blossomed into young womanhood, she had discovered, and indulged, a taste for dangerous men and the darker side of life, safe in the knowledge that if things got too real she could run back from her little flat above a greengrocer's shop to the family home, where her parents would cosset her and she could shock any visiting sisters with tales of her unusual sex life and recreational drug use.

Tallulah was a sweet girl who had been spoiled all her life because of her radiant good looks, but underneath the sweetness simmered a masochistic streak and a need to feel soiled – to assuage her guilty suspicion that she had had it all too easy.

Of course, there were plenty of wild young – and not so young – men only too willing to help her in these matters, and if sometimes one of them went too far and she had to go in to work with a split lip or a black eye, then it was no more than she deserved, she felt, and if, more often than not, she wept as she showered away the semen, flushed with shame as she remembered the oafish laughter, and winced as she numbered the bruises and welts so carelessly given, she felt excitement too and looked forward to the next time.

On this particular morning it was raining steadily as Tallulah walked to work nursing a fat lip courtesy of a pair of drunken bricklayers. She had been drunk too but not drunk enough to easily forget their casual discussion of City's new striker as they tore away at the tatters of her resentful innocence. She tilted her head back and closed her eyes momentarily to let the raindrops kiss her battered face, and Cubby, watching from across the road as he opened his pottery, felt her ethereal beauty wrench desperately at his tender heart. She must have felt his gaze on her because she looked round suddenly and gave him a tentative smile. His heart started leaping about in his chest like a landed fish and her spell wrapped around him like a golden cloak and held him there transfixed.

In his Parisian penthouse, the man with the antique ivory ear shudders and bares his teeth. Something is wrong. Random flashes of happiness from the cosmos are interfering with his enjoyment of human misery. Snippets of kindness, courtesy, and – foul belch of a word – *love* keep mingling incongruously with the usual pain and woe on which he thrives. He undoes the chased silver buckle and removes his ear, hissing when he feels the blood returning to his face as the straps fall away. He scowls at the ear, blows into it, mutters some kind of dark incantation and presses it to his chest, where his black and twisted heart beats out its rhythm of cruelty.

The intense heat again, interminable, but the pain is more bearable now somehow. Just as his body is hardening, so his mind is hardening too, perhaps. For this eternal suffering, he vows, there shall be a reckoning...

Woodhouse parked his car on a stretch of heathland owned by the Ministry of Defence. He needed to consider his next move and he needed to acquaint himself with the modifications that had been made to the Jag. Was it possible that the theft of the helicopter was linked to this shadowy Lomax character? And if so, what did he intend to do with it, and when?

Woodhouse removed the list of modifications from the glovebox and cursed bitterly: the print was so blurred that it was completely illegible. Useless bastards! He shrugged and reached out to the console that had been mounted unobtrusively beneath the dashboard. He flicked a switch at random. There was a click and a whoosh as a small rocket streaked out – from behind the number plate, Woodhouse guessed – and decimated a stunted pine tree some thirty metres ahead of the parked Jaguar. Not bad! He pressed a red button that looked interesting and twin streams of machine-gun fire arced out from either wing, converging to strike chips and splinters from the stump of the same tree. They stopped when he took his finger off the button. Nice! This was fun! He jiggled a toggle and a jet of oil spurted out to the rear of the vehicle. Bit boring... Now a button under the driver's seat – fucking hell! The sun roof shot back and, with a springy clunk and a loud roar, the passenger seat ejected, flying high into the air and spinning slowly in the sunlight before falling lazily back to earth, where it landed with a thump and a rustle in a gorse bush some distance away. Woodhouse supposed he should think himself lucky it hadn't come straight back down and killed him.

Getting out of the car he slipped on the oil and fell on his backside, ruining his trousers. Bollocks! He limped over to the bush and lifted out the seat, scratching himself quite badly in the process. The vintage tan leather upholstery was a mess, scuffed and scraped to buggery. Someone would pay for this, he vowed. Walking back to the car he fell in the oil again. He fitted the seat roughly back into place and, not wishing to get oil on the driver's seat, took off his trousers and underpants and rolled them up in the passenger footwell, on top of the cassettes. This was turning into a bad day. He started the car and began the journey back to London. The soft leather of the seat felt cool on his bare scrotum.

As he negotiated the journey home, Woodhouse's mind gently slipped its moorings like a neglected rowing boat with a coots' nest on board and, accompanied by the comical cries of the bewildered birds, gradually picked up speed until – with one broken oar poking crazily up through a rusted rowlock, and filling with water as it went – it spun into the turbulent waters of his childhood, where it began to fall apart.

The sunset bestows a benevolent glow on the bedroom of young Woodhouse. All is well with the rocking horse, the teddy bear's fur gleams complacently and under the covers the sleepy boy wriggles his toes contentedly. Soon Mother would be up to read him another chapter of *The Wind in the Willows*. Rat and Mole were on their way to Badger's house. Woodhouse liked Badger best: he was so gruff and stern and yet, it seemed to the innocent mind of the infant, beneath the regimental exterior there beat the passionate heart of a romantic. Yes: Badger, he is best. The warm feeling seemed to intensify as the boy contemplated his feelings for the anthropomorphic woodland creature and, as the light died, his hand slipped quietly beneath the bedclothes.

Gloriously entangled in furious consideration of the militaristic yet kind-hearted animal, the enraptured boy fails to notice his mother enter the darkened room.

'Darling,' she coos. 'Are you awake?' Placing her martini glass on the blanket box with only a slight stumble, she takes the book from under her arm and approaches. 'Darling, is there something wrong? What are you doing under there? Let Mummy see.'

She puts the book on the bedside table and pulls back the covers just as the onanistic boy realises that he has inadvertently been offending God.

'Ooh!' they exclaim simultaneously, the mother in shocked surprise, the son in badger-fuelled pre-pubescent ecstasy.

'Really!' she scolds. 'You are a naughty rancid *pelican* boy and you have made Mummy cross.'

The guilt-ridden boy hastily covers himself.

'Badger,' he blurts. 'Badger made me.'

'Badger?' repeats Maude disbelievingly. *'Badger?'*

She switches on the bedside light and Woodhouse can see that her demeanour is altering. The elegantly tipsy and gracefully maternal figure he loves so dearly seems to be changing, becoming hunched and gnarled and somehow much less pleasant than before. Her classically beautiful facial features are rearranging themselves into an expression that seems to comprise sinister elements of retardation and animal cunning, together with a disturbing undercurrent of probable sexual deviancy, although to the child, of course, she just looks scary. She is still some months away from the accident that will cost her her eye and her leg, yet her body seems, somehow, to anticipate her future disabilities and tip a knowing wink to them.

'Badger?' she snarls, rolling one eye and stamping her foot. 'Nothing will come of *Badger.*' She places her hands on her hips. 'The wind in the willows blows cold as the grave, young man.' She pauses then smiles conspiratorially. 'The banqueting hall is full of weasels and the canary-yellow caravan is smashed beyond repair.'

The boy pulls the bedclothes up over his face until only his wide eyes remain uncovered, fixed unwaveringly on his mother, who now wags her finger at him knowingly.

'I suppose,' she says silkily, 'you think you can dress up as a washerwoman and escape the consequences of these actions. I *suppose*,' she cries, 'you think you can ride up front with the engine driver, you horrible little toad!'

'We haven't got to that bit yet,' mumbles Woodhouse through the covers.

Maude runs her hands roughly through her dark hair, disordering it. Her eyes narrow and glitter at the cowering boy.

'You've got broken motorcars in your coach house,' she insinuates. 'And I daresay you maltreat the old grey horse.'

'I wouldn't,' protests the boy indistinctly from beneath the eiderdown. 'Honestly, Mum.'

'And spare a thought for poor Mole,' insists his mother, her voice thrumming with emotion. 'Sobbing on a tree stump because you kept him from his spring cleaning and he misses his little home. Poor, loyal, honest, innocent Mole, sobbing his homesick heart out on a tree stump because of *you*. For shame, Richard, for shame…' She brushes a tear from her eye and her expression hardens. 'I think you are not a *nice* animal, Richard. I think you are a filthy weasel, or a stoat, perhaps, skulking there with yourself. I think to the Wild Wood you must go, to seek out the patronage of your beloved Badger. And then we shall see… Oh yes, indeed… (She grimaces disgustedly.) Faugh! Badger, indeed! Fiddlesticks!'

She snatches the book up from the bedside table and sweeps angrily from the room, knocking her martini glass off the blanket box and slamming the door behind her.

All is no longer well with the rocking horse: its expression is sullen, verging on mutinous. And the teddy bear looks like shit. But Woodhouse is a child and he is tired so he sleeps.

And so Tallulah turned her ankle opposite Cubby's cat pottery. It was inevitable really: fate had to lend a hand or the boy would never have dared approach her. He was putting out his A-board and he watched her fall, spellbound, as passing traffic blurred between them. Her ankle buckled and she tumbled gracefully to the pavement in a beautiful heap, her grey eyes startled, her damp blonde curls extravagantly dishevelled and her clothes and limbs in seductive disarray. She gave just the slightest gasp and then came to rest like an angel in the rain, biting her already painful lip.

Cubby ran straight out into the traffic without looking and across the road without a scratch, oblivious to the screeching tyres and shouted curse. As he approached the girl she seemed to come into very sharp focus and, incongruously, he thought he heard the cry of a peacock.

'Can you stand up?' he heard himself say through the sound of the blood roaring in his ears.

She took his arm and he helped her to stand, painfully aware of the soft curves beneath her clothes.

'Try and put some weight on it,' he suggested.

Gingerly she tried the ankle.

'Ow! It really hurts!' she exclaimed. 'I can't walk.'

'I'll carry you,' said Cubby, astonishing himself with his bravery. 'It's only over there. You can sit down once we get inside and I'll make some tea while we work out what to do.'

She looked at him as if noticing him for the first time, which in a sense she was.

'Okay, then,' she said, giving him a look that warned on more than one level. 'But don't drop me.'

'I won't,' said Cubby, unable to believe his luck. 'I promise.'

Cubby might have been somewhat overweight but he was young and strong, and he picked Tallulah Grimes up as though she weighed nothing and carried her carefully across the road, making sure to look both ways first this time, and over the threshold of the pottery. She caught her breath and her eyes grew very large as she took in the ranks of cats staring at her from every conceivable angle.

'My God,' she said reverently, 'they're beautiful!'

'I made them myself,' said Cubby foolishly, 'in the workshop.'

Very gently he put Tallulah down into Grandfather's old wing-backed armchair and looked at the cats anew. Perhaps they really *were* beautiful; was it possible…? No, they were definitely ugly and menacing. Clearly this girl was so beautiful in herself that where others saw only misery and torment in poorly rendered feline form, she beheld hope and the possibility of redemption. That she might be a little crazy never crossed his mind. She was his muse, after all.

'My name is Pendleton Arbuthnot,' blurted Cubby. 'But I'm called Cubby.' He held out his hand stiffly.

'I'm Tallulah,' said Tallulah, taking his hand momentarily. 'Some people call me T or Taz but those people sicken and disgust me.'

'Hahahahaha,' laughed Cubby nervously, thinking she had made a joke. 'Tallulah is a beautiful name. Would you like some tea?'

'That would be nice.' She looked around at the cats and flexed her sore ankle as Cubby busied himself round the corner with the gas hob. 'Pendleton Arbuthnot is not a very beautiful name. Why are you called Cubby?'

'I don't know,' said Cubby, who didn't.

'I've seen you in the shop, haven't I? You asked me for a cream horn and then dropped all your change on the floor.'

In his confusion, Cubby fumbled with the tea caddy and knocked a mean-spirited looking tabby off a shelf with his elbow, managing to break its fall with his foot. He was glad she couldn't see him blushing.

'Oh, uh, yeah, I was a bit drunk that day,' he improvised. 'I'd been playing cards with my friends and drinking, uh, tequila. And stuff.'

What was he saying? Cubby used to feel drunk if he smelt sherry on Grandmother's breath. Why was he lying? Oh God! He had been doing so well up until now. There was a pause while the water heated.

'Do you often get drunk with your friends in the morning, Cubby?' Tallulah asked.

He could hear the amusement in her voice. The old kettle began to rattle and wheeze on the hob. His hands were shaking as he spooned tea from the caddy into the pot.

'We were up all night, you know. It was, uh, Moose's birthday.'

Moose! Why had he said that? No English person could have a friend called Moose.

'Moose? I don't think I know him. Is he a local boy?'

The kettle was emitting preparatory squeaks and wisps of steam. The palms of Cubby's hands were sweating. He fixed his eyes desperately on the Chinese lacquered tea tray: an old man in baggy clothes was fishing by a little wooden bridge, under a willow tree.

'No, he's, uh, he's an American-type boy. From Omaha, I think.'

He couldn't hear her reply, as the kettle started shrieking and jumping about as if in panic. He filled the teapot and carried the things through on the tray to where Tallulah sat among the cats, frowning at her phone.

'I need to call work,' she said as Cubby placed the tray on a small table next to her chair.

He went across to the kitchen of the house to get some milk while she made the call. From the freezer he took a bag of frozen peas, for her ankle.

'I told them I'm not coming in,' she said when he returned. 'Claire can manage.'

He handed her the peas and placed a footstool in front of her.

'You need to elevate it and get some ice on there,' he explained in response to her quizzical look. 'To reduce the swelling.'

She took off her shoe and, with a grimace, lifted her leg on to the stool and placed the peas on her ankle, which was starting to turn blue. Her skirt momentarily revealed her knees, which were shapely. She saw him looking and smiled slightly.

'Thanks,' she said, presumably with reference to his consideration rather than his lechery.

Cubby felt himself blush. She was beautiful. They looked at each other for a moment. The cats looked at both of them.

'Your friend Moose,' she ventured mischievously. 'Was he on the high school football team back in Omaha? In movies the guy called Moose is always a jock. Not a Scotsman – I mean an athlete. He always wears one of those jackets with a number on the back and he's none too bright. Very often he's a bully too. Is your friend like that?'

'Um, no, not really,' mumbled Cubby, unable to meet her eye. 'He's quite nice.'

'Do you have a friend called Skeeter too? Kind of a half-wit? Always laughs at Moose's jokes?' She was laughing herself and Cubby couldn't help joining in.

'I don't really have a friend called Moose,' he admitted.

'I'm glad to hear it,' said Tallulah. 'He would've been a dick.'

'Yes,' said Cubby. 'Yes he would.' He began to pour the tea; they were still laughing. 'What happened to your lip?' he asked, and regretted it immediately.

The smile vanished from her face and she froze in the act of lifting her mug of tea from the tray. She put it back down hard and the tea slopped over.

'That's none of your business. None of your fucking business, mate.'

'I'm sorry,' said Cubby miserably. 'I didn't mean anything.' There was an awkward pause.

They heard the *ting-a-ling-a-ling* of the bell above the shop door and the sound of laughter, which was immediately stilled. Cubby got up and went through. A young woman and a child stood in the shop doorway, gazing open-mouthed at the cats. Cubby could hear Tallulah speaking in urgent tones, presumably on the phone.

'Good morning,' he said brightly to the prospective customers. 'Can I help you?'

'We're just… *looking*…' the woman replied, unable to take her eyes from the horror of Cubby's creations.

There was a rising wail like the commencement of a Chrysler air raid siren attack tone. The child, a grimy faced boy, was preparing to signal his discontent.

'Waaaaaaah!' he bawled. 'Scareeeeeeee! Mummeeeeee! Scareeeeeeee! Waaaaaaah!'

'It's all right, darling, we're leaving.'

She picked up the boy, shot Cubby a look of mingled fear and loathing, and then they were gone, setting the bell jingling again. As the jingling died away it was replaced by a funereal silence, heavy as velvet, and then a distant muffled thudding, increasing in volume as it grew closer. It proved to be emanating from a menacing looking black car which pulled up outside. Evidently the thuds and accompanying shouts were part of some strange tribal rhythm.

The music stopped and an aggressive looking individual got out of the car and swaggered across the road, hitching up his tracksuit bottoms, flicking away his cigarette end and spitting eloquently. He entered the pottery, shouldering Cubby out of the way and sneering. He smelt of cooking lager, marijuana and chip fat, and his demeanour was Neanderthal in the extreme.

'Oi, Taz,' he roared. 'Tazza, move your arse, girl! Time is money, innit.'

Tallulah hop-hobbled through from the back, glowering and pulling her hair back into a pony tail. Cubby stood aside to let her pass.

'I hope your ankle gets better soon,' he said weakly.

'Yeah, whatever – bell end!' she replied nastily, tossing her head.

The unpleasant character half-helped, half-dragged her across the road to his threatening looking vehicle as the bell jingled again, and with a squeal of tyres they were gone, the diminishing thuds and shouts fading away to leave Cubby disconsolate and bereft. Without looking he reached for the nearest cat, a demented tortoiseshell, and dashed it to pieces on the floor. Dolefully he went to fetch a brush and dustpan.

He sits very still in the large claw-footed bath as the manservant shaves his head with a gold safety razor. His precious ivory ear rests nearby on a purple velvet cushion; he never lets it out of his sight. He is not a small man: in his youth he was a bare-knuckle fighter and he is still heavily muscled, although running slightly to fat as he approaches sixty. He has many tattoos. On his back is a scene like a painting by Hieronymus Bosch, a vision of hell. The figures depicted there seem to writhe in the flames as his musculature flexes when he soaps himself. The manservant does not like to see this. The massive arms are covered in runes and symbols, dark incantations to a bitter god. He has many scars, great slashes, some with the marks of stitches. There is one on his shoulder that is obviously a bullet wound and down one thigh a grouping that could well be the spread of a shotgun blast. He has fought hard and overcome many obstacles to be where he is today, in this massive marble bathroom.

He bares his teeth and gives a satisfied hiss. Without his ear he cannot hear the pain of the fallen, but he senses the echoes and is well satisfied. It marches. A sharp pain: the imbecile has cut him. He puts a finger to his head and it comes away red. The servant begins to stammer an apology as his boss takes hold of his wrist. The huge knuckles are covered in scar tissue; maybe there is still a tooth or two in there? He begins to twist the servant's arm, still hissing. The tattoos flicker and dance and the razor clatters to the floor. He turns his head slowly and looks into the servant's eyes as he continues to twist. The wrist fractures with a sharp crack and the man throws back his head and laughs with the sheer exultation of it all and the terrified servant with the broken wrist joins in.

On the table, by the cushion on which the ivory ear sits, a telephone rings. The man in the bath reaches out a huge hand and lifts the receiver. He listens intently to the voice on the other end.

'Good,' he says. 'Very good. This is pleasing to me.'

He replaces the handset and rises from the bath. The servant averts his eyes and hands him a towel with his unbroken arm. Lomax takes the towel with his left hand and knocks the servant unconscious with a backhanded blow from his right. His head is still bleeding. He dries himself, hissing and humming something that might be Bach, and carefully straps on his ear. He dons a large white towelling dressing gown and, with the bloodstained towel draped round his neck, walks barefoot from the bathroom, ignoring the motionless form stretched out on the marble floor.

He glances at the banks of screens as he passes through his office. All is well: cruelty and misery abound. Smiling, he walks into the living area of his suite, nodding to a muscular flunky who stands guard there. Two sides of the room are glass and the night-time lights of the great city are spread out around and below. On one of the several sofas a dishevelled girl in her underwear sits cross-legged, snorting the closest of the lines of powder racked neatly up on the table in front of her. In a large tank behind her a rattlesnake watches and sounds its warning. Without breaking stride, Lomax snaps his fingers at the flunky and gestures towards the girl. As he ascends the stone staircase at the end of the room, he can hear her slurred wails of protest behind him as she is escorted away.

At the top of the wide stairs he feels the night breeze and smells the heavy scent of jasmine as he steps out into the roof garden. Two men approach. Both are dressed in faded combat gear and one is carrying a flying helmet. Lomax joins them and together they walk through the fruit trees, some of which are in flower.

In a central area, crouched on the mosaic tiles as if ready to spring, engine ticking gently as it cools, sits the Sikorsky Stealth Hawk. The angled planes of its black fuselage seem to soak up the light from the surrounding Chinese lanterns, and white cherry blossom falls lightly through the rotor blades. Lomax gives a satisfied hiss as he takes in the scene.

'Beautiful,' he says. 'Truly beautiful. You have done well, my good boys, very well. She is no good for the fruit, perhaps, but still.'

He puts his great arms around the shoulders of the two men and hugs them to him, and they are careful not to notice that his dressing gown has fallen open.

'Cover her up,' he says, releasing them. 'She must wait her time.'

The pilots hurry away and begin to unroll a huge tarpaulin which has been waiting to one side, already roped to one of the high pergolas that surround the area on which the stolen helicopter stands. The tarpaulin is circular like the mosaic and bears the exact same pattern. Lomax makes a minute adjustment to the straps holding his ivory ear and turns to go back inside. There is much to be done and his head is still bleeding.

In the streets surrounding the building topped by Lomax's penthouse there is sudden confusion: it is a warm night but it appears to be snowing. On closer inspection, however, the snowflakes prove to be petals falling mysteriously from who knows where. One young man is so overwhelmed by the beauty and the romance of it all that he drops to one knee amid the blossom and proposes marriage to his girlfriend of seven months. Sadly for him, she is more pragmatic and demurs.

A fumbling at his eye socket and then a sudden pressure followed by the blurred image of an enormous bumbling figure, gradually becoming clearer as it turns away and then back to face him again. An impression of a huge face hanging over him and of a hand approaching his own unknown physiognomy. A hand, between the thumb and forefinger of which is an eye. He feels fumbling and pressure at his other eye socket now, and then the figure draws back. He uses his new eyes to glare at it as it seems to consider him.

'Hideous,' it says ruefully. 'Oh well...'

In the days following Tallulah's mishap Cubby loses weight. Not only is he sick at heart but he is too afraid to visit the bakery, so his diet improves by default. Once or twice he sees Tallulah walk haltingly by but more often she is driven by the troglodyte in the thudding black car. The cats Cubby produces during this time wear a more plaintive aspect than previously. He even sells one, to a doddery old woman reminiscent of Parma Violets and urine. He misses Tallulah and he misses pastry. It's a shame.

Woodhouse's drive back to town was relatively uneventful until some children in a people carrier next to him at the junction of a roundabout noticed his state of undress from their elevated viewpoint. They loudly brought it to the attention of their parents but Woodhouse was able to end their furious pursuit with a judicious touch of the oil-release toggle on a bend in the road. He only heard a slight bang after they spun out of sight and, as the bang was unaccompanied by a smash or explosion, he assumed the family would be relatively unhurt. Such incidents of collateral damage were unfortunate but unavoidable, he felt. The chain of events that had led to his semi-naked motoring had to do with matters of national security and sometimes it was necessary to take immediate action rather than waste time with awkward explanations. That's what Woodhouse told himself, anyway, and he was pretty sure he was right.

He managed to park and let himself into his flat without any further alarms. His neighbours were used to his ways and had learned to turn a blind eye to unusual goings-on. After putting the oily clothes in the washing machine and showering, Woodhouse dressed in the black silk kung fu suit he liked to wear to relax and poured himself a large gin and tonic. He switched on the answering machine and settled into the sofa with a satisfied sigh. There were a couple of messages from a disgruntled ex-girlfriend, another about an unpaid bill, and then this:

'Oh God, Richard! Not this bloody machine again. It's your aunt – it's Rosalind. He's done it again – John, I mean. I'm at my wits' end. We had some people from the neighbourhood watch over and he drank too much sherry. He followed Judy Warren into the bathroom, Richard, and seized her breasts! Like some wild beast! It was awful. She screamed the place down and I didn't know where to put myself, I was that mortified. Then Carl Warren punched John on the nose and they had a fight and broke the standard lamp and I can't get the blood out of the pile. I'll never live it down, Richard, never! Phone me. It's your aunt – it's Rosalind. Like a wild animal he was…'

There was a click as she disconnected, and Woodhouse took a sip of his drink as he digested the message. There were no such people as Aunt Rosalind and Uncle John; it was a coded message from control. Rosalind's continual complaints about John's fictional misdemeanours were the way in which Woodhouse's superiors chose to contact him. He wondered why they couldn't just call his mobile. Neighbourhood watch was MI5; the bathroom represented the location where Woodhouse was ordered to report; and the fact that John had seized Mrs Warren's breasts like a wild beast meant that Woodhouse should attend at ten-thirty the following morning. If John had lunged at her vagina like a crazy person it would have signified eleven forty-five that same night. That John had drunk sherry meant that Woodhouse should consider himself on standby and be ready to travel within the EU. The broken standard lamp was bad: it meant there had been some fatalities. The cuckoo clock would have been worse but the standard lamp was bad enough. Shit! Blood on the carpet was bad too... It was a complicated code but it kept them all amused, Woodhouse supposed. He switched on the television. One of the *Rocky* films was on; Woodhouse couldn't tell which one. Paulie was swigging from a bottle and seemed angry about something. Rocky mumbled something that Woodhouse couldn't quite catch. Fuck it!

Tallulah didn't really know why she hung around with Craig – unless it was for the free drugs. He spent his days driving around listening to hip-hop and delivering weed, coke and rock to other, lowlier, lowlifes. Often he would stop for a beer and help the customer smoke or otherwise inhale the merchandise in some shithole of a flat or filthy council house. When she wasn't working in the bakery, Tallulah would tag along and sit getting wasted and feeling superior to whatever loser they were rinsing at the time. Even though her own flat wasn't much to shout about, she knew it was only temporary with her; she wasn't in it for the long haul. Most of Craig's customers were intimidated by him, so his fee for delivery might end up being as much as half their gear, and Tallulah was included in the rounds of whatever substance was being abused, by virtue of being his companion. Plus he always had plenty of personal to hand as well.

She didn't fancy him much, although they had sex sometimes, more for something to do than anything else. He didn't have a particularly subtle sense of humour and his personal hygiene wasn't always the best, but he wasn't too difficult to be around and his forbidding presence kept other men at bay, which was useful, as sometimes Tallulah's one-night stands came around for another go, and they didn't always want to take no for an answer.

She didn't often think of Cubby, although she had noticed that he hadn't been into the shop. She was reminded of him whenever someone asked for a cream horn and it always made her smile and then feel unaccountably annoyed. It wasn't Cubby's fault that some bricklayers had knocked her about but she couldn't seem to forgive him for asking about her wounded lip. She remembered too the way he had been looking at her legs, the dirty bugger. He wasn't a bad looking lad but he was a bit too fat and a bit too nice. Tallulah didn't really do nice; she liked her men with a dash of menace.

Probably she would have been more attracted to Cubby's fictional friend Moose, the all-American jock. She would have given him a birthday to remember, all right. They could have made out in the back of his car, and maybe the idiot

Skeeter could have watched and whacked off... Tallulah smiled: maybe it was her that was the dirty bugger after all.

'Well, young Richard,' began Woodhouse's father kindly. 'What are we going to do with you, eh?'

The boy shrugged diffidently and fixed his eyes on the Art Nouveau fire screen in front of him. A peacock motif was embossed on the brass. Since the unfortunate incident at story time some weeks previously, Woodhouse's mother had begun to drink more heavily, and the drawing room in which they sat bore mute testament to the fact. She had used the poker to gouge the eyes out of the Victorian oil painting of a stern looking matriarch, viciously muttering something about ancestral invasions of privacy. Both china dogs on the mantle had been beheaded, and she had taken a hatchet to the front leg of the grand piano, which was now propped up with leather-bound volumes of Thackeray and Trollope. The word "WANER" had been carved roughly into the Jacobean panelling above the fireplace, although Mother hotly denied responsibility for this, perhaps because of the presumable misspelling and the rudeness of the workmanship.

'Your mother's not been well,' said Father unnecessarily.

There was a fresh ding and a scratch on the fire screen to the left of the peacock's tail where the brass shone more brightly, Mother having hurled her high-ball glass at it in a flamboyant fit of pique after Woodhouse had unwisely asked her to read him a story.

'No, Father,' replied Woodhouse, hanging his head and fighting back tears.

'Sometimes in a young man's life there comes a time when he must step forward into the breach and embrace the splendid adventure. All his life lies before him, filled with great promise and myriad possibilities. Truly, Richard, the best days of one's life.'

'Yes, Father.' He concentrated on preventing his lip wobbling. He could hardly see the fire screen through the tears welling in his eyes.

'One day, my boy, you will sit here as I do now, perhaps with a fine son of your own, and you will say to that boy: "Play up, play up and play the game, my boy, and have no fear. Follow in the footsteps of your father, and your father's father, and his father before him, and it will make you the man I am today!" And your fine manly son will reply: "Yes, Father, I will perform many brave deeds, and in the fullness of time I will become the man you are today and instruct my own fine manly son to have the courage of his convictions and be of stout heart in order that he, in turn, shall one day become the man I intend to be and father to a fine manly son of his own." Do you understand, Richard?'

'No, Father.'

'We're sending you to boarding school.'

The boy's whole life was swept away in a tsunami of tears, one of which even landed on the fire screen, where it ran down the face of the peacock as though the bird itself were weeping. Woodhouse couldn't see it though; his eyes were full of tears.

A legal assistant for Grandfather's lawyers looked in on Cubby every couple of months or so to ensure that he was meeting the conditions of the will. He always arrived unexpectedly, and at first the inspections had been fairly thorough. It soon became apparent, though, that since Cubby was compelled to produce fifty cats a week and sold virtually none, there were now so many of the things that it was impossible to keep track of them. Not only that, but the creatures were so disturbing that to inspect them in any detail would be to actively court psychosis.

Mr Gruber was a quiet young-ish gentleman of serious aspect, always impeccably groomed, his wispy blond hair side-parted and plastered to his egg-shaped head and his gaze intent through gold-rimmed glasses. He did not believe himself to be an imaginative man but he had had several vivid nightmares about Cubby's cats and, as he approached the pottery, he could feel his palms begin to sweat and feelings of panic rose in his chest like birds alarmed by a predator. He shouldn't have come back. Oh God!

He steeled himself and pushed open the door. He had anticipated the jingling of the bell but it made him jump nonetheless. Inside the shop it was dark, occasional spotlights revealing the looming ranks of inhospitable cats. Gruber tried not to make eye contact with any of them. Cubby wandered through from the back wearing a potter's smock. He looked as if he had been crying.

'Good morning, Mr Arbuthnot,' said Gruber. 'I trust I find you in good health?'

'As well as can be expected I suppose,' returned the potter mournfully.

'Just popped in to cast an eye over your latest, er, creations.'

Cubby led the way through to the pottery and gestured vaguely towards some shapes huddled on a large work surface near the kiln. Gruber took a deep shuddering breath and moved to examine them more – but hopefully not too – closely. There were thirty or forty cats arranged in a rough circle, some sitting up, some recumbent or frozen in attitudes of play, but all facing inwards to where one particular cat sat. He was the *leader*, realised Gruber, and his mind gave a horrible sinking lurch.

The leader of Cubby's latest batch was a Japanese waving cat. It was black and white and bore a striking resemblance to Adolf Hitler. It sat in the middle of a ring of adherents with one of its front paws raised in an approximation of a Nazi salute. The black smudge under its nose and lopsided black patch on its head lent credence to this unpleasant impression, although Hitler's comic pomposity was replaced by ceramic feline menace. The Hitler-cat appeared to be glaring at a tabby which was lying on its back with a ball of yarn and a lovesick expression. Gruber's perspective seemed to distort and zoom in to the circle of cats until he was surrounded by them. He felt nauseated. Cubby was looking at him curiously.

'I've got my eye on you, Gruber,' said the Führer of the Cats. Its voice was like rats in a tin bath and Gruber's mind shrank away in horror. 'I've got my eye on you and I don't like what I see.'

Reluctantly Gruber looked at its eyes. The awful cathedral-glass gaze went into his brain like a chisel and there seemed to be a murmur from the assembled throng. *Adolf Kitler,* he thought wildly: *Adolf Kitler – the Furred Reich.* He didn't care for this thought at all. A terrible laugh was forming deep down in the bowels of his psyche and he knew that if he gave voice to it, it would grow into a scream that would go on forever.

'I'm going to scratch you, Gruber. I'm going to tear your tiny mind to ribbons. *Ribbons*, Gruber.'

His mouth was dry. The remorseless glass stare seemed to turn in his brain like an auger and still the laugh was building inside, beginning to bubble as it came to the boil. Now all the cats in the circle were looking at him. His eyes rolled back in his head and he opened his mouth to let out the laughter. Goodbye sanity, goodbye forever…

'Would you like a cup of tea, Mr Gruber?' asked Cubby solicitously. 'You look a bit tired.'

The cats turned their eyes away in disgust and the laugh was quelled, but Gruber knew its echo would abide in him always.

'No, thank you just the same, Mr Arbuthnot, I really should be getting along. Everything seems to be in order here.'

Could anything be further from the truth? He bobbed his head at Cubby in lieu of a handshake – his hands were soaked with sweat – and forced himself to walk slowly out of the shop. As he moved between the rows of cats he could almost, but not quite, hear them laughing at him in horrid squeaky, scratchy voices.

Woodhouse awoke early in a jaunty mood. He disliked being summoned by the old man but he wasn't prepared to let it spoil his day. Whatever the problem was he would be equal to it. He drew back the curtains and the sun streamed in through the cane blind. Yawning, he dressed in the tracksuit bottoms and T-shirt he wore for working out and went sleepily downstairs to his gym.

Woodhouse's gym was one of his vanities: the machines had been made from various vehicles he had crashed in the line of duty or recreationally. He turned on the stereo. It amused him to listen to heavy metal music while he lifted weights, and Anthrax's ebullient debut *Fistful of Metal* was a favourite. As the guitar intro to *Deathrider* progressed through bass and drum stabs, he settled himself into the driver's seat of his first car (a customised Ford Capri he had wrapped round a tree while pursuing an arms dealer), took hold of the handlebars of his old Triumph Bonneville (stacked into the back of a removal van on the North Circular) and began to lift the weights: two V6 engine blocks.

Even the pulley system utilised parts from the wrecked vehicles: cables, pistons, the back wheel of the Bonneville. The ceiling fan was fashioned from the tail rotor of a Lynx that Woodhouse had crashed in Armagh. As a ceiling fan it was rubbish but it looked cool, even if it did wobble about alarmingly and dislodge plaster. He hated and feared helicopters and hoped he never had to go up in another one, much less pilot it. Even looking at the rotor made the old injury at the base of his spine ache, but still he kept it there. Woodhouse supposed he must be sentimental.

Workout over, he shat, showered and shaved and, wearing his vintage Chinese dressing gown (lingering garden motif), made coffee and scrambled eggs for breakfast. He allowed himself to smoke a roll-up with the coffee though he knew he should give them up. Sighing ever so slightly, he dressed in a navy pinstripe suit and ran his fingers through his blond hair, which had a tendency toward unruliness. If he had to go into the city he might as well look the part, he supposed. At the last moment he remembered that he might need his passport. His photo made him look like a serial killer, which he supposed he was, albeit sanctioned by HM government.

As he left the flat, carrying a tightly furled umbrella despite the sunshine, he saw his car being taken away for yet more work and gave the technical boys a cheery wave. He had planned to go in on the Tube anyway, but he hoped the Jag wouldn't become part of his workout equipment anytime soon.

He walked the short distance to the St John's Wood Tube station among the commuters and took a train, disliking the crowds and the invasion of his personal space but still retaining his good mood. Alighting at Green Park he ascended, emerging blinded by the sudden sunlight near The Ritz. He had once fallen down the stairs in there, having drunk too many cocktails in the bar. Extremely embarrassing… It was the Ritz 100s that had done the damage – they were lethal! He was a little early for his appointment so he got a coffee and sat in the park and smoked another roll-up. The sunshine was warm on his face and life wasn't so bad, perhaps.

He checked his watch. Bollocks! Better go and see what the old man wants. He left the park and walked down Piccadilly, through dithering tourists, into a side street where he rapped on a tatty grey door with his brolly.

The door was opened by a man wearing high visibility gear and a hard hat. He glanced at Woodhouse's proffered ID card and ushered him in, closing the door behind them.

'Morning, sir,' he said in surprisingly well-bred tones. 'Bit of a hike, I'm afraid.'

They walked across a dimly lit area and descended an aluminium spiral staircase. The walls around them were tiled in the Art Deco style, and grimy apart from occasional finger marks. The clang of their footsteps echoed in the stairwell and as they neared the bottom Woodhouse could hear the rattle and rush of a distant Tube train. The man dressed as a workman led the way down a narrow corridor and Woodhouse's shoulder brushed against the wall, making a dirty smudge on his jacket.

'Cleaner's day off, is it?' he inquired irritably.

They turned right, down a flight of stairs and emerged into a large tunnel. On a raised section of the disused platform were a desk, a filing cabinet and a standard lamp, and at the desk sat Greaves, fiddling with his pipe as usual. As if this were not incongruous enough, he was wearing a blazer, Panama hat and the egg and bacon tie of the Marylebone Cricket Club.

'Ah, there you are,' he said, tamping tobacco into his pipe bowl. 'Good weather for batting.'

Woodhouse wondered wryly whether he was referring to cricket or a planned hunting expedition.

'No movement and a nice quick outfield,' he agreed, assuming it was the former, given the man's attire.

Greaves struck a match and puffed fiercely, disappearing momentarily among wreathes of smoke.

'Mm,' he grunted, through his teeth and the pipe stem. 'Once the dew dries out.'

'I gather there's been a development, sir,' ventured Woodhouse, tiring of the small talk.

Greaves opened a file on the desk and leafed through it. He took off his hat.

'Two nights ago, a fishing boat out of Boulogne disappeared. The, ah, *Adrienne*. Three hands on board. It was a calm night, clear but with no moon.' He looked up to make sure Woodhouse was following him, and his glance through the smoke was shrewd. 'Two people on the beach at Cayeux-sur-Mer, further down the coast, saw and heard an explosion out at sea. They had spent the day kite-surfing, whatever that might be, and were relaxing with a bottle of wine.'

'Some kind of mechanical fault?' suggested Woodhouse.

'Well, that would be the obvious conclusion to draw, were it not for the fact that they also say they saw a black shape in the sky.'

'A helicopter-shaped shape.'

'Exactly that.'

'So, somebody spirited a stealth helicopter away from the airbase and for no apparent reason they attacked a fishing boat.'

'Possibly they realised they had been seen by the fishermen. Or they just wanted to make sure the weapons systems were working.'

They looked at each other for a moment. Greaves's pipe had gone out.

'Do you think these witnesses are reliable?' asked Woodhouse.

Greaves consulted the file.

'A brace of young lovers drinking wine under the stars, by the sound of it. All very romantic, and they were doubtless away with the fairies, but it has a ring of truth about it nonetheless, and there's oil on the water in the area where they say they saw the blast, and one or two pieces of wreckage have cropped up.'

'Well, at least we know they have no more than seventeen missiles left.'

'Those fishermen had families, Woodhouse,' said Greaves sternly.

'Of course, sir. I meant no disrespect.'

'The question is: how do we find the damn thing before they use it again? If this was just a weapons check and three people are presumably dead in the water somewhere, then what the hell is going to happen when they get down to business?'

'Realistically, sir, it seems to me that rather than physically searching for the Stealth Hawk, which could be almost anywhere by now, we would do better to concentrate our energies on finding the scent of the people who took it. This Lomax character, for instance, who's been sending these lunatics to kill me – what do we know about him?'

'The short answer to that is nothing. Either your informant was lying or Lomax is not the chap's real name. We looked into it and found nothing, not even whispers.'

'What about the people he hired? Some of them must have had a past. Dental records, tattoos, fingerprints, DNA, all that sort of business. I gave you several corpses, sir.'

'Don't get snippy with me, Woodhouse. I'm a busy man. If you're so interested in corpses perhaps you had better run along to the mortuary and have a little chat with them about it. I believe your friends are still on ice, so to speak.'

Greaves pulled a large gold half-hunter pocket watch from his waistcoat and consulted it meaningfully, which Woodhouse considered the height of affectation. The old boy was worried about missing the start of play at Lord's, no doubt.

'I suppose they're over at Westminster, are they, sir, the deceased?'

'That's right; we've kept them all together for you, Woodhouse, all in the same place. They'll be naming a wing after you soon, I shouldn't wonder.'

Greaves was so pleased with this witticism that he began to laugh wheezily and this soon escalated into a fit of coughing, some of which was channelled into his pipe, causing a small eruption and subsequent ash cloud. He wiped away the tears and, as the ash began to settle on his desk, said:

'Nice of you to drop in, dear boy, don't let me keep you. Come and see me again soon.'

'Absolutely, sir,' said Woodhouse. 'Enjoy your batting.'

Greaves looked momentarily confused.

'Ah, yes, batting… quite so. Good weather for it.'

'Indeed,' replied Woodhouse and, feeling that a circle had been completed, he left.

Woodhouse's mother had become lackadaisical. She roamed the house listlessly, unable to summon the enthusiasm even for vandalism. Dressed in her white silk dressing gown she was wraith-like. The boy was distraught; he loved his mother and wanted her back. The house was beginning to look neglected and the maid had given notice and left.

'For heaven's sake, buck up, Maude,' said Lockhart crossly. She was reclining on the ottoman, twisting her fingers in her hair absently and gazing into space as if posing for a painting by Rossetti or Waterhouse.

'The sudden appearance of a dachshund was a cause of some consternation to them all,' she replied coolly.

'Come on, old girl, snap out of it. What's happened to the beautiful girl I married, eh?'

'They rode roughshod through the roses, regardless of the thorns that furrowed their flesh,' she remarked, sipping her martini.

'Will you do a puzzle with me, Mummy?' ventured the boy.

She turned her eyes towards him.

'They have torn me and I bleed,' she sighed. 'I should have known what fruit would spring from such a seed.'

Woodhouse swallowed nervously.

'It's HMS *Victory*,' he pleaded.

'The only lasting victory is death. Kiss me, Hardy.' She began to laugh.

'Come away, Richard,' said Father disgustedly. 'Let's go and stencil your tuck box. Perhaps when you're feeling better, Maude, you could sew some name tapes on the boy's uniform – if it's not too much trouble.'

'The salamander sallied forth and farted in the sun,' she sang after them.

Preparations for Woodhouse's departure to boarding school had been going on for some time now. He had been forced to accompany Father to the local department store where they had spent what seemed like days in the school section picking out uniform, sports equipment, a trunk, tuck box and all the other details that bring it home to a child that he is being sent away. It was like making a condemned man choose the timber for construction of the gallows and expecting him to look happy about it.

'Marston Hall will be fun,' said Father brightly as he placed the tuck box on the kitchen table. 'All boys together, midnight feasts and rugger and all that sort of thing. Make a man of you.'

'Can't I just stay at home and be a boy for a bit longer?'

'Now, Richard, we had a talk about this. One day you will have a fine son of your own, with his own tuck box, and you will stand at the table here, in this same kitchen, holding a stencil with that fine son's name on it—'

'I wouldn't send him away.'

'Look here, old chap, your mother's really not well, you know. It's not normal for people to babble on about dachshunds and salamanders and all the rest of it, is it? It's not healthy for a growing boy to listen to a lot of damn gibberish, pardon my French. Now… we put the stencil on the lid like this, I'll hold it steady and you draw round the inside of the letters. That's it. No, wait, not like that… Blast!'

Eventually the job was done. The tuck box was a rectangular box about the size of a bedside cabinet lying on its back. It had handles on either end, riveted plastic protecting its edges, and metal corners and clasps (like a flight case for gluttons), and on the lid it now read, in large outlined capital letters, "R. A. WOODHOUSE". Apparently tuck meant food. Why couldn't they just say so? The whole business was a complete mystery to the boy.

Father sat down at the kitchen table and opened a book called *On Northern Dialect*. Woodhouse noticed that he had started to grow a moustache.

Mr Gruber's work began to suffer. He became careless and untidy in his appearance. The law seemed unimportant to him now and he constantly wore the aspect of one who is listening, often failing to respond when someone spoke to him. In the end the firm had no choice but to send him home, despite the fact that he had been a model employee until then.

His home life suffered too. The voice of his wife sounded unpleasantly cat-like and he was forced to speak harshly to her.

It wasn't long before she left to go and stay at her sister's, and Gruber found himself alone with his thoughts, which were increasingly disturbed. The Führer of the Cats spoke to him and its voice was like a whiplash, galvanising him to terror.

'You are weak, Gruber, and disgusting to me (it said). You are not a Christian, I think. I shall unwind your brain like a ball of yarn and tangle it round the furniture. Your mind is like a little butterfly in the sunshine, Gruber, and I will catch it and toy with it and tear its wings away.'

Gruber began to sob. How could this be happening to him?

'Please, sir,' he said brokenly, alone in his kitchen. 'I *am* a Christian. I'm a Methodist.'

'A *Methodist*,' repeated the Führer of the Cats mockingly, its voice sounding the sibilants lovingly. 'No, Gruber, not a Methodist. You are a Jew; your father was a Jew and your grandfather was a Jew. Your great-grandfather also, and back and back and back... *Alle Jüdischen schweine!*'

The terrible voice grew louder and louder until it filled Gruber's head, and he put his hands over his ears and rocked backwards and forwards, tears rolling down his face, but still it went on, a gentle sing-song now but equally as threatening.

'Your mind is like a little frightened mouse running from the truth, but I can catch it, Gruber, I can catch it in my claws. Oh, such fun we will have, such games to play. Can you feel your heart beat, Gruber? I will catch the little mouse of the mind and squeeze out the sanity like toothpaste.'

'No, sir,' sobbed Gruber. 'Please don't – I'll do anything.'

'Ah, yes. This is better, Gruber. Perhaps we will be friends. You would like to be my friend, Gruber, I think? To wear a little bow in your hair and go to the party?'

'Yes! Yes! To the party!' cried Gruber desperately.

'Attend me then, Gruber,' said the Führer of the Cats and was gone.

Adolf Kitler, thought Gruber, *the Furred Reich*. But thankfully the awful laugh was frozen deep inside him for the time being, so he sat looking at the kitchen clock. His eyes followed the second hand round and round and round and round and round and round and round but he saw nothing there but pain.

Tallulah pushed open the door of the cat pottery. She was on her way home after a Saturday morning shift at the bakery. Craig's phone was switched off but she was tired of his company anyway, and Cubby's obvious adoration was good for her self-esteem. Accompanied by the jangling of the bell he shuffled through from the workshop looking sorry for himself until he saw who it was.

'Tallulah!' he exclaimed, wishing he had bothered to shave.

'That's me,' she said, smiling.

'I thought you'd forgotten about me.'

'I tried but I missed the cats.' She looked around at them. They were so sweet: there was even one that looked a bit like Hitler, bless it! 'They're gorgeous.'

Cubby tried to look at the cats as anything but a burden and a chore and failed completely. That one over there looked like Adolf Hitler: disgusting! What the hell had he been thinking when he painted that?

'I'm glad you like them,' he said carefully. 'Just say the word if you see one you want – as a gift, of course.'

'Perhaps you could make one for me 'specially?' she suggested, fluttering her eyelashes at him playfully.

He blushed.

'There's no way I could make one beautiful enough for you,' he said, avoiding her eye.

'It's very kind of you to say so, Cubby,' she said, and there was genuine warmth in her smile.

'But it wouldn't have to be beautiful, just special and for me.'

'Would you like some tea?' he offered nervously.

'Tea would be nice.'

He led the way through to the workshop and she sat down on some bags of clay. Cubby was careful not to look at her legs this time, but he did anyway. Tallulah pretended not to notice. As he busied himself with the kettle she looked around the workshop at the cats in various stages of creation and said:

'Is it hard to make a cat?'

'It is for me,' said Cubby. 'I'm rubbish at it. Grandfather was the expert.'

'Nonsense, your cats are very fine.' She paused. 'You haven't been into the bakery for ages – you're wasting away.'

'I thought you'd still be angry with me.'

'I was more angry with myself really. It wasn't your fault, Cubby; sometimes I'm – difficult.'

'Maybe we could work on a cat together,' said Cubby suddenly, fully expecting her to refuse.

'What, now?'

'Only if you want to.'

'That would be fun.'

They smiled at each other and the kettle started clamouring for attention. Cubby wondered whether he should buy a less neurotic one. He took it off the heat and gestured at some damp cats on a nearby shelf unit.

'You could pick out one of those and knife the seams off it before we dry it ready for biscuit firing. I sometimes forget because I'm a bit absent-minded. There's an apron over there on the side.'

Tallulah had noticed one or two painted and glazed cats still with seams but had assumed it to be deliberate, a rustic look. She wandered over and inspected the ones on the shelving, tying the apron over her work clothes as she did so.

'I like this one,' she said.

The cat was sitting up straight, in a haughty posture, though this effect was marred by a crooked ear and furtive expression. Cubby looked at it sadly and wondered how it was possible for an animal that as yet had no eyes to appear boss-eyed. However it was done, he reflected ruefully, he had managed to achieve it. He finished stirring the tea and then lifted the cat carefully on its platform and placed it on a worktop.

'This one it is, then,' he said, handing Tallulah a short-bladed knife and placing a mug of tea on the worktop for her. 'Be careful, the clay's still quite soft.'

She tested the keenness of the blade gingerly with the ball of her thumb.

'It's sharp!'

'I'm always cutting myself,' said Cubby cheerfully. 'I'm ever so clumsy.'

Very gently, and with a look of fierce concentration that made Cubby's heart hurt, Tallulah began to slice off the seam that ran from the cat's left ear, down the side of its neck and round the curve of its back. She sipped her tea and considered.

'It's satisfying,' she said after a while. 'Where did you get the moulds from? Did you make them?'

'Grandfather made them from cats he sculpted. He used to let me help him with them when I was little – the ears were my speciality. The originals are in the house.'

'Was he nice, your grandfather?' She started to remove another seam, pausing to tie her hair back with a scrunchy. Cubby admired the curve of her throat.

'He was quite quiet. Thoughtful, I suppose. I used to like coming in here when he was here.'

'But you don't like it now because I'm here?' She stopped cutting, to look at him mischievously.

In his confusion Cubby took refuge behind his mug of tea and then accidentally slurped it too loudly and made her laugh.

'I like it very much with you here,' he said simply.

'That's good,' said Tallulah, resuming her fettling. 'You can still see the marks – of the seams, I mean.'

'We'll just go over them with a damp sponge when you've finished. You're making a nice job of it.'

'Thanks. I've never knifed a seam before – it reminds me of the crimping on pasties.'

Cubby filled a bowl with water and stood next to her to admire her work, conscious not only of the proximity of her beauty but also the forbidden swell of her cleavage. She finished cutting away the last seam and looked up at him. A blonde curl had fallen over her eyes. Unable to help himself he reached out with trembling fingers and carefully smoothed it back. She looked at him seriously with her wistful grey eyes.

'Are you going to kiss me now?'

As Cubby took his life in his hands and moved dreamily towards her, there was the most tremendous smash from the shop. Tallulah threw up her hands and gave a piercing shriek well worthy of a B-movie starlet. Cubby found it difficult to imagine Emmeline Pankhurst reacting in such a way but it was not without a certain ear-splitting charm.

'It's just a cat,' he told her. 'A real one – it must have followed you in. It's always coming in here.'

They went through to the shop, Tallulah peering round Cubby nervously. One of Cubby's cats lay in pieces on the floor. A big black tom, clearly an arbiter of good taste, stood poised on a shelf. At the sight of them it made a mad dash, dislodging several more cats as it went. They too smashed loudly. Cubby made a hissing noise and waved his hands impotently. The cat hissed back. It had nowhere to go since they were blocking the doorway. It was a stand-off.

'It's just frightened,' said Tallulah.

'Bloody thing,' said Cubby, oblivious to the probability of his grandmother turning in her grave at such foul language.

He lunged at the cat, which looked at him with naked hatred in its eyes then gave a low growl and sprang acrobatically to the top of some shelves where it dangled by its front paws, miaowing loudly. The cats on the shelves began to rock as the weight of the scrabbling feline pulled the top of the unit away from the wall. It teetered. It toppled.

'No—!' cried Cubby, running towards it.

Tallulah screamed again: another bravura performance. Cubby arrived just too late. The tomcat leapt to the safety of the top of the shelves opposite and the falling unit crashed down on top of the despairing potter. So, this is how it ends, he had time to think as the ceramic avalanche engulfed him: crushed by cats and never been kissed.

The falling shelving was a big unit, but luckily so was Cubby. Nothing was really hurt but his pride and his stock, but he emerged from under the shelves, covered in dust and blood and bits of broken pottery, thirsting for revenge. The tomcat could see it in his eyes and it pelted round the room frantically looking for a way out. Cubby hurled a simpering tabby at it. The tomcat dodged and the tabby exploded on the wall. Cubby picked up a one-eyed tortoiseshell. He was smiling a grim smile and nodding his head now.

'You made a big mistake coming in here, my friend,' he said conversationally to the tom. 'The biggest mistake of your life, and the *last* one. I'm going to make a pair of mittens out of your miserable hide and wear them on cold winter mornings. And when I do I'll think of you and the big mistake you made coming into my shop – and my hands will be nice and warm while I'm thinking it.'

The cat looked up at him and hissed. Cubby took careful aim with the monocular tortie; he was a man who meant business. Tallulah walked across the room, heels crunching on broken china, and opened the door of the shop. *Ting-a-ling-a-ling-a-ling* went the bell and the tomcat was gone, zig-zagging frantically down the road.

'Thanks for the tea,' said Tallulah coldly, 'and for the insight into your true character.'

With a disdainful look she too was gone, still wearing the apron, and Cubby's dreams went snivelling after her like orphans.

Woodhouse disliked visiting the mortuary but Greaves seemed to delight in sending him to view his kills. What a waste of time. The attendant, a man who looked like a cadaver himself, recognised Woodhouse from previous visits.

'Your colleague is waiting for you,' he said.

Colleague – what the fuck? The attendant led the way through the reception area into the small private room where they generally showed Woodhouse the results of his handiwork. There was a not entirely pleasant odour.

Standing by the mortuary drawers was a flame-haired temptress. Her lipstick was fire-engine red and the tailored suit she wore served only to emphasise the lavish curves that lay in wait beneath.

'Hey, Richie,' she said, smiling. 'How's it hangin'?'

'Well, well,' he said, returning her smile. 'Sweetcakes! What the hell are you doing here?'

'It's Maryanne,' she reminded him. 'I've been sent to liaise wit' you.'

'What, from the base?'

'I don't really work at the base, hun. I was placed there to keep an eye on you.'

'You were very thorough,' he said, grinning.

'I'm a very conscientious girl, Richie. I love my country.' She blew a bubble with her gum and considered him thoughtfully.

'God bless America,' agreed Woodhouse fervently.

It was hard to tell if she was blushing beneath the blusher. Woodhouse thought probably not. She was smiling though, and that was good enough.

'So,' he said reluctantly, 'down to business. Pleased to meet you, Miss—?'

'Carter – Maryanne Carter.' They shook hands.

'So, what we have here, Miss Carter, is some deceased miscreants who may or may not have been working for a helicopter thief.'

'Agreed, Mr Woodhouse, but please call me Maryanne.'

The attendant, who had been looming in the corner like a coat stand, stepped forward gloomily and slid out one of the drawers. An unattractive and very dead individual lay within, his pockmarked blue skin smoking slightly as the warm air hit it. Maryanne consulted a clipboard.

'No ID, nothing on prints as yet, or DNA or dental. Death due to ingestion of cyanide – cuts on his face caused by busting a windshield with it.'

'Windscreen, Maryanne, over here it's a windscreen. He should have worn his seat belt.'

'He had a couple things in his pocket but we'll get to those in a moment.' She gestured to the attendant, who closed the drawer and opened the one next to it.

This corpse made the previous one look like a matinee idol.

'Nothing on this guy either – died from blood loss caused by partial flaying and disembowelment. I don't even wanna know, Richie.'

'He was the one who gave up Lomax.'

'I'm not surprised! Jesus Christ – look at him!'

'He exhibits great dignity in death.'

'You *think?*'

'No…' Woodhouse smiled at her. 'What about the other one?'

'What, the one they had to pick up with a grass rake and a shovel? They didn't find any fingers or teeth and nothing came up when we ran the DNA.'

'Okay, well we know that neither of these other two spoke English as their first language. What about clothes labels? Any clues as to country of origin?'

'They're looking into it but nothing obvious from the clothes, same with the weapons.'

'I was about to ask about the weapons.'

'The guys that ambushed you were using Heckler & Koch MP5s – both clean – and the cyanide guy had a Welrod pistol in the glovebox of his automobile. Also clean.'

'A Welrod!' Woodhouse was impressed. 'That's your proper assassin's weapon to go with his poison tooth. Pretty cool to get shot with a Welrod; they're collectors' items.'

'He had something interesting in his pocket too.' Maryanne took something from the inside pocket of her suit jacket. 'Apart from some English money, a disposable lighter and a pack of *Gitanes* with a French health warning, we found this.'

She held out a slip of paper. Woodhouse took it and saw this:

ADDSAAXXOSDAXADDDAXOSSAO
XADDDAXOJGGGDGDDDDXOSOSO

He looked up. She was watching him with an amused expression.

'How's your code-breaking skills, Richie?'

'Rusty. We used to have a separate section for that nerdy stuff – MI1.'

'Guess the days gone by are always the best, huh, Rich?'

'What about the girl?' he asked.

Maryanne nodded to the attendant. The girl looked peaceful and almost glamorous, in an Edgar Allan Poe-ish, Hammer Horror sort of way.

'Illegal immigrant,' said Maryanne, frowning disapprovingly at the corpse. 'Kind of a tramp by the looks of her – nothing useful to be learned.'

'What do you say we grab a spot of lunch somewhere, Maryanne,' suggested Woodhouse, 'and have a closer look at this cipher?'

She grinned at him.

'Sure, I like to eat. I gots to feed my fig-ure, don't I?'

'What was all that Sweetcakes stuff about anyway?'

'Aw.' She pouted. 'I was just fuckin' witcha, Richie – it was all part of my cover. But I do got a good butt though, right?'

'Indeed you do,' he agreed wholeheartedly, and they departed that place of death together smiling.

William Gruber had been deeply affected by his conversation with the Cat-Führer. The combination of intricate threats and the promise of a party had left him desperate to impress. But how? How to please his ceramic overlord? He must be allowed to attend the party. The party! He hugged himself and giggled with glee: how beautiful he would be!

The firm let Gruber go. He barely turned up for work and when he did he frightened the other employees. He muttered to himself and behind the gold-rimmed glasses dwelt the wild eyes of a fanatic. He became increasingly dishevelled and people began to cross the street to avoid him. His formerly neat blond hair hung down in front of his crazy eyes. You might say it was a lunatic fringe.

'Gruber,' said the disembodied voice of the Cat-Führer to him one afternoon in the bookmakers. 'Gruber, I wish you to wager on the 12.40 at Kempton.'

'Yes, my Führer,' said Gruber, looking around frantically to see if the Führer would manifest himself. 'Which horse do you like?'

'I am thinking to back Thundercat in this race, Gruber. I am thinking he is a course and distance winner and that the firm ground will be suitable to him. Also I am liking the name. You will place a large wager on this horse immediately, Gruber, and there will be no mistakes this time, verstehst du?'

'Yes, my Führer – Thundercat in the 12.40 at Kempton. I understand.'

Gruber filled out the slip and took it up to the counter. Seventy-five pounds was as much as he could afford but he could feel the Führer's displeasure at the small amount as a momentary pressure on the inside of his skull. He took the odds at twelve to one in case they shortened as the race approached. The clerk looked at him suspiciously but made no comment. He was used to dishevelled men who muttered to themselves; they made up a significant minority of his custom.

Fifteen minutes before the race, Gruber went outside to get a can of beer from the nearby shop. Standing outside the bookies he lit a cigarette and drank the beer in three large gulps. There were tears in his eyes.

Back inside he saw that the odds on Thundercat had drifted out to sixteen to one. He hoped the Führer wouldn't notice. He sat down just as the TV coverage flicked over to Kempton. The horses were being manoeuvred into the starting gate. He saw Thundercat's pink and yellow silks; the jockey was laughing and exchanging banter with his tiny peers. There was a pause, then a clang as the gate opened, and the horses surged out. Gruber could hear their hooves drumming on the turf. The crowd on the television roared and a man in the bookies shouted something unintelligible.

The horses rounded the first bend. Thundercat was handily placed among the bunch immediately behind the early leaders.

'Yes,' hissed the voice of the Cat-Führer. 'This is good, Gruber. He shows well, I am thinking.'

They took a jump. There were no casualties but Show No Mercy stumbled and was cast further adrift at the back. They jumped again, Thundercat looking comfortable and moving up a place or two on the rail. The early leader, a horse called John o' Groats, continued to make the pace without pulling any further clear.

'He will fade, Gruber, and victory will be mine. How sweet it will be, yes?'

They jumped again and one of the back markers fell.

'Now to shooting this one, I think,' gloated the Führer as the horses took the straight for the first time.

As they started the second circuit, John o' Groats still led, followed by Clancy's Dream, then three or four lengths back was the bunch that included Thundercat. They jumped again and one of the bunch fell: it was Thundercat – no, he was safe. Gruber dug his fingernails into his palms; he was not enjoying himself. They jumped again. Thundercat stumbled slightly but recovered and went on without losing much ground. A drunken man in the bookies shouted something in a Scottish accent. Gruber felt ill.

John o' Groats was tiring. He was pulling to the left, and as they approached the final fence Clancy's Dream drew level with him. The crowd on the television roared and the commentator's voice ascended another semi-tone in pitch. They took the jump. John o' Groats landed badly and Clancy's Dream moved into the lead. One of the horses around Thundercat fell, but he jumped cleanly and, as they came into the home straight, began to move up on the leaders.

'Reminding him,' snarled the Cat-Führer in his horrible scratchy voice. 'Reminding him with the whip, you swine! Whip to him immediately!'

As if in response, the jockey gave Thundercat three or four cuts with the whip and he burst clear of the bunch and passed John o' Groats on the inside. He was about two lengths behind Clancy's Dream, who was fading, and closing steadily. The jockey gave him some more of the whip. He was running raggedly now but drawing level with Clancy's Dream. The roar of the crowd was constant and Gruber wondered whether he might faint and possibly die.

Thundercat drew clear of Clancy's Dream but he was tired and stumbling now and suddenly another horse was absolutely tearing down the outside. It was only a question of whether Thundercat could reach the post before being caught.

'Run, you lazy beast,' hissed the Führer. 'Run, or it will to being the glue factory for you.'

Men in the bookies roared and gesticulated at the screen, some tearing up betting slips. Thundercat was being caught; he was covered in foam, and staggering. The other horse, Lover's Rock, was running cleanly, and they passed the post together, Lover's Rock winning by a neck, Clancy's Dream a distant third.

'Ah well, Gruber, this is not so bad, eh? Second place one quarter the odds I am thinking, yes?'

Gruber stared miserably at the betting slip:

Kempton 12.40, Thundercat £75 to win @ 12/1.

'What is this, Gruber – to win? To win! You filthy imbecile! To win? You incompetent swine! You imbecilic moron; there will be no party for you, you dog! You must bet this race each-way, you cretinous villain!' The Führer began to quieten, which was worse. 'Oh, Gruber, what have you done? What have you done, with your small, weak mind?'

Gruber put his head in his hands and began to cry.

'Oh, Gruber,' continued the Führer of the Cats silkily. 'There would have been jelly and ice cream at the party and you could have worn a bow in your hair. But now I am going to have to hurt you. Now I am going to disembowel your slimy little mind like a frog and play with the bits.'

'Aaaaaaaaaargh!' screamed Gruber. 'I want to go to the party! I want to go to the Nazi party!'

'No party for you, Gruber,' taunted the Führer. 'No Jews allowed at the party. No jelly and ice cream and no presents for you, Gruber.'

'I'm not a Jew, I'm a Methodist! I want my presents! It isn't fair! Aaaaaaaargh!'

There was pandemonium in the bookies. Gruber was screaming and tearing at his hair. A man at the counter panicked and dropped his winnings on the floor and there was a scramble for the money. With the strength of the insane, Gruber wrenched the television off the wall and hurled it through the window.

'I want to wear a bow in my hair and go to the party!' he shrieked. 'I'm not a Jew!'

'Run, you fool,' ordered the Führer. 'Get away from this place at once. Once again you have failed, Gruber. Tell your puny brain to instruct your cowardly Jewish legs to run away from this place immediately.'

'My legs are Methodists!' shouted Gruber defiantly and made good his escape on them.

The police arrived ten minutes later and took a description of Gruber from the clerk. They searched the area and looked in some of the pubs but the madman was gone.

Lomax takes the plush private elevator down from his penthouse. Django Reinhardt is playing the guitar on the speakers as the lift descends. Lomax smiles and hums a little: he likes this gypsy jazz.

The elevator stops at the basement and the doors open. Lomax strides into the underground car park where his limousine awaits, engine already running. He wears a dark suit and his shoes echo crisply on the concrete. A chauffeur in full uniform opens the back door of the sleek black car and Lomax gets in. He pours himself a brandy as they move smoothly up the ramp and sighs with satisfaction. It is night and the streets of the bustling city are lit with sodium and neon. Lomax opens the window so he can hear the laughter and snatches of music as they pass slowly along.

He hears other things too, some past, some present and some still to come: the ringing of sabre blades on some far distant battlefield; the thump of the cannon ball and the scream of an injured horse; the wet smack of the cat-o'-nine-tails on ruined flesh; and – he shivers a little although he knows no real fear – the voice of a man, one particular man whose existence is a threat. And that terrible, inexplicable metallic laughter that seems to come from inside his own head. Somehow they are linked – this laughter and this man.

Lomax hears the whispers winding back to him across the water, over the land, through the dark span of the days, the cold arch of the nights and the mighty grind and wheel of the planetary gears: a challenge! He likes this. This man must be eliminated for he is dangerous, but there is still time. He is as yet almost oblivious, this threatening man, but he begins to awaken. Lomax hears the echoes. Soon the battle will be joined! Lomax exults. His blood sings! He throws his cigar butt out of the window, narrowly missing a baby in a pushchair. He curses his poor marksmanship but he is smiling. Making an adjustment to the calfskin straps that hold his ear, he hisses just a little then pours another brandy and begins to laugh. Magnificent! The power and the glory!

The chauffeur is very careful not to accidentally make eye contact in the rear-view mirror. He has heard tales of the fate of inferiors who dared to bandy looks with their leader. He keeps his eyes on the road and tries not to hear the laughter.

They all fear Lomax, all these hard men and bad men. His powers are legendary in the Paris underworld. He is brilliant and ruthless and he knows everything; he *hears* everything.

Nobody knows his real name or his history. He appeared from nowhere when in his early or mid-thirties and effortlessly overwhelmed the underground fight circuit. Opponents were maimed, even killed. He fought with ultimate savagery married to brilliant spite, toying with opponents and never, ever, displaying even the slightest weakness.

When the gypsy, Jean-Jacques Baptiste, was unwise enough to mock his missing ear, he just grinned and went to work on him slowly and thoroughly and with obvious relish. Nobody who was there ever forgot it – except the gypsy.

Baptiste still lives, but he has never spoken since that night twenty-five years ago. He is brain-damaged: a drooling, grinning idiot. Lomax sends someone once a month to pick him up from the nursing home and take him to the zoo. He likes the monkeys.

The origins of the ivory ear are shrouded in mystery. Some say its runes are diabolic scrimshaw: that the ear was carved from the ivory of a cursed narwhal, harpooned by a madman during a lunar eclipse. That it shattered from the tusk of one of Hannibal's elephants, struck by dark lightning as they traversed the Alps. They say Lomax stole it from the Louvre, from the Vatican, the British Museum. That it belonged to Napoleon, Genghis Khan, Alexander the Great. But they say these things quietly, oh so quietly, for what is not in dispute is that Lomax hears everything and, when he dislikes what he hears, he acts swiftly and decisively and punishes without compunction.

He owns the underworld: it rests in the palm of his hand and pays tribute. Even without his extra abilities he would have been a great man and with them he has the absolute edge. How can you plot against a man who discerns the earliest glimmer of a treacherous thought at the moment of its conception? To be around this man and survive is to learn to keep your mind clear and fill it only with his will.

They draw to a halt outside Notre-Dame-du-Travail. Lomax gets out of the car and walks up the steps into the church. Inside, the clean lines of the exposed structural ironwork please his eye and soothe his mind. He pauses to light a candle but does not say a prayer. The organist is playing Bach. Lomax takes a seat at the back and closes his eyes, and the music washes away the whispers and brings solace. God, however, is not apparent.

PART TWO

SPIRAL DESCENT

The boy Woodhouse stood forlornly on the front steps of Marston Hall and watched his father's car disappear round the bend of the drive. A cold wind whipped cruelly at his knobbly young knees, exposed as they were between his grey school socks and his grey school shorts. His shirt collar and tie were choking him and the sleeves of his blazer hung down to his fingertips. His cap was a cruel imposition.

He puzzled over Father's parting words: Remember, Richard, the boy is father to the man. What boy? What man? This was no time for riddles, thought Woodhouse angrily. Father's pronouncements were becoming increasingly impenetrable, he felt.

Various children and parents were saying their farewells. There were some tears, and one demonstrative boy was clinging to his mother and screaming. Here and there stalked a teacher, smiling and shaking hands solicitously with the departing parents and casting proprietary glances at the boys.

'You – boy!' came a peremptory voice. 'What is your name?'

Woodhouse looked up. A shaggy haired ogre loomed over him, brows beetling, eyes goggling and cruel mouth twisted in a quizzical leer beneath a nicotine-stained moustache.

'Richard,' he replied stoically.

'I do not require your Christian name, boy. At this establishment boys are addressed by their surname and when a boy is speaking to a master, to which august body I have the privilege of belonging, he will employ the honorific "sir" or his breach of etiquette will be punished corporally – the Latin word corpus, of course, meaning body and the word punish deriving, incidentally, from the French verb punir. Now, I will enquire of you again – in the hopes that this brief explanation may have clarified matters for you to some extent – what is your name, boy?'

'Woodhouse – sir.'

'Better... Woodhouse, eh?' He consulted a list that he held in his huge strangler's hands.

'RAFFERTY!' he roared at a passing ginger-haired boy, making Woodhouse flinch. 'Kindly conduct Woodhouse here to his dormitory, which I believe is the one infested by you and your grimy little cohorts, ensuring – if you would – that he is not burned at the stake or eaten by cannibals en route.'

'Yes, sir,' said Rafferty, hustling Woodhouse up the steps into the school.

'We're not allowed to use the front stairs,' said Rafferty as they passed them. 'Only prefects and masters can use the front stairs. If you get caught on the front stairs you get six.'

'Six what?' asked Woodhouse.

'Six on the arse, you div, and if you cry or struggle you get another six. It hurts, especially if he uses the whippy cane.'

This news did nothing to lighten Woodhouse's spirits and, as they hurried through dimly lit corridors that smelt of floor polish, and up two flights of wooden stairs, the dreadful hollow feeling in his stomach intensified. It's just butterflies, Father had said. It seemed a very gentle name for the worst feeling Woodhouse had ever had in his life.

'Who was that teacher?' he asked.

'Master,' corrected Rafferty as they passed two boys fighting on a landing. 'You call them masters. That's Beastly – Mr Beazley – he takes Latin. He's a pig; he likes picking people up by the hair. This is us – it's a seven-dorm.'

They entered the dormitory. It was a large square room lit by the setting sunlight through sash windows. There were three tubular steel-framed bunk beds and one single bed near the door.

'Who's this, Raffles?' asked a boy with unruly hair and eyes that went in different directions behind thick glasses.

'This is Woodlouse,' said Rafferty, who had obviously given the matter of a nickname some thought. 'He's a new bug.'

'How pathetic,' sighed a boy who was reclining on a top bunk with his hands behind his head. 'I hate new bugs – they're so wet, always crying for their mammas and keeping people awake.'

'I won't cry,' vowed Woodhouse fiercely.

'We'll see,' said the reclining boy, smiling. 'I'm Sketchley – you can call me Sketch. The four-eyes there is Gunton – we call him Gubbins; I can't remember why.'

'I think it's because he's a complete spaz,' suggested Rafferty, which led to a semi-good-humoured scuffle with cries of 'Mind my glasses!' from Gunton.

'Break it up, girls,' said an older boy, coming in and sitting on the bed by the door. 'Who's this, then?'

'I think he's called Earwig,' said Sketchley. 'Or perhaps it was Beetle. Some kind of insect anyway.'

'It's Woodhouse,' said Woodhouse.

'Ah, Woodlouse – I see. My name's Carrigan. I'm the dorm captain here. If I get any cheek from you you'll get a cuff.' He demonstrated by bringing the palm of his hand sharply up across the back of Gunton's head at an angle of about thirty degrees. This obviously well-practised assault produced a sharp crack and Gunton's glasses fell to the floor. He picked them up, muttering darkly.

'Someone's missing,' said Carrigan, looking around the room. 'Where are Drinkley and Catford?'

'Drippy got a nose bleed so Pussy took him to the sick bay,' explained Rafferty.

'Drinkley is a delicate child,' said Carrigan to Woodhouse. 'He has asthma and allergies and doesn't have to play rugby.'

'He's pathetic,' added Sketchley scornfully.

'He's a flid,' agreed Gunton with relish.

A stocky dark-haired boy ushered in a sickly looking individual who was holding a bloodstained handkerchief to his nose.

'Drippy's in love with Matron,' Catford announced. 'I saw him looking at her tits.'

This was greeted with general hilarity and Drinkley mumbled something into the handkerchief.

'Now that we're all here,' said Carrigan, looking at his watch, 'you'd better get into your pyjamas; it's time for prayers. That bottom bunk's yours, Woodhouse. Your stuff should be in the locker.'

They started to get changed in silence that was broken by an electric bell ringing loudly. Woodhouse jumped.

'Whenever the bell rings,' said Carrigan to him, 'it means you have to do something. That one means prayers.'

They knelt beside their beds, the boys from the top bunks kneeling at the bunk below. Woodhouse found Sketchley next to him. There was silence and Woodhouse could hear a grown-up's voice doing a head count in one of the other dormitories. Don't let me cry after the lights go out, he prayed: don't let them hear me crying.

Later in the darkness a voice whispered:

'Earwig!' There was silence.

'Earwig!' Louder this time.

'What?' hissed Woodhouse.

'You know your name, then!'

There were muffled sniggers.

'Shut up, Sketchley,' said Carrigan.

There was quiet for a while and then sounds of stifled weeping.

'Shut up, Drinkley,' said Carrigan.

Woodhouse slept.

Monday morning dawned cruelly on the lovelorn Cubby. He had been unable to face clearing up the mess in the shop and had spent most of the previous day in bed, bemoaning an existence that was continually blighted by cats. Kissing Tallulah would have been the most glorious moment of his life and it had been ruined by a mangy interloping moggy. Tears of self-pity squeezed painfully from his downcast eyes as he chewed miserably at a piece of cold toast.

In the shop he stood the fallen shelves back up and began slowly sweeping up the broken cats, all the while seeing Tallulah's face and hearing the scorn in her parting remark.

A loud knocking came at the locked door. Cubby leant his broom against the wall and went to open it. Two uniformed police officers were there, a man and a woman.

'Pendleton Arbuthnot?' asked the male officer.

'Yes,' said Cubby.

'We would like to speak to you about a missing person – a Miss Tallulah Grimes.'

Cubby was unable to respond; he just stood there with his mouth hanging open, looking at them.

'Perhaps we could come in,' said the woman, suiting action to the words. 'You seem to have had a bit of trouble here,' she observed, looking around.

'Tallulah – missing?'

'You do know her, then,' said the man – a sergeant – pushing at a broken cat's head with the toe of his Dr Martens shoe. 'Perhaps you would like to tell us exactly what happened in here.'

'It was a cat.'

'Yes, I can see that it was a cat, but what I want to know is how it got broken, Mr Arbuthnot.' He stressed the first syllable of the "Mr" and accompanied it with a hard look.

'It looks as though there was a struggle of some sort,' suggested the female officer, a rangy brunette.

Cubby made a desperate effort to marshal his thoughts.

'A stray cat came in and got up on the shelves,' he said finally.

'A stray cat,' repeated the sergeant disbelievingly.

'A black one,' Cubby elaborated.

'When did you last see Tallulah Grimes?' asked the female officer briskly.

'She came in on Saturday – to visit me.'

'Did she buy a cat?' inquired the sergeant sarcastically, regarding the broken ones with obvious disgust.

'We had a cup of tea and she helped me in the workshop.' Cubby was beginning to realise that he was in some trouble. 'What's happened to her?'

'That's what we're trying to find out, Mr Arbuthnot,' said the woman sternly. 'She was supposed to have Sunday dinner at her parents' house but she never turned up. She didn't turn up for work this morning either, and she didn't phone in. Her mobile's been off since Saturday. What time was she here?'

Cubby thought about it.

'She must have come in around one and stayed for – I don't know – an hour, hour and a half?'

'She worked at the bakery until one o'clock on Saturday and nobody's seen her since.' She looked at him carefully. 'Apart from you.' She wrote something in her notebook.

'Workshop through here, is it?' The sergeant went through and they followed. The mug Tallulah had used was still on the side where she had left it and Cubby could see a pink lipstick mark on the rim. The sergeant looked at it but didn't pick it up. 'What was the argument about?' he asked.

'We didn't have an argument,' said Cubby desperately. 'She was working on that cat over there and then the black cat came in and frightened her and she left.'

'A witness reports hearing screams and the sound of breaking china at two fifteen on Saturday afternoon. I'm going to ask you again – what was the argument about?' The sergeant got right up close to Cubby's face. His breath was horrendous.

'The cat was breaking the stock and Tallulah screamed because she was startled.' Cubby was sweating; this was not going well.

'I've heard just about enough bollocks about this imaginary cat. What happened? Did she say no? You touched her, she said no and you lost your temper. Where did you get those cuts on your face?' The sergeant was shouting. The woman looked on impassively.

'The cat pulled the shelves over and they fell on me. I never touched her – she was my friend.'

There was a long silence, broken only by Cubby's sobs.

'Did you say she "was" your friend – past tense?' The sergeant's voice was quiet now.

'I meant that she *was* my friend but she doesn't like me anymore so now she's probably not.' Renewed sobbing.

'So, you *did* have an argument. I think you'd better come along with us, old mate. I hope you aren't going to be any trouble.'

Cubby was absolutely no trouble at all. He was a broken man.

Maryanne had used public transport to get to the mortuary so they got into Woodhouse's car together. The upholstery had been cleaned but the oil stains on the passenger seat still showed up. Maryanne either didn't notice or withheld comment. She placed her feet carefully amongst the loose cassettes in the footwell and they drove for a few minutes in comfortable silence before Woodhouse pulled into a pub car park. He got out and walked round to open the door for her but she was already out and waiting for him.

'I'm hungry, Richie,' she said, rubbing her stomach thoughtfully.

'I've eaten here before,' he said, smiling at her. 'It's not too bad.'

They walked across the gravel and went in. Inside it was dark and redolent of stale beer and chips. *Dreadlock Holiday* by 10cc was playing faintly, and the line about cricket made Woodhouse think of Greaves and his batting. They approached the bar, behind which a lugubrious individual was polishing a glass. Every now and then his head gave a twitch, as though he were nodding greetings to a succession of invisible customers. Maryanne began to giggle and Woodhouse gave her a stern look.

'A pint of your best bitter please, Landlord.' he said loudly, with a flourish.

'And I'll have a glass of orange,' said Maryanne, trying not to laugh.

'Awnge?' queried the landlord.

'Orange,' confirmed Woodhouse. 'She's American, aren't you, darling?'

'Why, certainly,' she agreed proudly in her Brooklyn accent.

The landlord went away to pour the drinks, nodding disgustedly to a whole array of non-existent alcoholics clustered round the bar. When he returned, Woodhouse and Maryanne both ordered steak and ale pie from the specials board and Woodhouse paid. They took their drinks and sat at a window table as far as possible from the bar. Maryanne took her gum out of her mouth and stuck it surreptitiously to the underside of the table. They looked at each other. Woodhouse remembered things about her from that night at the air base. Keep your mind on the job, he told himself, trying not to think about the softness of her skin and the dangerous luxury of handling her shape.

'Cheers,' he forced himself to say, and raised his glass.

'Cheers,' said Maryanne and they touched glasses. In the sunlight falling through the window, her eyes were the colour of amber, he noticed reluctantly.

'To business. Let's break some code,' he suggested.

'Sure.' She got the slip of paper out of her wallet and they looked at it again.

ADDSAAXXOSDAXADDDAXOSSAO
XADDDAXOJGGGDGDDDDXOSOSO

Woodhouse copied it into his phone and they looked at it some more.

'You think the Xs could be dummies?' he asked finally.

'You mean like spaces between words and they just put the Xs in to complicate it?'

'Yeah, maybe. Shit, we've got our work cut out here!'

'Okay,' said Maryanne briskly. 'What we got here – we got a slip of paper, no watermark. It's been folded into four where the Welrod guy had it in his pants pocket. No fingerprints that flagged up, capital letters, kinda wobbly, maybe done on a typewriter.'

'Edges not quite straight,' added Woodhouse. 'Like it's been cut from a bigger sheet of paper.'

Just then, a blushing teenage waitress arrived with the food.

'Jeez, Richie, these fries taste like crap,' complained Maryanne when the girl had gone.

'They're chips and they taste like shit.'

'Hell, Richie, potato chips come in a bag and they're crunchy.'

'No, Sweetcakes, crisps come in a packet and they're crispy.'

'Crazy Limey bullshit! The pie's good though.'

'Yeah, the pie's all right.'

'The thing I don't get, Richie,' said Maryanne, putting down her fork and dabbing delicately at her mouth with a serviette, 'is how comes this Lomax guy's got beef wit' you. You think he's someone you know, maybe?'

Woodhouse considered.

'I hadn't thought of that,' he admitted, 'but he could be.'

He told her about the car chase, the girl in the hotel room (he left out certain parts of this) and the ambush (skipping over the interrogation).

'So, you knew this girl, huh?' Unnervingly, Maryanne got straight to the heart of the matter.

'I'd met her before.'

'How did you meet her?'

'We got talking in a bar and hit it off.' He wasn't enjoying this.

'You approached her, or she approached you?'

'She approached me, Maryanne. She said she liked my shoes or some lame shit like that. She reminded me of someone I used to know and we got talking.'

'She was a hooker.' She looked at him with her amber eyes.

'She did turn out to be an escort, but I didn't know that until later. I liked her.'

'Jeez, Richie, I hope you wore a rubber. I don't need no goddamn diseases.'

Woodhouse squirmed.

'Look, the first time I was too drunk, so I met her again in the same bar the following week, and yes, I used a condom. Are you happy now?'

'Good boy.' Maryanne smiled at him fondly. 'I wonder why she didn't try to kill you that first time, while you were drunk.'

Woodhouse swallowed his injured pride and thought about it.

'Maybe she wasn't sure I was the right guy, or she hadn't been hired yet.'

'See if you can remember anything that seemed weird, out of place.'

'You mean weirder than some brass trying to stab me and then flinging herself out of a third-floor window?'

'Yeah, Richie, weirder than that.'

He looked at her angrily and then began to laugh. She was a cool customer, this Maryanne Carter! He thought about the time when he had been drunk with the escort. He had passed out on the bed for a short time and when he'd come to he had wondered if she'd been through his wallet. He was careful about these things and he had noticed that it hadn't been at quite the same angle to the lamp on the bedside table as he had left it. When he checked, nothing was missing so he had thought no more about it – until now.

'I think she went through my wallet,' he admitted.

'Guess you're kind of a sucker for the ladies, huh?' She was smiling sympathetically.

'I fell for your concerned act at the base, anyhow,' he said testily.

'I wasn't acting, honey,' she said mildly, making him feel like a heel. 'I better get going, Richie. Have a think about the code. It's obviously some kind of substitution cipher, judging by the plaintext, so we need to figure the algorithm and then we can work out the key.'

'Algorithm, absolutely,' he agreed.

She passed him a card.

'Here's my number. Give me a call now, so I have yours, and we'll talk soon.' He keyed in the number and a phone rang in her bag.

'Can I drop you somewhere?' he asked.

'Sure, just drop me at the subway.'

On the way out, Woodhouse nodded to the landlord, who nodded back several times.

When he dropped Maryanne at the Tube station Woodhouse didn't watch her walk away. He made a point not to.

They were rudely awakened by the bell while it was still dark outside.

'Time to get up, Earwig,' said Sketchley from the bunk above.

Drinkley sat on the edge of his bottom bunk looking pale and frightened. His pyjamas were wet.

'Drippy's wet the bed again,' said Catford to Carrigan. 'Shall I go and get Matron?'

'I think it's you that's in love with Matron,' said Carrigan. 'Off you go, then.'

Catford put on his dressing gown and slippers and left, while Drinkley stayed sitting sadly on the edge of his wet bed. The rest of them took their sponge bags and towels and

Carrigan led the way to the bathroom, where they queued for the rows of child-sized sinks. There seemed to be a lot of people.

'How many children are there here?' Woodhouse asked Rafferty, who was brushing his teeth.

'There's eighty boarders,' said Rafferty indistinctly. 'And about forty day bugs, I think. They start arriving after breakfast.'

'They're pathetic,' said Sketchley joyfully. 'They have to go home to their mammas every night because they're scared of the Grey Lady. Whooooooo!' He capered in front of Woodhouse, grimacing and waving his hands.

'Who's the Grey Lady?' Woodhouse asked.

'The Grey Lady is the Marston Hall ghost,' explained Carrigan, who was standing nearby looking very tall compared to the younger boys. 'Her spirit cannot rest and sometimes, at night, you can hear her stick tapping upstairs in the attic, where no one ever goes. They say she once came for a boy in the night and they never found him until years later when they discovered his mouldy old bones.'

'She's going to come for you, Earwig,' exulted Sketchley, reprising his ghost dance. 'Mouldy old bones – whoooooooo!'

'Huh,' said Woodhouse. 'I'm not scared – we've got a ghost at home. He's a gardener who got run over by a steamroller in the olden days, and you can hear him moaning outside in the night-time, looking for his lost parsnips.'

'He sounds rubbish,' said Sketchley, looking impressed despite himself.

'Come on,' said Carrigan, smiling. 'We'd better go and get dressed.'

They filed back to their room and got dressed. Woodhouse had a bit of trouble with his tie, but Father had taught him how to do it and he managed in the end. Catford had returned and they all went out and down the stairs and waited in a large hallway for the bell to signal breakfast. All the boarders were there and most of the masters and there was a considerable hubbub.

Suddenly there was silence, and Woodhouse looked up to see a handsome, buxom woman, whom he rightly assumed to be the matron, leading a procession of three miserable little boys who were carrying piles of wet bedding. Drinkley was among them.

'The walk of shame,' whispered Rafferty. 'They have to carry it to the laundry room.'

As the bed-wetters disappeared forlornly round a corner, the bell rang – there were bells everywhere, Woodhouse realised – and the rest of them trooped into the dining room.

The dining room seemed huge to Woodhouse: a great high-ceilinged rectangular room with rows of large tables either side of a central aisle. One of the long walls was filled with windows looking out to landscaped gardens, above which the dawn was breaking, and the opposite wall with scholarship boards: carved wooden rolls of honour filled with names going back to the 1880s. The most recent board was only half filled and included names from the previous year.

It seemed that they would stay together as a dormitory at mealtimes, and Carrigan led the way to their table; as prefect, he stood in his place at the head of it while they waited for grace to be said. Woodhouse, the new boy, was jostled down to the foot.

At one end of the room was a table on a dais and, as they all stood waiting in silence, the headmaster came in, wearing his gown, and took his place there. He was quite a small man but he looked powerful, Woodhouse noted with alarm, and pugnacious – like a bull terrier. Being beaten by him would not be likely to be a pleasant experience. Woodhouse decided to avoid it if at all possible.

Two other masters entered, and a pale woman who seemed to be the headmaster's wife. Lastly, the matron rushed in, ushering the bed-wetters before her. Drinkley came and stood next to Woodhouse. He was wheezing and took a blast of his inhaler.

'GOOD MORNING, BOYS,' roared the headmaster.

'Good morning, Mr Campion,' they replied as one.

'WE HAVE A NEW BOY WITH US TODAY. HIS NAME IS WOODFORDE.' Matron whispered something to him. 'HIS NAME IS WOODHOUSE. I TRUST THAT YOU WILL ALL MAKE HIM WELCOME.'

There was a pause while everyone stared at Woodhouse.

'GRACE THIS MORNING WILL BE SAID BY –' the headmaster consulted a note – 'SEWELL MINOR.'

A small boy at the next table to Woodhouse began to shake with fear, and mumble.

'SPEAK UP, BOY!' bellowed the headmaster, turning purple with rage.

'For-what-we-are-about-to-receive-may-the-Lord-make-us-truly-thankful-amen.'

'Amen,' echoed everyone.

The headmaster sat down, looking disgusted, and everyone else followed suit. A boy from each table went and collected a huge tureen from a side table near the door to the kitchen and struggled back with it. Carrigan sent Rafferty. He lifted it onto the table, grunting with the effort, and Carrigan began dolefully ladling the contents into bowls and passing them down the table. The first one arrived in front of Woodhouse, who was seated in his junior position at the far end. He looked into it. A great glutinous steaming lumpy grey mass assaulted his senses.

'What is it?' he enquired fearfully.

'It's porridge,' said Drinkley sadly. 'If you don't eat it all you get whacked.'

Woodhouse looked around: everyone was eating the stuff, one or two with seeming enjoyment, but most with clear misery or stoical resignation. He picked up his spoon and broke the skin. A lump the size of a golf ball was lurking there.

'Eat up, Woodhouse,' called Carrigan. 'It's good for you… *allegedly*,' he added more quietly.

Woodhouse took a deep breath and began to eat.

After his meltdown in the bookies, Gruber got into his car and drove around for a time, finally parking opposite the cat pottery. He needed to prove himself to the Führer. As he watched, a beautiful blonde example of Aryan womanhood went into the shop. From across the road, Gruber could hear the doorbell.

'Ach so, Gruber, this is good breeding stock, yes?' said the Führer lecherously.

Gruber waited for a few minutes but the girl didn't come back out. He got out of the car and went over to the shop and looked through the side window. Through a throng of cats he could see her talking to that fool Arbuthnot. She fluttered her eyelashes, the hussy. Ah! There he was – the Führer – on a shelf slightly apart from lesser cats, waiting for Gruber to liberate him.

'Yes, Gruber,' said the voice of the Cat-Führer softly.

As he watched, Arbuthnot and the girl went through into the workshop. Gruber was seized by irrational jealousy.

'Wait a little, Gruber – calm yourself. All in the goodness of time.'

Gruber got back into the car and sat for what seemed like hours. The girl still did not emerge. At last he could wait no more. He was filled with religious fervour. The power of the old gods sang in his veins.

Gruber walked across the road to the shop door, turned the handle and very, very slowly, so as not to disturb the bell, pushed it open. He could hear their voices in the workshop and the bell gave one faint *ting*. He wedged the door open with a large marmalade cat and advanced slowly towards the Führer. Its head seemed to turn slightly as he approached and the light caught the cathedral glass of its eyes.

'Softly softly, Gruber, catches a monkey.'

Gruber crept through the shop and started to reach up his hand to where the Führer sat, regal as he was in his magnificence. A noise behind him. Gruber froze with outstretched arm and looked round. A horrible great black cat was advancing through the open door. Gruber glared at it, trying to will it to leave. It walked casually across the shop and started winding itself round his legs and purring. Gruber shrugged and his hand closed around the Führer. The glaze was cold and smooth to the touch.

'Are you going to kiss me now?' The girl's voice from the workshop.

A huge rush of jealous rage caused Gruber to twitch, and the hand holding his precious Führer knocked another cat off the shelf. Helplessly, Gruber watched it fall. It hit the concrete floor and exploded. There was a shrill scream from the other room – probably Arbuthnot, thought Gruber spitefully – and the startled black cat jumped up on to a shelf. Clutching the Führer, Gruber crossed the room, removed the cat that was propping the door open, went outside and slowly – don't panic – pulled the door closed behind him.

Gruber got into his car and placed the Führer on the passenger seat. He wound down the window. From the pottery he heard more crashes. Two old women who were passing paused to listen and there was a scream and then a huge bang. The old women hurried slowly on and, as they disappeared round the corner, the shop door opened and the black cat came streaking out and ran down the road. The girl and Arbuthnot appeared. She turned and said something to him angrily and then strutted off with her nose in the air. Arbuthnot stood looking after her helplessly for a few moments and then went back inside and closed the door. Gruber sat in the car watching the girl walk away.

'Take her, Gruber,' said the Führer, and Gruber was not at all surprised to see its mouth and eyes move. 'Your destiny awaits – attend me, Gruber.'

Gruber started the engine of the car and moved off, listening carefully to the cat's instructions.

Tallulah was furious with Cubby. What if he had hurt that poor cat? It was probably just hungry and frightened and he had started throwing things at it. Cats – he had started throwing cats at it! And what was it he had said? Something about making it into mittens and his hands being warm while he was thinking something. The horrible brute!

Tallulah was a sensitive girl who wept if she saw an advert on TV about an overworked donkey or a beaten dog, but she started to smile in spite of herself. She was discovering that it was impossible for her to stay angry with Cubby for any length of time. He must have been hurt when those shelves fell on him. He was bleeding – no wonder he was angry! That was it: he had said his hands would be warm while he was thinking about the mistake that the cat had made coming into the pottery!

Tallulah started to giggle as she took the shortcut through the pungent alley. Maybe she would go back and make sure he was all right, and perhaps he would get to kiss her after all. She had been quite looking forward to seeing what it would be like. When she emerged from the alley and realised she was still wearing Cubby's apron, it clinched it for her. She was about to turn and go back when a man stepped in front of her. She hesitated. He had crazy blond hair and crooked glasses and he smelt of beer and cigarettes.

'Excuse me, miss,' he said politely, 'I wonder if you could help me with this cat.'

He gestured towards a shape in the open boot of his car. Tallulah could see the eyes. She moved closer to see better and the man stood aside.

'That's one of Cubby's cats,' she exclaimed, reaching out for it. 'It's the one that looks like Adolf Hit—'

Gruber tipped her neatly into the boot and, after snatching the Führer away, slammed it shut, got into the car and drove calmly off. Tallulah was too shocked even to scream.

Woodhouse sat at his kitchen table. He carefully copied the cipher from his phone on to a sheet of paper and sat looking at it.

ADDSAAXXOSDAXADDDAXOSSAO
XADDDAXOJGGGDGDDDDXOSOSO

His heart sank. He had absolutely no idea where to begin with this. The cat barged in through the cat flap and complained loudly for food, even though there was already some in the bowl.

'Shut up, Walther,' Woodhouse said. He phoned Maryanne.

'Hello?'

'Hello – Maryanne?'

'Oh, hey, Richie. How's it going?'

'Pretty average. I'm looking at this cipher and it's giving me a migraine.'

'Hold on while I get it.' He could hear her rustling about. 'Okay, Richie, I've got it here. What are you thinking?'

'Well, it can't be words – we've got three Ds in a row twice, three Gs once, and even four Ds in there near the end. If it was words you'd expect to see something more recognisable – more familiar structures.'

'Yeah, you'd take a guess at where the Es might be and get some kind of starting point to work from there. I'm with you, Richie – I don't see any words in there. So, we got two rows of – what? – twenty-four numbers, you think?'

Woodhouse made some notes on the paper.

'Yeah, but we've got forty-eight letters here and only seven different ones: A, D, S, X, O, J and G. You'd expect to see ten numbers: one to nine and a zero.'

'Shit, Richie!' They were silent for a moment. The cat miaowed. 'You got a cat there, big boy?'

'Yeah, I've got a cat.'

'What's his name?'

'He's called Walther.'

'Walther – what, like the guns?'

'Yeah, that's right – like the guns.'

Woodhouse was impressed: most people just called the cat Walter.

'Walther… I like that, Richie. Is he cute?'

'Christ, no! He's fat and ugly and thick as two short planks!'

The cat miaowed again, as if in protest, and they both laughed.

'Maybe I'll get to meet him some day,' she said, and Woodhouse thought she sounded a little wistful.

'Maybe so,' he agreed. There was a pause.

'You think they could be international phone numbers, hun?'

'I suppose it's possible but, again, you'd expect to see ten different digits occurring and we've only got seven. Fuck!'

'There's something about the Xs, Richie – see the way they're spaced out? Six letters, then two Xs, then four, then an X; five, then X; five, then X; five, then X; then eleven, an X, and five again.'

'Sets of six,' said Woodhouse thoughtfully. 'Sets of six, with one of twelve. The Xs always occur at the beginning of the sets.' A very faint bell was beginning to chime at the back of his mind. 'And the other letters come in little clumps, in clusters, like – like…' He reached for it, that little elusive chiming bell.

'Like herpes?' suggested Maryanne innocently.

He had to put the phone on the table and rest his head on his forearms. He was laughing so hard he couldn't breathe. The cat ran away in disgust.

'What? What'd I say?' She was laughing too on speakerphone.

'Oh shit, woman! I almost had it there. You've got a dirty mind!' His arms were wet from tears.

'Aw, Jeez, Richie, I was just trying to help, y'know? I'm a helpful kinda girl.'

'You're beautiful, I—'

He couldn't continue and had to put his head on his arms again, but even through the laughter he knew that he had been close to a breakthrough with the cipher, and he knew that he would get there. It's something to do with the Xs; just remember: it's something to do with the Xs. Herpes… Christ!

The world outside school was soon all but forgotten. School was such a complete world in itself that there was no room for nostalgia. In most cases, homesickness lingered for a day or two and then the boys participated wholeheartedly in school life. Those who persisted in fruitless yearning for their previous lives placed themselves at a disadvantage and were likely to become targets for bullies.

The bottom of the food chain at boarding school is not a good place to be. The majority, of course, find their place somewhere in the middle: if someone gives them a dead leg, for instance, they find someone weaker and pass it along and the problem – for them – goes away.

Prefects, sports stars and natural performers make up the ten per cent who rule the roost. Few of them are bullies.

They have no need to be, they already command the respect. The bullies come from the herd. They aspire to belong to the top tier but lack the skills or personality to make it there on merit. The dead leg originates with them and makes its way down through the eighty per cent majority or, very often, goes directly to the other ten per cent: the perennial victims.

Physical weakness, stupidity, homesickness, a stutter, a ridiculous name: any of these things or a hundred others could result in a boy finding himself at the bottom of the pecking order and, once down there, it is very difficult to get out. Over time you might develop your sense of humour, for instance, and joke your way to safety. Or you might just grow physically and become strong enough to fight your way out, but usually once you're down there you're stuck and your life is likely to be a misery. Anyone who has a problem can come and torture you for a while and then go away feeling better. And you? You just have to take it. Don't even think about telling a teacher – chances are they despise you just as much as the boys. You'll get the cane for sneaking and the boys will get you afterwards. There's nowhere to turn.

The seven boys from dormitory three fitted into this hierarchy just like anyone else. As a prefect and a pretty decent sportsman, Carrigan was one of the elect and he was quite protective of his six charges, which was just as well since as first years they were naturally at the bottom of the pile and all were likely to be bullied at some point.

Rafferty was a happy-go-lucky character and a natural survivor. Sketchley had a quick tongue which, although it sometimes got him into trouble, could also help him out of it. Catford was strongly built and enjoyed fighting, which left Woodhouse, Gunton and Drinkley.

Woodhouse was quite small, quiet and sensitive looking and he had joined the school in the middle of the term, which placed him at a disadvantage. He was being watched and before long he would be tested.

Gunton looked like a natural target, with his boss-eyes and thick glasses, but he had a surprisingly vicious temper. He had borne the bullying for a few weeks and then suddenly snapped and attacked a third year, making his nose bleed and loosening a tooth. This had afforded him instant hero status, although he was oblivious to it.

Drinkley, however, had all the odds stacked against him. He was small, weak and sickly and constantly homesick. He was excused rugby and often wet the bed. Even his friends belittled him, calling him Drippy, or The Drip. The boy was a complete weed and an utter tick and Woodhouse felt sorry for him even though he was fully occupied with his own problems. Drinkley never fought back: he was seemingly too miserable and too weak. Carrigan would chase off the bullies but all too often he just wasn't there. Even among the victims, Drinkley's status was low. He was in a bad place, with no foreseeable means of escape.

Tallulah came out fighting but Gruber was ready for her. He had backed the car into his garage and closed the door behind it. The moment he opened the boot Tallulah swung at him with the wheel brace but he was too quick. The Führer had warned him that she would be spirited. Their children would be brave and strong and in time her defiance would become submission, and finally adoration.

Gruber took hold of her wrist and twisted until she dropped the weapon. He was smiling. She scratched his face with the nails of her other hand. He slapped her quite hard, spun her round and picked her up. They were both breathing heavily but it was not in the least erotic. He carried her through the door into the house. Her hair was in his face and she was kicking at his shins with her heels. His glasses had fallen off.

'Let. Me. Go,' she kept saying, but he intended to hold on to her forever. It was their destiny.

At the foot of the stairs she kicked over the telephone table and the phone fell on to the carpet and lay there bleating electronically. Gruber closed his eyes and took a deep breath. Her hair smelt wonderful. The stairs were narrow and she fought him all the way up. Halfway up she screamed and then bit his hand when he covered her mouth. After that, she saved her breath for struggling and by the time they got to the bedroom they were both tired and sweaty.

He pushed her to the floor and, holding her down with his knee in the small of her back, tied her hands behind her with a paisley necktie that he took from the wardrobe.

'Let me go,' she said. 'Let me go now and I won't say anything. I promise.'

'I'm afraid I can't do that,' he said, as he fastened her ankles with one of his wife's belts. 'It has to be this way.' He took her shoes off gently and considered her feet. They were dainty.

'My friends will find me, and when they do they'll fuck you up.'

'I'm already fucked up,' he said, and she didn't like the way he said it. She didn't like it at all.

'It's just a mistake – I know you don't mean it. Let me go and I promise I won't tell anyone.'

He got off her and sat down next to her to rest. He pushed her hair out of her face to see her better, reminding her of Cubby. She rolled on to her side. The carpet had left an impression of its weft on the skin over her cheekbone. They looked at each other. It was an unusual situation for both.

'You have strong bone structure,' he said. 'Is there any history of mental illness in your family?'

'You're asking *me* about mental illness? You sick fuck! Where the hell did *you* escape from?'

He considered for a moment.

'I escaped from the darkness, into the light. Together we will walk the paths of righteousness with our fingers entwined – and truth and beauty will be our guide. You will see – it is ordained.'

In the light from the bedroom window his face was serene despite the bloody furrows down one side. Oh shit, thought Tallulah. Oh. Fucking. Shit. He's a maniac. It went through her head in the form of a song: He's a ma-niac, ma-niac… What the hell was that from? *Flashdance* – Jesus Christ! Horrified, Tallulah started to laugh and Gruber joined in.

Tallulah's phone rang and they stopped laughing immediately. Gruber reached over and took it out of the pocket of her cardigan. It said "Mum calling". He switched it off and put it in his pocket. Standing up, he lifted Tallulah with only slight difficulty and put her on the bed. His expression was hungry as he looked at her legs and, for the first time in her life, she wished they were less shapely. Or that she had worn trousers to work. She had worn the skirt because she had known she would go to see Cubby, she could admit it to herself now. She liked it when Cubby looked at her legs. But not this kidnapping maniac (maniac, ma-niac...).

'I have to go and get my glasses,' said Gruber, peeling his eyes off her legs.

The moment he was out of the room Tallulah started trying the knots. The tie round her wrists was tight and there was no give in the knot. The belt fastening her ankles had been cinched tight through the buckle and then knotted. She bent her legs to bring it within reach of her fingers. No good – fuck!

She looked round the room. On the far wall was a large window. The curtains were closed (an unpleasant geometric motif), and a chest of drawers stood underneath. To her right was a large wardrobe and a cane chair heaped with cheap stuffed toys. To her left crouched a grubby white dressing table and beyond that the door stood open. On the wall hung a large velvet picture of a peacock which Tallulah hated immediately and wholeheartedly.

The maniac returned. He was wearing his glasses and carrying a coil of blue rope, a hunting knife, and the cat that resembled Adolf Hitler. As he came in he was looking at the cat and nodding seriously. Christ! thought Tallulah: the fucking thing's talking to him! Gruber put his Führer carefully on the dressing table. Turning to Tallulah he said:

'You're going to go to the toilet now, and then I'm going to tie you to the bed properly.'

She made no reply. He sat down next to her and, taking the knife from its sheath, cut through the tie and then the belt. He motioned to the door with the knife and she stood up, rubbing her wrists. She had pins and needles in her legs too so she stamped her feet.

'I liked that tie,' said Gruber accusingly.

He walked her along the landing to the bathroom and prised the bolt off the door with the tip of the knife blade. He put the bolt in his pocket and pointed at her meaningfully with the knife.

'You've got two minutes,' he said. 'And then I'm coming in.'

Tallulah sat on the toilet with her skirt round her waist and her knickers round her knees and looked around the room. She couldn't see anything helpful: the window was too small to climb out of and, when she got up and tried to open it, it was locked, anyway. The toilet roll holder was crocheted, as were the seat cover and the brush holder, and there was a picture of a posturing bullfighter on the wall. She wondered where the maniac's wife was: not buried under the patio, she hoped, although to judge by her taste in décor and men she was deserving of a savage beating at the very least.

Tallulah smiled. She knew she was a resourceful girl and was reasonably confident that she would find a way to confound the maniac. He was only a man, after all.

'Hurry up,' said Gruber outside the door.

Back in the bedroom Tallulah sat on the bed while Gruber cut four lengths of rope from the coil.

'Sorry about this,' he said. 'It's only till we get to know each other.'

His smile made her shudder but she forced herself to smile back.

'You don't have to tie me up,' she said. 'We could just sit and talk for a while. My name's Tallulah.'

'That's a pretty name but I'm afraid that I am still going to tie you up, Tallulah, so if you could lie down on your back that would be very helpful.'

She suddenly felt very much like crying and lay down helplessly. Gruber sat astride her and, resting the knife on top of the headboard, began tying her wrists to the bedposts. He left some length in the ropes so she would have limited movement. His fingers were deft and the knots looked assured.

'I was in the Sea Scouts,' he said, guessing her train of thought.

'Shame you didn't drown.'

Their faces were very close as he leant over her and their eyes met for a long moment. He got off her and knelt further down the bed to tie her ankles. Her skirt was too tight for him to part her legs sufficiently so he pushed it up around her thighs. She waited until he was distracted by the flesh on display and kicked him efficiently in the side of the head. His glasses flew across the room and so did he, landing on the floor with a thump. The glasses landed neatly on the dressing table, next to the Cat-Führer.

Gruber was up quickly. His hair was hanging in front of his eyes and his face had started bleeding again. He pushed his hair back and stepped forward. His eyes were empty. Suddenly he turned his head.

It's saying something to him, thought Tallulah. That fucking cat is *saying* something to him. Gruber went over to the dressing table and put his glasses on. He leant over to the cat attentively and Tallulah could hear whispering. She thought how sweet it would be to take the cat and smash it over the maniac's head. Gruber straightened up and took the knife from the headboard.

'No more games,' he said. He licked his lips just once then smiled.

'I'm sorry,' Tallulah said desperately. She was terrified. Whatever the cat had said to him, it wasn't good. He was suddenly far more menacing. 'I'll be still.'

With the knife in his left hand he ran his right hand over her bare legs. She froze. Gently he stroked her thighs, watching her expression intently, and then moved his hand slowly down her legs to her feet. Taking his eyes from her face, he leant over and softly kissed first one foot and then the other before tying her ankles to the bedposts, leaving some play in the ropes as before. Tallulah was still frozen.

'I'm going to have to gag you now,' he said, pulling open one of the drawers in the chest.

He took out a yellow scarf which might have been silk and gagged her with it. She was too frightened to struggle. It tasted awful and smelt of cheap perfume. Taking the cat from the dressing table, he smiled at her again and left the room. Tallulah let the tears come.

'Hello? Are you there? Oh God, Richard, not this ghastly machine again. It really is the *absolute* end. Look, I'm sorry to bother you – oh dear – Richard? It's Rosalind – your aunt. It's John, you see – he's attacked Rowena Wainthrop. It really is too bad of him. They invited us round for dinner, you see, the Wainthrops, and John drank too much wine. He *promised,* Richard! He absolutely *promised!* After dinner Rowena went outside for a cigarette. Their garden's lovely, by the way, Richard – they have a fountain with coloured lights and a pond with beautiful Japanese fish in it.

'Anyway, Rowena was in the garden having her cigarette and John pounced on her! He was lurking in the pampas grass, Richard, and he absolutely *leapt* on her, like a filthy tiger or something! She said he started kneading her buttocks and groaning. *Kneading* them like some beastly baker! And *groaning* as if he was in pain! She screamed like anything and Peter Wainthrop and I came to the rescue. It was awful, Richard – John was all red and sweaty and his tie was crooked. I think he was *aroused!* It's just too terrible for words. Well, of course, Peter and John started fighting and fell into the fishpond, but to be honest, Richard, I couldn't help but notice that she *was* wearing rather revealing slacks and *far* too much blusher. Anyway, I must go – my programme is starting. Bye, darling. Love you.'

The answering machine gave a couple of clicks as she disconnected and the cat leapt suddenly onto Woodhouse's lap, landing heavily on his groin.

'Piss off, Walther!' he cried indignantly, pushing him away.

He quite enjoyed the messages from his fictional aunt but wondered if they were strictly necessary. There must be an office somewhere with a crazy woman in it who spent all day making these calls. Perhaps an ex-operative whose mind had been crippled in the line of duty and they had invented this code to keep her busy. He smiled and topped up his drink.

The Wainthrops' garden represented Highgate Cemetery. The kneading of the buttocks and groaning meant 11.30 the next morning, and that John had been drinking wine signified that it was a routine meeting. Woodhouse supposed that Greaves would want to know how he was getting on with deciphering the code. He considered calling Maryanne but it was a bit late.

He rolled a cigarette and turned on the television. One of the *Rocky* films was on. Adrian was crying and Paulie was shouting at her and waving his arms. He looked drunk. Rocky mumbled something at him angrily and shrugged. Woodhouse changed the channel.

'So, what *is* hare and hounds?' asked Woodhouse.

'It's sort of like a cross-country,' said Rafferty. 'But three boys set off ten minutes ahead of the rest of us. They're the hares. They scatter pieces of paper as they go and we have to follow the trail and try and catch them. We're all the hounds. It's an old game – I think it's in Shakespeare.'

'Do they always get caught?'

'Not always, but they usually do. They use first or second years for the hares so they usually get caught cos the older boys are faster. Sometimes they get beaten up – it depends who catches them first.'

Woodhouse was silent while he thought about it. He sat down to lace up his plimsolls. They were in the changing room. Virtually the whole school was in there and it was noisy and quite smelly.

'They're even making Drippy run,' said Rafferty. 'Matron says we've got to look after him.'

Woodhouse looked in the direction indicated by the scornful jut of Rafferty's chin and saw Drinkley sitting alone, eyes rolling back as he sucked despairingly on his inhaler.

'I don't suppose we'll catch them, then.'

Rafferty laughed.

'No chance. We'll just stay near the back and try not to get back last. If you get back last, sometimes you get whacked.'

'That's not fair!' Woodhouse was incensed.

'Nothing's fair here. Gubbins'll probably get whacked – he nearly always comes in last. He doesn't care though,'

Rafferty's tone was admiring. 'He says he finds the whackings invigorating.'

'I don't much fancy getting whacked.'

'It's not that bad. The worst bit's waiting outside while he's caning someone else. You can hear it. And there's the lights – do you know about the lights?'

'What lights?'

'When you're waiting outside the head's study there's two lights above the door – a red one and a green one. When the green light goes on it means he's ready for the next person to go in. The red light means he's whacking someone.'

'How many times have you been whacked, Raffles?'

'Loads of times,' Rafferty said airily. 'Well, twice anyway. I got slippered for laughing in prayers, and then, just before half term, I got caned for fighting. It was supposed to be six but I struggled and he gave me another six. I'll keep still next time!'

'Does it hurt much?'

'It hurts when he's doing it and it's really sore for about an hour afterwards, then it just feels hot till the next day. It kills when you sit down though.'

A master in a tracksuit came in and blew a whistle and they started to file outside. It was windy and the sky was black. Drinkley came and found them. He was shivering and looked on the verge of tears as they walked from the gym up to a farm track behind the school. The boys were only wearing shorts and rugby shirts so Woodhouse was looking forward to running if only to keep warm.

The master called for quiet and blew two sharp blasts on his whistle. Three boys wearing white pushed through the crowd and ran off up the track, sliding now and again in the mud. They each had canvas shoulder bags and every twenty paces or so one of them would take out a handful of paper scraps and throw them behind. The paper swirled around in the wind. The track was long and straight, inclining upwards, and it took quite a while before the hares disappeared out of sight. Woodhouse could see a treeline there in the distance.

They stood around shivering and it started to rain, big heavy drops that hurt. Finally the master looked at his stopwatch and blew the same two blasts on his whistle. About thirty of the fourth and fifth years sprinted away immediately and were halfway up the track while the rest were still jostling and grumbling. Woodhouse saw Carrigan among the frontrunners, elbowing his way through.

Woodhouse and Rafferty got either side of Drinkley and did their best to hurry him along but it was slow progress, what with the wind, the rain and the mud. They struggled up the incline, Drinkley gasping for breath, and gradually fell further behind the main pack, who themselves were already far behind the leaders. Woodhouse kept his eyes on his feet as he ran and could see scraps of white paper here and there, trampled into the mud. He looked round and was reassured to see a forlorn collective of non-athletes shambling along, the master haranguing them furiously. Woodhouse saw Gunton there, running awkwardly with his arms straight out by his sides and fingers splayed, like an escaping scarecrow or, indeed, a crow.

They eventually reached the top of the track and the ground levelled out and grew firmer underfoot as they turned left and ran alongside deciduous woodland to their right, the overhanging branches too bare to keep the rain off. To their left, ploughed fields sloped down to the school and, behind that, although Woodhouse couldn't see it through the rain, was the sea.

They went a little faster now and Drinkley even managed a watery smile. The others grinned and patted him on the back and they ran on, pulling further away from the hectoring master and his unsportsmanlike companions.

The trail of trampled paper led them up into the woods, where the track narrowed and they had to run in single file. Woodhouse led the way; he was surprised to find that he was enjoying himself. Drops of water fell from the trees and there was silence apart from their running footsteps and Drinkley's laboured breathing. Woodhouse heard the whirr and gasp of the inhaler behind him.

The track twisted and undulated and their footing became treacherous. There were muddy patches and exposed tree roots. In places it was so steep that they had to use their hands to pull themselves up, only to find themselves sliding and tumbling down the other side moments later.

'Stop,' said Drinkley. 'Can we just stop for a minute? I've got a stitch.'

They stopped.

'Pull your knee up to your chest,' said Rafferty. 'Like this.' He demonstrated, standing on one leg while bending the other and pulling it to him with his hands. 'It helps with a stitch.'

The others tried it. Woodhouse's foot slipped and he fell, landing startled on his back in the mud. Rafferty burst out laughing and Drinkley looked surprised and then joined in.

The master appeared on the brow of the rise behind them. He had a long thin face, permanently set in a sneer, and looked about ten feet tall.

'Get up, boy!' he shouted. 'This is no time for fun and games. And you, Drinkley, what the bloody hell do you think you're laughing at?'

'Nothing, sir,' said Drinkley, looking at his feet.

Woodhouse got up and they started to run again. The master pushed past them and ran on ahead, muttering something under his breath. Drinkley waited until he was gone and said with feeling:

'Wanker!'

The track had widened enough for them to be running abreast again and they looked at him in amazement. He was showing hitherto unsuspected spirit.

'He hates me,' continued Drinkley breathlessly, 'the bastard.'

'It's true,' said Rafferty; 'Sidebottom really does hate Drippy. And he is a bastard.'

They ran on in silence. The track straightened and inclined downwards and they naturally picked up the pace. The rain had stopped and, as they emerged from the trees, the sun tried to push through the clouds, but they were obdurate. They saw two figures waiting up ahead and as they grew closer they resolved themselves into Catford and Sketchley.

'Frontbottom went steaming past us in a right snot,' said Sketchley, 'so we thought we'd hang back and see how you lot were getting on.'

'We're all right,' said Rafferty. 'Earwig fell in the mud – it was brilliant! And Drippy called Frontbum a wanker. He didn't hear though.'

'He *is* a wanker,' said Catford to general agreement, and they continued on, past a derelict barn and soggy meadows where grubby cows were grazing, towards the cliffs.

In the distance the sea spread out like a dirty grey blanket and the sun continued to cower behind the busy black clouds. Maybe everything will be all right after all, thought Woodhouse, and felt unexpectedly happy.

Gruber went into the sex shop wearing a full-face crash helmet to hide the wounds on his face. He had untied Tallulah, escorted her to the bathroom and given her breakfast before he left: scrambled eggs, toast and warm coffee. Warm and not hot in case she threw it in his face. She had finished all of it and then lain down quietly while he tied and gagged her again. He was already tired of all the rope work.

The sex shop was predictably seedy, though hopefully not literally. There were no windows, for obvious reasons, and the lights cast a sickly yellow glow, like diseased urine. Rows of DVDs with bold titles like *Gangbang Apocalypse* and *Fist-Fuck Slut-Whores Two* filled one wall. There were racks full of vibrators of various shapes, sizes and colours – some of them were the size of Gruber's forearm and one of them actually had a fist instead of a glans – butt plugs, whips, masks, crotch-less panties, pant-less crotches, rubber vaginas, blow-up dolls, prophylactics to suit all sizes and intentions, and boxes and boxes full of dirty books. The kind of books a man keeps secret and reads when he's alone, and if he weeps a little afterwards then it's nobody's business but his own.

The man behind the counter was flabby and pasty. His hair was greasy and curly and his stubble was patchy and grey. He wore a soiled cardigan and a pained expression and he did not look pleased to see Gruber, who pushed back the visor of his helmet because it was starting to steam up.

'Good morning,' he said through the padding of the crash helmet. 'I would like four pairs of handcuffs and a ball-gag – one of the ones with a buckle if you have them.'

'You what, mate? I can't hear you, can I? What is it you want?'

Gruber adjusted the helmet. The material was sticking to the scratches on his face.

'Four pairs of handcuffs and a ball-gag with a buckle,' he said, as distinctly as he could.

The sex shop proprietor – he must be the proprietor; surely no one would have hired him – raised his upper lip quizzically, revealing brown teeth, and wrinkled his greasy nose in puzzlement.

'Handcuffs and a what?'

'A BALL-GAG! A BUCKLE BALL-GAG!' shouted Gruber desperately through the padding.

The proprietor's dewlap quivered indignantly.

'Who are you calling a ball-bag?' he demanded. 'Just who do you think you're calling a fucking ball-bag?' He put his hands on his hips and shook his head disgustedly. 'You people, you come into my shop, with your innocent expressions and your ill-concealed erections, and you give me no respect. None! Do you think I enjoy this? I'm losing money hand over speeding fist here. Job satisfaction? Job satis-bloody-faction? My arse! Don't make me laugh! Peddling plastic pricks to perverts, that's my bloody game, and a losing game it is too.'

He leant over the counter and Gruber could see the veins in his yellowy eyeballs.

'And you have the *cheek* to come in here with that sodding thing on your head like a bloody armed robber or something, swearing at me and calling *me* a ball-bag! In my own bloody shop! I'll tell you who's the fucking ball-bag, mate: *YOU*, that's who. *YOU'RE* a fucking ball-bag! *THERE!* So get out of my shop, you fucking *BALL-BAG!*'

He advanced on Gruber menacingly, waving a huge rubber penis that he had produced from under the counter. Gruber backed away.

'I'll *show* you who's the bloody ball-bag, mate: *YOU! BALL-BAG! BALL-BAG! GET – OUT – OF – MY – FUCKING – SHOP!*' And he began raining down blows on Gruber's crash helmet with the unwieldy purple phallus.

Realising that the situation had deteriorated beyond recovery, Gruber left quickly and ran off down the road. The Führer would not be pleased.

Woodhouse saw Greaves from a distance. He was half-sitting, half-leaning on the keys of a stone baby grand piano set back slightly from the main path, smoking his pipe and wearing what appeared to be cricket whites. He looked as if he was posing for a photograph. The famous old graveyard was beautiful in the late morning sunshine, shafts of sunlight slanting through the trees and lighting the tumbledown gravestones like a stage set. Wood pigeons called and a passenger jet roared ponderously across the blue sky above.

As Woodhouse got closer he was able to deduce that Greaves was wearing bowling whites rather than cricket. On the ground by the leg of the piano was a canvas bag shaped to contain the woods and a jack or two. Woodhouse remembered playing the game at school. It was less dangerous than most.

'Good morning,' said Greaves looking at his watch. 'Punctual, I see.'

'One does one's best, sir,' said Woodhouse, smiling.

Greaves re-lit his pipe, looking up at Woodhouse through the smoke. As usual his glance was shrewd. There was silence for a moment apart from a distant woodpecker drumming, and Woodhouse took tobacco and papers from his pocket and rolled a cigarette. The sun was hot on his back.

'How are you getting on with the code?' Greaves asked, tossing away a spent match. 'And that American girl they sent us.'

'I'm close to cracking it, I think. I can feel it.' Woodhouse lit his cigarette with a Zippo. 'Miss Carter seems very capable,' he added carefully.

'Attractive girl, like a 1950s' film starlet.' Greaves was smiling.

'Indeed, sir.' Woodhouse kept his face deadpan.

'Very, ah, pneumatic.'

You dirty old man! thought Woodhouse.

'Extremely voluptuous, sir,' he agreed.

Greaves bridled.

'Steady on now, Woodhouse, she's a very well respected operative. One of their best – so keep your mind on your work, there's a good fellow. We can't have the poor girl getting a bun in the oven, can we now?'

'No, sir,' said Woodhouse through gritted teeth.

Greaves stood up and Woodhouse could see that the name in the stone above the moss-covered piano keys was Thornton. He'd had some piano lessons at school but had shown more aptitude for the guitar. He still had one at home; perhaps he should dig it out and strum a few – a few – my God, that's it! It's so simple! He shook his head in disbelief: he should have solved it ages ago.

He took out his phone and hurriedly accessed the cipher:

ADDSAAXXOSDAXADDDAXOSSAO
XADDDAXOJGGGDGDDDDXOSOSO

Fingers shaking, he inserted some spaces:

ADDSAA XXOSDA XADDDA XOSSAO
XADDDA XOJGGG DGDDDD XOSOSO

'Do you mind, Woodhouse – we're in a meeting,' said Greaves testily.

'It's the code, sir. I think I've got it – it's guitar tab!'

He showed the screen to Greaves, who was clearly nonplussed.

'Stop talking gobbledygook, man. Explain yourself!'

'Each set of six letters represents the six strings on a guitar. They've substituted letters for the fret numbers, but the Xs represent strings in the chord that you don't sound and the Os are open strings. You can see that the third set is the same as the fifth – that's because it's the same chord!'

'So, you're telling me that this is a tune?'

'Part of a tune, at any rate. I just need to work out which fret numbers are represented by which letter and then I should be able to play it.' He thought for a moment. 'If it turns out to be a song it could be that there's some kind of clue in the lyrics.'

Greaves looked doubtful.

'Seems a funny old business to me. Are you sure about this?'

'I'm certain, sir. I knew there was something familiar about the groupings.' He remembered Maryanne's suggestion about herpes and smiled.

'Well, crack on with it. Perhaps when you've finished you can give us a concert, eh?' Greaves picked up his canvas bag and motioned Woodhouse to walk with him. 'I'm away next week but the office will be able to contact me. Good work, Woodhouse.'

'Thank you, sir.' Woodhouse re-lit his roll-up. 'Going anywhere nice?'

'Bit of a golfing break in Scotland. Get away from all the hurly-burly.'

They paused by an ivy-clad angel on a plinth. Her expression was serene despite the fact that she was missing an arm.

'Well, good luck with that, sir – and with the bowls.'

'Ah yes, bowls. Nothing wrong with your deductive powers then, Woodhouse. Conan Doyle would be proud. Not buried here, is he?'

'I don't know, sir. I don't think so.'

They shook hands. Greaves's grip was firm and dry.

'Try not to impregnate young – what's-her-name? – Carter.'

'I'll do my best, sir.'

Woodhouse watched Greaves walk slowly away, past a man photographing a statue of a sleeping dog. The woodpecker drummed again and there was a cry that most likely wasn't a peacock. The old man's getting old, thought Woodhouse, probably time he retired.

Cubby discovered that helping the police with their enquiries was a lot less civilised than it sounded. They didn't charge him with anything but they asked him unpleasant questions and they kept on asking them for an unreasonably long time.

When they got to the station they made him empty his pockets and put the contents on the custody sergeant's desk. Then they took away his belt and shoelaces, all the time looking at him as if he was the worst man in the world, led him downstairs, chalked his surname on a cell door and locked him away inside. Cubby had never been in a cell before and he didn't care for it at all. They left him there for a long time. At first he walked around, then he sat down on the wooden bench that served as a bed, and finally he lay down and pulled the thin blanket over his face.

When they finally came for him he was almost pleased to see them. The custody officer led him to an interview room. Cubby had to shuffle and his trousers kept slipping down. He was left alone in there for a little while and then two plain clothes officers came in and the questions began. They recorded the interview on a cassette machine.

It was straightforward at first. Name, address, date of birth; how long had he known Tallulah Grimes; how would he describe their relationship (Cubby blushed and said 'friends', to the obvious amusement of the jaded-looking officers); did he and Tallulah often argue (Cubby hesitated before saying no). Then they started to increase the pressure. The dynamic between them was beginning to become apparent: it wasn't as simple as "good cop, bad cop" but they did have different roles. The taller and older of the two, the one with the shaved head, cold eyes and the scar on his chin, asked the questions and maintained eye contact with Cubby. His colleague – unshaven, curly black hair, unpleasant Cupid's bow mouth – yawned, stretched, sneered and made insinuations.

They took him through the events of Saturday lunchtime over and over again, coming at it from all kinds of angles, firing questions faster than he could answer them, messing with his equilibrium, breaking him down, looking to get under his skin and hit him where he lived so as to gauge his reaction.

They gave his psyche a good kicking then they made him a cup of tea and chatted with him until he felt better. Then they started in again, harder than ever. To his credit, Cubby took it well. He did his best to remain calm, understanding that, to a certain extent, it was a performance, a tried and trusted routine designed to crack the veneer of people who were hiding something. Cubby had the huge advantage that he was telling the truth and his conscience was clear. He didn't have to remember to stick to his story because it wasn't a story, and however oblique the angle from which they attacked him they found him solid, unshakeable.

They kept at him for three and a half hours then put him back in his cell and discussed it. It seemed clear that he was telling the truth. His story was so stupid that it *had* to be true. And his behaviour and body language were those of an innocent man. Even the scratches on his face told in his favour, being more consistent with shards of pottery than fingernails. They debated whether to keep him overnight and decided there was no need. They got him out of the cell, gave him his possessions back and, while he was lacing up his shoes, warned him not to leave town and told him to contact them if he heard from Tallulah. Then they let him go. It was four in the afternoon and he walked home through a hailstorm, wondering where she was.

Lomax sat at his desk and issued instructions into the phone. As he talked he sipped brandy and looked at the images on his monitors. A woman was being raped on the roof of a tower block. He watched disinterestedly for a while and then turned his chair and looked out of the window instead. The late afternoon sun was low behind the Eiffel Tower and a skein of geese flew past. Lomax put down the receiver and opened his ledger.

He considered the list of names there and wondered whether his opponent had deciphered his message yet. He didn't think so: he would have heard through the ether – or from his spies. The man would puzzle it out soon, and receive another, more definite message. He noticed that the ink bottle was almost empty – he would have to get some more. He lit a cigar, took another sip of brandy and got up from the chair, stretching and rolling his shoulders. He didn't get enough exercise these days and he was getting old.

He left the office and went into the room next to it. A stained-glass window shed soft diffused light of many colours. This window was an imposing eight-foot-by-twelve representation of a peacock displaying its tail, executed after the style of Irish stained-glass maestro Harry Clarke. On its breast was a bleeding heart surmounted by a crown of thorns. The work had cost a great deal of money and Lomax was very proud of it.

In the centre of the room, set into a purpose-built base in the floor, stood a nine-foot crucifix made of railway sleepers. The blue, green and gold of the peacock's tail were projected on to the flesh of the naked figure that hung there, creating dazzling patterns that shifted slowly. It was hauntingly beautiful. Lomax stood and took in the scene for a time, still smoking his cigar. There was silence apart from a slow drip.

'Crucifixion must be a very great honour for you, Father,' he said after a while. 'To experience the agonies suffered by your precious messiah. You must be proud, yes?'

The man on the cross groaned and the speed of the dripping increased slightly. Blood ran black from the razor-wire crown on his hanging head, from the wounds in his hands and in his feet, dark rivulets among the glorious kaleidoscope of colour, black streams running and dripping into ornate chalices positioned beneath. Lomax examined the chalices for a moment then said:

'Soon you will die, Father, but there will be no resurrection for you. No ascension either. You will suffer and you will die and you will be gone, and your corpse will be thrown in the river or buried in the woods or burnt. It matters not. There will be no heaven for you, if you are even worthy – which I doubt – just as there will be no hell for me, though I am certainly deserving of it. You have wasted your life, Father – I tell you this as one who knows. But you have, at least, provided me with some more ink for my pen, so you may find a little comfort in that.'

The priest groaned again and Lomax took the chalice from the foot of the cross, replacing it with an empty one. He looked up into the priest's face for a moment then left the room.

'I forgive you, my son,' said the priest quietly.

Up on the roof the air is fragrant and the sounds of the city are distant. The crew are busy with the Stealth Hawk, performing checks. She has work to do soon. Lomax watches. He is satisfied.

Woodhouse woke with a start: something was holding his nose closed. He struggled and opened his mouth to cry out but the hand let go of his nose and covered his mouth instead.

'Come with me,' whispered a voice close to his ear. 'I want to show you something.'

The hand was withdrawn from his mouth and Woodhouse opened his eyes. He could just make out the figure of Rafferty wearing dressing gown and slippers.

'What is it, Raffles?'

'Shh! Come on.'

Woodhouse got out of bed and quietly put on his dressing gown. The room was filled with the sounds of sleep. Carrigan was snoring gently; Gunton stirred and mumbled something; Sketchley whimpered like a dog. Sliding his feet into his slippers, Woodhouse followed Rafferty out of the dormitory and on to the darkened landing. The emergency lights above the doors shed enough light to see that Rafferty was carrying an unlit torch.

By the stairwell they stopped and listened for a moment. They could hear quiet footsteps somewhere below them. A distant door opened and closed and all was silent again but for the faint ticking of a clock.

Woodhouse felt something tug at the sleeve of his dressing gown.

'I'm coming with you,' whispered Drinkley.

'Christ!' said Rafferty too loudly. 'Go back, Drippy.'

'No,' whispered Drinkley, jutting his chin, 'I won't!'

They all looked at each other for a moment then Rafferty shrugged his shoulders and led the way to a small panelled door in the wall. Slowly he turned the brass handle and pulled it open. He had to duck to go inside. Woodhouse followed and then Drinkley, who pulled the door closed behind him. Rafferty switched on the torch. They all blinked as their eyes adjusted to the sudden light.

They were standing in an empty cupboard about the size of a phone box. The back wall housed a couple of bare shelves. They looked at Rafferty.

'So?' asked Woodhouse.

Rafferty smiled.

'Watch this,' he said. Handing Woodhouse the torch he climbed up the shelves, gave a wriggle and disappeared from view. An arm stretched down.

'Hand me the torch.'

'You go next,' said Woodhouse to Drinkley. 'I'll give you a push if you need it.'

Rafferty shone the torch down and Drinkley climbed up. He was gone in no time. Woodhouse followed. He squeezed through the space above the shelf and found the others waiting in a crawl-space.

'Wow!' he said.

'This is nothing,' said Rafferty. 'Come on.'

They crawled. It was dusty and a bit splintery. They came to a short vertical section with hand and footholds, making it an easy climb, and then crawled again and arrived at another small door.

'Ready?' asked Rafferty, smiling proudly.

They squeezed together to see. He opened the door and shone in the torch beam.

It was amazing: a huge raftered space as far as the torchlight would let them see. Woodhouse could see aeroplanes hanging from the rafters, bicycles, a pantomime horse, folds of rich velvet drapery, clothes racks hung with brightly coloured costumes, and Persian carpets stacked in rolls. There were stage flats painted with woodland scenes, seascapes, a drawing room. His mouth hung open.

'Come on,' said Rafferty. He climbed in and stood up. The others followed. Woodhouse heard the gasp of Drinkley's inhaler.

Rafferty walked into the neglected wonderland, shining the torch around. They found a packing case full of wooden swords and rifles, and each took a sword but resisted the temptation to fight, knowing the need for silence. A trunk contained Regency era wigs: extravagant curls and ringlets. They each donned one, smiling at each other delightedly. Suddenly they found themselves in a forest of painted trees.

'This must be all the stuff for the school plays,' whispered Drinkley reverently.

'Duh!' said Rafferty.

There was scenery from a pirate ship and from a tropical island, and then they found the treasure chest. Crowding round as Woodhouse eased open the massive iron-banded lid they all gasped. There were goblets, gold and silver coins, strings of pearls, bejewelled rings and brooches, bracelets and bangles, crowns and tiaras, candlesticks, crucifixes, salvers and chargers: all piled together in a great glittering heap. It was astonishing. They looked at it for a while, taking turns to run their fingers through it, enjoying the shine and the weight of it.

'Look at this,' said Drinkley.

Lying on its side was a red and white striped canvas Punch and Judy booth, covered in dust. In a packing case next to it were the puppets. The treasure was forgotten, although Woodhouse slipped a gold coin into his dressing gown pocket.

'My great-grandfather was a Punch and Judy man,' said Drinkley, holding up the Punch puppet.

The cruel wooden face seemed to twist in the torchlight and Woodhouse was suddenly afraid. Rafferty hunted through the box. Here was the clown, the blackamoor, Judy, the curate, the convict, the devil, the gallows, the baby in its coffin and a string of sausages.

'What's this?' he asked, holding something small out on his palm.

In the torchlight Woodhouse saw a flattened oval shape, about an inch long. As Rafferty turned it over it became apparent that it comprised twin strips of silver wrapped in dusty material. Through the open centre of the oval ran a further strip of the same material.

'Chuck it away, Raffles,' said Woodhouse. 'It's manky.'

'That's the swazzle,' said Drinkley, snatching it and blowing through it to remove the dust. 'That's how you do the voice. It's a closely guarded secret among Punch and Judy men.'

'How does it work?' asked Rafferty.

'You put it in your mouth and talk through it, kind of like a kazoo.'

'Do it!' said Woodhouse.

'It's too dusty,' said Drinkley. 'It needs cleaning up and soaking first.'

The light grew suddenly dim.

'Shit,' said Rafferty. 'We better get back before the batteries run out.'

There was a bump. Then something that sounded like a gasp.

'What was that?' whispered Woodhouse. He could feel the hair trying to stand up on his head under the wig.

They looked at each other with fearful eyes.

'It's the Grey Lady!' sobbed Drinkley.

Mindless of the need to be quiet they ran panicking back to the door, hurling the wigs away as they went, and fought each other to get through. They climbed hurriedly down the vertical section, Drinkley almost falling, jostled each other along the crawl space and tumbled noisily into the cupboard, emerging shortly before the headmaster rounded the corner of the landing.

'Go to bed immediately,' he said coldly, 'and report to my study at nine o'clock tomorrow morning.'

'Oh, man,' said Rafferty sadly as they walked back to their dormitory. 'We're going to get whacked.'

'I've dropped my inhaler,' said Drinkley.

'So what?' said Rafferty. 'You've got a spare, haven't you?'

'Yes, but—'

'What, you want to go back up there? We're in enough trouble already.'

They went to bed.

Gruber got into the car and threw the crash helmet onto the back seat. The Cat-Führer looked at him disdainfully.

'You are pathetic, Gruber,' it said, making a clinking sound as it scratched its ear with a back foot. 'A shower of scheisse. Even this simple task you have failed to complete. Your inadequate brain angers me, Gruber. It is like the weak baby bird that has fallen from its nest and lies dying on the moss. Perhaps now I will to biting down upon the tiny soft bones of your feeble baby-bird mind – like so!'

The Führer's eyes grew large and Gruber felt the glassy glare tunnelling through the soft meat of his brain. He clasped his head in his hands and screamed. The Führer smiled and it was a most disconcerting sight. He clawed Gruber's psyche like the arm of a settee and Gruber began to cry.

'I grow weary, Gruber,' said the Führer eventually. 'Drive. She awaits.'

Still sobbing, Gruber drove home, his mind in tatters.

'Have you been crying?' asked Tallulah. 'You should.'

'It's hay fever,' said Gruber, placing the Führer on the dressing table.

'Untie me, Tiny Tears – I need the toilet.'

Gruber made sure that she could see the knife in its sheath on his belt and began to untie her. She looked particularly beautiful today and without warning his heart became entangled in the knots in her hair and he fell helplessly into her sad grey eyes and floundered there, drowning happily.

'Control yourself, Gruber,' snapped the Führer. 'You are not Cary Grant.'

Gruber swam to the surface and finished untying Tallulah. She sat up, rubbing her wrists.

'It's time you let me go,' she said. 'They'll be looking for me.'

'I told you: it's our destiny. It is written in the stars.'

'Oh, don't start all that shit again. You're as mad as a balloon, mate – you've been talking to a china cat and it talks back, doesn't it?' He nodded warily, trying not to look at the Führer. 'You took me and tied me to a bed, for reasons that I don't even want to think about, but it's not too late. Let me go now and you can get some help. Everything will be all right, I promise.'

She had been moving towards him during her little speech and now she smiled prettily and looked up at him. He jumped back, just as her hand was closing round the hilt of the knife.

'You little bitch!'

She smoothed down her skirt, reminding him suddenly of Raquel Welch in *One Million Years B.C.*

'It's our destiny,' she said huskily, thrusting her breasts together and pouting. 'It is written in the stars.' She narrowed her eyes and shook out the tangles in her hair. She smouldered at him.

'Stop that!'

'Theirs was a love that would burn for all eternity.' She fell to her knees, arms outstretched, her upturned face radiant. 'A shining beacon through the ages, giving hope to all mankind.' She began to crawl towards him. He backed away, horrified. 'But it was a tragic love—'

'Stop doing that!'

'A love that was doomed.' She stood up and looked him in the eye. 'Because he was a shitty kidnapping little pussy with a tiny misshapen penis!'

She feinted to run towards the doorway and he moved to block the way. She dodged back the other way and snatched the Cat-Führer triumphantly up from the dressing table.

'No!' cried Gruber.

'Yes!' she said. 'Oh yes.' She made as if to throw the cat through the window. 'Suppose I smash this thing to pieces? What then?' She smiled. 'Is that destined to happen?'

'Give it back to me, Tallulah. Give it back NOW!' He lunged for it.

'Ah-ah-ah-ah, naughty, naughty!' She shaped to dash the cat to the floor. 'Stand back!' He moved back, his mind racing. 'I think it's time for you to let me go now,' she said, beginning to edge towards the door.

'I can't do that, Tallulah. You know I can't.'

He jumped at her and the cat was knocked from her hand. Tallulah twisted, landing on top of Gruber, and immediately began punching him in the face, but he had eyes only for the Führer. It turned slowly in the air, gleaming in the light.

'Catch me, Gruber,' it warned. 'If I break, you break too.'

The Führer began its descent. Gruber stretched out a hand but Tallulah was still punching him, making it difficult for him to see. She kneed him hard in the testicles. It was agony, but the Führer dropped safely into his hand. He closed his eyes as nausea overwhelmed him.

'After her, you fool,' shouted the cat. 'She is escaping!'

Gruber staggered to his feet. His testicles were aflame and his left eye was already closing as a result of having Tallulah's dainty fist driven repeatedly into it.

'She can't get out,' he said groggily. 'Both the doors are locked.'

He put the Führer back on the dressing table and went gingerly downstairs, removing the knife from its sheath. Tallulah was on the floor, sitting by the front door with her chin in her hands.

'Come on,' he said. 'I'll make you a nice cup of tea and we'll have a chat.'

She got up slowly and they went into the kitchen together.

It was the kind of lie that could ruin your day. Greaves looked at it disgustedly. He had sliced his tee shot and then watched impotently as it curved away and struck the trunk of a small pine tree a hundred and fifty yards away in the edge of the rough. McTavish had laughed, damn him.

Greaves looked down at the ball nestling in the bracken. There was no room to address the thing, much less swing a club. He was being hampered by a gorse bush. Infuriating! He would have to waste a shot chipping the ball just to get back on to the fairway and he was four shots down on McTavish already. Damn and blast the bloody thing! He swiped moodily at the gorse bush with his nine iron.

It had taken him ten minutes just to find the bloody ball. McTavish had given up the search and played on, pledging to wait for Greaves to catch up after the next hole – the ninth.

For one terrible moment it crossed his mind to cheat: just pick the thing up and lob it into the fairway. Then a nice high iron over the rise that obscured his view of the flag and he should land within a chip of the green.

Greaves patted his pockets to make sure his pipe was safe and sighed. He couldn't do it: a man who cheats at golf is the lowest of the low, worse even than a child-molesting traffic warden. He focussed his mind and addressed the ball. There wasn't even room for a practise swing. Keep the wrists nice and loose, he reminded himself, and chop down under it so it pops up. Greaves made the shot. It popped up and then popped back down again, landing in the exact same place, just as a severed bracken frond dropped smugly on to the precise spot he had been aiming for on the fairway. Blast! Don't lose your temper – just a little more angle on the face and a bit more *oomph* in the swing. There! The ball jumped neatly out of the rough and skipped gladly along to the centre of the fairway. Beautiful!

He sat down on the turf by the ball and took out his pipe and tobacco tin. As he packed the bowl he looked around. It was a cloudy morning but the scenery was bright, the blues and purples of the heather and the yellow of the gorse flowers vivid. He could smell the pine, and as he looked up at the trees along the fairway he saw a red squirrel jump nimbly from one branch to another. The peace was marred by a nearby mechanical sound: must be the greenkeeper cutting the grass. A startled bird blundered away through the foliage nearby, protesting loudly.

He lit his pipe and stood up slowly, careful of his creaky knees. A good shot here and he could still make par. He elected to use his trusty seven iron. Walking back to his trolley he slipped the nine iron into the bag, taking out the seven. He stood over the ball, pipe clamped between his teeth and eyes narrowed against the smoke. He made a practise swing, and then another; it felt good.

He shuffled into position, pipe jutting belligerently, and took his shot. It was a belter! He watched delightedly as it climbed into the distance, straight and true, and began to fall towards the green, which he knew was hidden behind the rise. It disappeared from view and he heard a clunk. What the hell? Had he hit the greenkeeper's mower or something?

'Fore!' he called belatedly.

There was no response and then slowly, as if rising from the depths of hell, a great black helicopter lifted into view over the brow of the hill and hovered there, flattening the grass and stirring the trees with its downwash. Gradually it turned broadside to him.

The club fell from his hands and the pipe from his mouth as he reached for the pistol that he had left in the clubhouse. He watched the barrel of the gun in the cabin door angle towards him and saw the distorted face of the man behind it. The first fifty calibre rounds punched through him and then he heard the shots and the chatter of the ammunition belt feeding through.

Browning M2, he thought dreamily. Early retirement – bugger!

From the Stealth Hawk, Lomax watches Greaves perform an involuntary Charleston as the big shells tear through his body. The smell of hot oil and the jingle and shine of the shell casings are invigorating. He fires another burst at the now prone figure, just for the joy of it, and then orders the pilot down. As the wheels touch down on the green he lets go of the gun and jumps out. He picks up Greaves's ball for a souvenir: it is a Titleist. It had been a fine shot the old man had made; would have dropped close to the flag if it hadn't hit the helicopter. He inspects the nose of the Stealth Hawk: yes, there is the faintest of scuffs where the ball struck. He licks a finger and polishes out the mark, then puts the ball in his pocket, gets back into the cabin and they lift off and climb away into the clouds.

A message has been delivered and a round of golf terminally interrupted.

Cubby lay on the ottoman in his dusty drawing room. Mahler's first symphony was unfolding quietly on the radiogram and a pile of novels lay on the floor within easy reach. He couldn't read, though, because he couldn't concentrate for worrying about Tallulah. The music helped a little but not much. The doorbell rang and was followed immediately by loud banging. The police again, thought Cubby miserably.

He opened the front door. An unpleasant looking individual was there, wearing a bright green tracksuit and high-top trainers. It was Craig.

'I is got beefs wif you, innit,' he announced, making obscure hand signals. 'You is some sort of noncer or whatever – man come for ping you out, bruvs. What is you done wif my Tazza, you perv?'

'I haven't done anything to her. I'm worried about her as well.'

Craig began shuffling his feet and rolling his shoulders; clearly he was preparing to attack.

'You is well weird and that, cuz – I seen the way you lookin' at her. You done somefink to her, innit – I know you did. Man come for mash you up.'

'I would never harm a hair on her head,' said Cubby loftily.

'Is it though? Ha! I don't think so.' Craig advanced menacingly. 'You all rapey and that, innit, fam. Buried her in the garden for sure. Accept this!' He hit Cubby with a straight right-handed punch that knocked him off his feet. 'Where is she?' he demanded, following up with a kick in the ribs.

'I don't know!' shouted Cubby.

'Where is she, you pussy?' Another kick.

Cubby had never been hit before – or kicked. It stirred his blood. It invigorated him. The war cries of his ancestors sang in his ears: a woad-smeared berserker ripped to the tits on hallucinogenic mushroom wine; a blood-spattered crusader cleaving heathens with a broadsword for the glory of God; a proud hussar readying his lance for the charge and a gory but glorious death. He stood up, heedless of the blows. Craig's head morphed into that of a cat and enraged him.

'I told you – I don't know where she is, and I don't much care for your attitude.'

He stepped up to Craig and knocked him unconscious with a flawlessly executed uppercut. Despite all Grandmother's efforts to civilise him, Cubby was a warrior.

Craig came to on the carpet in the drawing room. He sat up rubbing his jaw.

'What d'you hit me with – baseball bat, is it?'

Cubby was sitting on the edge of the ottoman. He showed Craig his fist.

'I hit you with this. And you'll get another one if you don't behave yourself, my lad.'

'Chill out, bruv – squash the beef, innit, you get what I mean?'

'Not really, but I told you – I'm as worried about her as you are.'

They looked at each other. Mahler was still playing.

'Need to find that girl. Bad t'ing can happen, cuz, bad t'ing.'

'We should go and look for her. Have you got your car?'

'Tchah, man; man got to have him wheels for take care of him business.'

'Quite.'

Cubby helped Craig up and they went to look for Tallulah.

They sat outside the headmaster's study looking at the red light. Drinkley was shaking with fear and Woodhouse felt like he might be going to be sick. Rafferty seemed fine apart from a nervously tapping foot.

'I'll go in first if you like,' he said.

'Can I go first?' asked Drinkley. 'I really want to get it over with.'

The others looked at each other and nodded. The red light went out and after a moment the green one came on. A voice shouted:

'COME!'

Drinkley got up and went in. The red light replaced the green. They could hear the rumbling of the headmaster's voice then Drinkley came out again, looking even more miserable than before. He gave them a pitiful look then trudged off down the corridor. The red light stayed on.

'Raffles, what's happening?' whispered Woodhouse.

'He's sent him to the gym to get one of his gym shoes – for the slippering. If you can't find it he uses this massive one he keeps in the desk. It's a size fifteen or something.'

They waited. Woodhouse was starting to need the toilet. After a few minutes Drinkley returned carrying a plimsoll.

He knocked on the door and went in. They heard the headmaster's voice again and then the sound of a blow and a muffled cry.

'Keep quiet, Drippy,' muttered Rafferty, 'or you'll get six more.'

They counted the blows. Woodhouse could see why it was called whacking – it sounded like someone beating a carpet. After six it stopped. They heard the headmaster's voice again then Drinkley came out, biting his lip and holding his bottom with one hand and the plimsoll in the other. He went off down the corridor. They looked at each other and the green light came on.

'You go,' said Woodhouse without knowing why.

Rafferty shrugged and went in. The red light came on. Woodhouse heard the voice again and then a different sound: a rush of air and then a sharp crack. The cane, thought Woodhouse, he's getting the cane! His scrotum shrivelled with fear. He counted the strokes, sure that he would wet himself at any moment. After six he held his breath, listening to see if there would be more, but after the rumble of the headmaster's voice Rafferty emerged making a comical "ooh" face and, like Drinkley, holding his bottom. He rolled his eyes at Woodhouse and went off rubbing his bottom and groaning.

The green light came on and Woodhouse took a deep breath and went in. The headmaster sat behind his desk looking red-faced and angry.

'Woodforde, isn't it?' he said.

'Actually it's Woodh—'

'SILENCE, BOY!' The headmaster stood up, put his hands on the desk and leant forward. 'Go immediately to the gymnasium and fetch one of your plimsolls from your locker and then return. NOW, BOY!'

Woodhouse went out and down the corridor, turning once to see that the red light was on. At least he wasn't going to get the cane by the look of it. Cheered slightly by this thought, he went across the hall and out of the side entrance. Faces in the Portakabin windows turned to watch him pass. And he was missing French – that was good too. As he entered the changing room in the gym block he worried that his gym shoes wouldn't be in his locker, though he knew perfectly well that they were. He opened the locker and debated which one to take: left or right. He decided on the right one, reasoning that it might be softer because he was right-footed. He knew it was a vain hope.

He trudged back to the main building, looking up at the high white clouds scudding across the blue winter sky. Frost glittered on the concrete.

The red light was still on but he knocked and went in. The headmaster reached across the desk and took the gym shoe.

'I will not have boys mucking about after lights out, Woodforde.' The headmaster looked at him, weighing the plimsoll in his hand. 'Any excuses? – no – good. Bend over and face the window.'

He gestured to a dining chair with its back to the french windows. Woodhouse leant over its seat, placed his hands on its back and braced himself for the impact. The headmaster came and stood behind him. A blackbird was tugging a worm out of the lawn outside.

'Do not struggle or cry out,' warned the headmaster, adding unconvincingly: 'I can assure you that this will hurt me far more than it hurts you.'

Woodhouse heard him take a couple of steps back. God, he's taking a run-up! he thought.

The first one was painful but bearable. The second was in exactly the same place but harder and it really hurt. The third and fourth hurt so much that Woodhouse found that his hand had crept round to try and fend off the blows.

'KEEP STILL, BOY!' roared the headmaster, seizing his wrist and forcing his hand back on to the chair.

The fifth blow was agony and Woodhouse half-cried out. Through the tears he saw the blackbird triumph and fly away with the worm dangling from its beak.

The headmaster paused before delivering what Woodhouse hoped would be the final blow. He's enjoying himself, thought Woodhouse, and was filled with hatred so black that he could taste it like bile.

The headmaster put everything into the last blow and it hurt a lot. Woodhouse gritted his teeth and waited, praying that it was over. The headmaster stepped away.

'Let that be a lesson to you,' he said, handing Woodhouse the plimsoll. 'Put this back in your locker and then get to your class. Don't let me see you in here again, boy.'

Woodhouse got the call about Greaves on his mobile.

'It's Rosalind,' she said. 'Your grandfather has died. Can I come round and see you?'

'Of course,' said Woodhouse. He was stunned.

Twenty minutes later the doorbell rang. A serious looking woman in her forties was waiting there. She wore a dark suit and carried a briefcase.

'Good morning,' she said briskly. 'My name is Taylor – I will be taking over from Mr Greaves.'

'You'd better come in,' said Woodhouse.

He led the way to the kitchen and they sat down at the table. She steepled her fingers and regarded him soberly. Opening the briefcase she took out a file.

'What happened?' he asked.

'He was attacked while playing golf – on the eighth hole actually. Fourteen fifty-calibre bullet wounds – a very nasty business.'

'Christ!'

'I doubt whether *he* was involved. His golfing partner died too – of a heart attack. Several witnesses saw and heard a helicopter, as well as the sound of the gun. We've informed them that they were mistaken, naturally. Mr Greaves was struck by lightning and Mr –' she consulted the file – 'McTavish died of a heart attack brought on by shock.'

'The last part's true enough at any rate, I would imagine.'

'I'm told that you're working on deciphering a code that may give us some clues about the people who did this?'

'I'm more than halfway with it.'

'Well perhaps you could crack on with that as a matter of some urgency. We're quite keen to apprehend these people and recover or destroy this helicopter. You've been working with Miss –' she took another look at the file – 'Carter, yes?'

'That's right.' Woodhouse was starting to dislike Ms Taylor.

'Perhaps you could liaise with her – two heads better than one and all that.' She smiled brightly.

'You sound different to on the phone,' said Woodhouse. Less human, he thought.

'Oh, one of the girls does those. I expect we'll be replacing that ridiculous code now.'

'I rather like it.'

She seemed about to reprimand him when the cat barrelled in through the cat-flap, miaowing loudly, and approached her expectantly.

'Would you mind keeping it away from me? I'm allergic to them.' She began to sneeze.

'Come on, Walther.'

Woodhouse picked up the cat – Christ, he was heavy! – and shut him in the sitting room. The woman was still sneezing – what a drama queen! Woodhouse did his best to conceal his disgust.

'Would you like a cup of tea?' he asked.

'Do you have any Earl Grey?'

'Yes, I think so.' He rummaged in the cupboards.

'It's a great loss,' she said. 'Mr Greaves was very popular, although of course some of his methods were rather old-fashioned.'

You bitch! thought Woodhouse. You couldn't even pay him a compliment without qualifying it.

'Sometimes the old ways are the best, wouldn't you say? I worked with Greaves for the best part of twenty years. He was very astute.' He found a box of Earl Grey behind the cat biscuits.

'I'm sure he was. I meant no disrespect but times are changing. People don't get stabbed with poisoned umbrellas these days, Woodhouse. It's about satellites now, not dead letter drops.'

I'd like to stab *you* with a poisoned umbrella, he thought mutinously as he filled the kettle. Right up the jacksie!

'You don't think it's a mistake to rely too much on technology?' he asked.

'I think that it behoves us to use any and all means at our disposal,' she said pompously. 'Have you tried feeding the cipher into a computer? We have programs for code-breaking these days, you know. Our cryptography people at Cheltenham are very good.'

There was a crash and a yowl from the sitting room. Walther was making his displeasure known.

'I believe Miss Carter has been looking into the more technical side of it,' he said, willing the kettle to boil so he could get rid of her the sooner. 'We have it under control, ma'am.' He changed the subject. 'What's happening about the funeral?'

'We're making arrangements,' she said. 'His mother is very elderly and apparently his wife died some years ago.'

'I met her once or twice; she was a wonderful lady.' Unlike you, you old bag.

The kettle boiled.

'Would you like milk?' he asked.

'Do you have any lemon?'

He took a lemon from the fridge and sliced it irritably using the stiletto he had wrested from the homicidal escort.

'You don't have to like me, Woodhouse,' Taylor said as he put the mugs on the table. 'I'm not here to be your friend – I'm here to make the department run smoothly. There's no room for quirky characters these days – charm has to give way to efficiency. By the same token, there's no room for the traditional drunken, womanising operative as immortalised by Mr Fleming.' She shot him a stern look. 'Those days are gone, if they ever even existed.' She sipped her tea. 'Very nice. Thank you.'

'Don't mention it, ma'am.' He stressed the "ma'am" heavily.

She put the file back into her briefcase and snapped the catches shut.

'I must be off. We'll be in touch via the usual channels, until I come up with something better.' She gave a mirthless smile. 'Thank you again for the tea.'

He saw her to the door and, after letting the disgruntled cat out of the sitting room, sat down at the table again to finish his tea. Taylor had barely touched hers: charm had indeed given way to efficiency. She had left a card on the table. It said simply *Taylor* and there were two phone numbers. Woodhouse put it in his wallet and went to see what the cat had broken.

Woodhouse did not enjoy playing rugby. He was of slight build but lacked the turn of speed to get himself out of trouble, so whenever someone passed him the ball he tried to get rid of it quickly, before he was trampled into the mud by the pack. It was always raining or hailing or snowing when they played rugby, which just made it hurt all the more.

The tracksuited master shouted unintelligible orders and gave furious blasts on his whistle as little mud-covered boys with blue legs ran about or stood miserably, depending on their aptitude or lack of it.

Woodhouse had discovered that if you kicked the ball it was considered more acceptable than just throwing it away, so he spent time after school practising his kicking. You had to hold the ball with one end pointing down and drop it, connecting with it with your foot just as it hit the ground. If you could get the thing to go between the goal posts, why, so much the better, it seemed. The problem was that the opposing forwards didn't always stop. They sometimes didn't seem to notice if you had the ball or not, or perhaps they didn't care.

On this particular day, Woodhouse used his method on the occasions when he couldn't avoid possession of the ball and stayed out of the way when he could. On one occasion his kick even drew some applause from people on the touchline, though he had no idea why. Catford passed him the ball: thanks a bunch, Pussy! He executed his kick neatly but the forwards were too close to stop and he didn't see any evidence that they were trying. The first one knocked him down and the others just piled in – big heavy, husky lads all over-excited by their shared love of rugby and of violence. He was underneath a great pile of them, all boots and knees, elbows and fists, their panting heavy bodies pressing him into the cold mud. He got kicked in the mouth and tasted blood. After a while they all got up and ran off, leaving him spreadeagled like a starfish. He stood on wobbly legs and spat a tooth into his palm, along with some blood.

'You'd better go and see Matron,' said the master, walking him to the touchline. 'That was a nice kick – you should try out for the Colts.'

'Yes, sir. Thank you, sir.' Not in a million years!

He had to walk through the woods to get back to the school and as soon as they hid him from sight he sat down on a fallen tree to collect himself. He looked at the tooth: it was one of the front ones but it had been loose anyway. He could feel the edge of the new one in the squishy hole.

He heard a cry coming from further into the trees and stood up, grateful to find his legs were less wobbly now. The cry came again; it sounded like someone in pain. He walked towards the sound, dodging through the tree trunks, until he saw a flash of colour. There was a small clearing and there he found Drinkley at bay. A much bigger boy had him by the throat, pressed up against a tree, and another one was looking on and laughing. Drinkley's face was purple.

'Let him go,' said Woodhouse, without intending to.

He knew who they were: Jones and Bayliss, a bullying double act from the fourth year. Thus far Woodhouse had managed to avoid them but that looked set to change. They turned to face him, and Jones let go of Drinkley's throat but held him by the tie instead so he couldn't escape.

'Well, well, well,' said Bayliss, looking Woodhouse up and down. 'Who's this little hero?'

'It's Woodhouse,' whispered Drinkley through the bruises.

Jones took hold of his face, squashing his cheeks and forcing his mouth open.

'He wasn't talking to you, Drinkley. Speak when you're spoken to.'

Bayliss was short, blond and vicious. Jones was big, dark and brutal. Together they amounted to pain.

'We found this little weed hiding in here,' said Bayliss to Woodhouse, 'while everyone else has to play rugby. Hiding in here and making funny noises, isn't that right, Jones?'

'He was making funny noises with this,' said Jones, holding up something that Woodhouse recognised as the swazzle. 'He thinks he's Mr *Punch!*'

As he said the word "Punch", Jones punched Drinkley in the stomach. Drinkley made choking sounds.

'You must be Judy,' said Bayliss, coming close to

Woodhouse and leaning down so their faces were almost touching. 'Call to your girlfriend, Mr Punch.'

Jones forced the swazzle into Drinkley's mouth.

'Call your girlfriend,' he ordered.

'Judy! Judy!' sobbed Drinkley through the swazzle, tears running down his face.

The sound was so unearthly that they were all taken aback for a moment.

'Run to him,' said Bayliss, giving Woodhouse a shove that sent him sprawling.

'Give him a kiss,' commanded Jones, smiling.

Woodhouse got up and threw himself at Jones, arms flailing. In the confusion Drinkley got loose and ran away, thrusting the swazzle into his pocket.

'What's going on in there?' shouted someone grown-up from the path.

'This isn't over,' said Jones, pushing Woodhouse away.

'It's only just beginning,' added Bayliss. 'We'll make your life a living hell.'

'Piss off!' shouted Woodhouse and ran off after Drinkley. He discovered that he still had the tooth in his hand.

Tallulah was walking a tightrope, metaphorically speaking. She would, no doubt, have looked very fetching in a sequinned showgirl costume and tights, showing off her legs on the high-wire, as an enraptured crowd gazed up and marvelled at her beauty, skill and bravery; and there would have been only a very few twisted individuals willing her to fall. But the cable she trod so carefully was representative rather than actual and nobody was watching her legs other than the lunatic Gruber.

This deranged individual, seemingly acting under the instruction of a stolen ceramic cat strongly reminiscent of an even more deranged Nazi despot, had abducted her, apparently with a view to winning her affections and embarking on some kind of ill-advised Aryan breeding programme.

While Tallulah had every intention of one day settling down and raising a family, her present circumstances were as far from her romantic ideal as it was possible to get, and her immediate objective was survival with a view to escape.

She knew that she was reasonably safe as long as Gruber thought he could eventually win her over, but, at the same time, if he thought he actually *had* won her over then he was likely to make unpleasant demands of her – physical demands. This, then, was the wire she walked: she had to offer encouragement while remaining out of reach; and her balancing act was all the more delicate because he was so completely *un*balanced.

Her plan was far from perfect; she was still feeling her way into the situation. She had established that he was no match for her womanly wiles, but what then? Distracting him and then attacking him was dangerous: she needed to keep him off balance but within parameters. She had tested the limits as far as she dared and put him on his guard. Now she had to find a way of making him relax again without endangering herself.

If she inclined too far one way she ran the risk of being raped; the other, murdered. She didn't think her captor was a rapist or a murderer by inclination, but that cat, on the other hand, was a seriously dangerous influence. She would have to do something about that but, in the meantime, if she trod carefully and kept her head, maybe she could find her way to safety, risking nothing more than an unwelcome kiss or a slap. She would keep her balance. She had to, or she was lost.

They sat in Gruber's kitchen with the blind down. Tallulah's tea was warmer than her breakfast coffee but still not hot enough to scald. Gruber was taking no more chances.

'I'm sorry about your eye,' she said. 'You frightened me.'

He looked at her doubtfully with the eye that could still fully open. The other one was getting blacker by the minute.

'You didn't seem very frightened.'

'I didn't mean the things I said – I panicked.'

'We need to find a way to make this relationship work, Tallulah.'

She looked at him, careful of the expression on her face.

'You can't blame me for being confused – I don't even know your name.'

'William,' said Gruber. 'My name's William.'

'That's good... William.' She paused. 'Well, William, perhaps you have a pair of jogging bottoms I could wear? My legs are cold. You wouldn't want me to catch cold, would you?'

'I'll find you some when we go back upstairs. I want you to be happy.'

'Thank you.'

There was silence while they sipped their tea.

'The police will be looking for me, William,' she said.

'They won't find you – you're safe here.'

She considered this.

'I miss my family. They'll be worried about me.'

'You can call them when things settle down. Everything will be all right, Tallulah.'

'It's dangerous for you, William. People wouldn't understand.'

This was uncharted territory and she knew it was risky.

'Do you understand me, Tallulah?'

'I think I'm beginning to. With time perhaps I could learn.'

She lowered her eyes.

'I've been so lonely,' he admitted.

He laid his head on the table and started to weep, wincing from the pain in his eye. Suddenly he jerked upright, obviously listening. He wiped the tears from his face and looked at her angrily. That fucking cat, she thought. That fucking cat is calling him! The room seemed to turn slightly – to judder – as though the gears of an enormous machine were slipping. Gruber's eyes grew distant and the sunlight falling on the checked tablecloth appeared to fade.

'We have to go back upstairs now, Tallulah,' he said, and his voice was hollow.

The surface tension of her tea was disturbed as if by a tremor deep in the earth. She stood up, feeling deeply uneasy. Something bad was happening here. They went upstairs.

'My name's Cubby, by the way,' said Cubby as their feet crunched on the gravel drive outside his house.

'Craig,' replied Craig, initiating a complicated handshake.

'She went off that way,' Cubby said, pointing as they rounded the corner of the building that housed the pottery. 'Maybe we should walk it in case there's any clues?'

'Man fear for the safety of that girl, fam.' Craig gave his car a pat on the wing as they passed it.

'Can I ask you a question, Craig?'

'Axe me anyt'ing you like, bruvs.'

'Why do you talk like that?'

Craig stopped dead. He looked genuinely shocked.

'That's how the yout' him speak,' he said indignantly. 'It's a street t'ing, innit. Don't be chattin' shit about the way man speak, man!'

'I mean no disrespect, Craig,' said Cubby hastily. 'It's just that I can't understand very much of what you're saying. I mean, are you a youth really? You look a bit old to be a youth.'

Craig was horrified.

'I'm only thirty-two! That's not old!'

'It's old for a youth,' suggested Cubby.

There was silence while Craig digested this. They came to the mouth of the alley.

'I'll cut through here,' said Cubby, 'and you walk round and meet me at the other end.'

'Fine,' said Craig sulkily.

The alley stunk of piss and was studded with dogshit. Cubby breathed as shallowly as possible and picked his way through. He thought he saw a clue but it turned out to be a used condom. Clue or no clue, he wasn't touching it. He emerged from the alley and waited for Craig.

'Did you find anything?' he asked.

Craig still looked sulky.

'Nah, man.' Cubby gave him a look. 'No,' said Craig, bridling, 'I did not find anything, old chap.'

Cubby grinned.

'That's better! I can understand you now.'

Craig muttered something. His phone blared drum and bass.

'Wha' 'appen, cuz,' he said into it. 'It's a youth,' he mouthed to Cubby. 'Nah, man – gotta re-load, innit. Check me later, blood – bare Balboa an' t'ing.' He put the phone away. 'I have to talk their language – it's a business thing. What's that?' He pointed.

Crumpled at the foot of a chain-link fence, wet from the recent rain, was a piece of dirty grey material. Cubby picked it up.

'It's my apron!' he exclaimed. 'Tallulah was still wearing it when she left.'

'Why was she wearing your apron? That's *my* woman!'

'She was helping me, Craig – calm down.' They looked at the apron and up and down the road. 'Someone must have grabbed her and put her into a car or a van.'

'And it came off in the struggle. Shit!' Craig bent down and picked something up from the gutter. 'Look at this!'

It was a sheet of folded paper, grimy and wet. He unfolded it and it revealed itself to be an MOT receipt from a garage on the outskirts of town.

'It's fallen out of his car!' shouted Cubby. 'There's a plate number – look!'

'Got you, you bastard!' said Craig, smiling. 'Let's get over there and find out where the cunt lives.'

They ran back to Craig's car. Inside there was a distinctive odour – acrid and sickly sweet.

'What on earth is that horrendous smell?' asked Cubby.

'That's cheese, man – weed.' Craig took a joint from the glovebox and lit it, inhaling deeply. He turned the key in the ignition and the engine started. A moment later the stereo kicked in. Amongst the tribal rhythms (it seemed to Cubby) the vocalist, beset by demons, was searching for a menagerie from which he had become separated in thick fog. The tune was strangely hypnotic.

Craig nodded his head and mouthed along with it, blazing intermittently on his joint.

'DMX,' he shouted, gesturing at the stereo. 'Old school – man a bad man!'

'It's very, er, interesting!' Cubby shouted back and was pressed into his seat as Craig floored the accelerator.

PART THREE

DEVIL IN THE DOWNWASH

Woodhouse was feeding the cat when he heard a knock at the door. It was Maryanne, looking fetching in a charcoal-grey pencil skirt and tight yellow jumper. They smiled at each other.

'Come in,' he said, standing aside.

She teetered in on stack heels. Parts of her wiggled and other parts wobbled. She was magnificent.

'I heard about your boss, Richie,' she said over her shoulder as she went through to the living room. 'We need to catch this guy. I liked your Mr Greaves, even if he did stare at my rack.'

'Can't blame the old boy for that – it's a very fine one.'

'Well, thanks, big boy.'

She sat down on the sofa and smoothed down her skirt. Woodhouse took a seat opposite her, in the armchair. She blew a pink bubble with her gum and popped it. She was looking fresh-faced and young with her red hair in a jaunty ponytail, her freckles charmingly in evidence. Woodhouse had been working out and felt scruffy and smelly in his tracksuit bottoms and T-shirt. Maryanne took a laptop from her leather shoulder bag and put it on her knees. She looked at him.

'You got big muscles, Richie, huh?'

'Working out's boring but I have to be able to beat up the bad guys so that good can triumph over evil.'

'I guess so. I'm pretty tough too.' She smiled. She had good teeth: not too big like those of so many Americans but straight and white. Woodhouse found her worryingly distracting.

'Can I make you some tea or coffee?' he asked.

'Maybe later, hun. We should talk about the code a little.'

'Sure,' said Woodhouse, beguiled into the Americanism.

'You said on the phone you figure it for guitar tab?'

'I'm certain of it.'

The cat marched in with his tail held high and rubbed himself on Maryanne's bare calves.

'This must be Walther – hey there, mister.' She chucked him under the chin and he looked up at her and purred. 'I was checking it out on here and I noticed something.' She opened the laptop and booted it up. She giggled. 'That tickles, Walther! Come and sit by me, Richie.'

Woodhouse sat down next to her.

'Sorry, I'm a bit sweaty.'

'That's fine, baby, you smell manly. I like that.'

She brought the code up on screen:

ADDSAA XXOSDA XADDDA XOSSAO
XADDDA XOJGGG DGDDDD XOSOSO

'So, we got eight chords here – right?' Woodhouse nodded. 'But the fret numbers have been replaced by letters.

We can disregard the Xs and Os, cos the Xs mean you don't play that string and the Os mean open string. Am I right so far, Richie?'

'Absolutely – do you play?'

'I'm from Virginia, honey – even the dogs and hogs and frogs play guitar. So, if we take out the Xs and Os, we're left with A, D, S, J and G. Have a look at the keyboard, Richie.'

He leant in so their heads were almost touching. There was that smell he remembered from the base: her hair, like hay or a sleeping cat – a happy childhood smell. He wanted to close the laptop and kiss her...Christ! Concentrate, man! She pointed at the keys and her nail varnish was pink, like the bubble-gum she chewed.

'We got the numbers along the top here: one to zero, going left to right. Underneath them we have a row of letters: Q, W, E, R, T, Y, U, I, O and P. Now, looky-here, Richie – look at the next row down.' She pointed again. She didn't wear any rings, he noticed. 'A, S, D, F, G, H, J, K, L: all the letters we're looking for, all in the same row.'

'Shit – a keyboard code!' He sat up. Maryanne smiled at him and blew a pink bubble that matched her nails.

'So,' she continued, after bursting the bubble, 'if we substitute the letters for the numbers two rows above, A becomes one, S becomes two, and so on and,' she scrolled down, 'we get this.'

133211 XXO231 X13331 XO221O
X13331 XO7555 353333 XO2O2O

Woodhouse looked at it and experienced a presentiment – an unpleasant jolt.

'Yeah,' he said slowly, 'they're chords all right.'

They both looked up at the acoustic guitar that hung on the opposite wall. Reluctantly, Woodhouse got up and took it down. The strings rang faintly and – it must be his imagination – the atmosphere seemed suddenly oppressive. The cat, which had been sleeping by Maryanne's feet, ran out of the room bristling.

'He's not a fan,' said Woodhouse weakly.

He sat down and strummed the open strings softly. His hands were sweating. The top E was flat and he adjusted the corresponding machine head until it was in tune. He looked at the chords and shakily fretted the first one. The strings were old and lined with black residue – like toe-jam, he thought queasily. He sounded the chord, a barred F, and then a D minor. He stopped, still holding down the strings. The D minor shimmered in the air like a sword blade. Oh fuck! It can't be – it's not possible. How could anyone possibly fucking know?

'You okay, Richie? You want I should play it?'

He forced a smile.

'Would you? I'm a bit rusty.'

She put the laptop on the floor and he handed her the guitar. He wiped his palms on his trousers then ran his fingers through his hair. Maryanne played the chords. The sequence yearned cruelly and he fought against unwanted tears and unwelcome memories. She paused and then ran through it again, and this time she sang. Her voice was clear and light as a mountain stream and it pierced his heart. *Moon River* was a song of deep and terrible significance to Woodhouse. Dark threads of guilt and childhood pain were inextricably interwoven within its familiar melody and the down-home longing of the lyrics was tainted by shame.

Maryanne stopped. Woodhouse was ashen-faced. She leant the guitar against the wall.

'What's wrong, honey?' she asked. 'You're worrying me, baby.'

He couldn't answer, just shook his head. How could someone know that – that song? How could some bastard *know* about the song and fucking send it at him like this? Maryanne put her arms round him and he rested his head on her shoulder. The scent of her hair lent added poignancy to the pain and he closed his eyes as the memories overwhelmed him.

It was Christmas morning and Woodhouse was home for the school holidays, sitting on the floor in the drawing room unwrapping presents. His parents were half talking to him and half watching *Breakfast at Tiffany's* on television. The sun was warm through the french windows and he was happy to be away from school. Mother seemed better too – happier and more like her old self. Father's recently cultivated moustache was peculiar but only vaguely disturbing and he seemed pleased with his new job at the abattoir. They had decorated the tree together, as a family, and it filled the corner of the room, resplendent with the Victorian ornaments that they had unpacked from boxes carefully labelled in faded Indian ink.

Woodhouse took a bite of a mince pie and began to open a present that was nearly as long as he was, heavy, slim and shaped like a crucifix. The paper was patterned with mistletoe and he tore at it impatiently. A gleam of chrome was revealed. He tore some more.

'Oh wow!' he exclaimed delightedly. 'A pogo stick!'

His parents smiled at him.

'Happy Christmas, lad,' said Father in the strange accent he increasingly affected.

Mother took a sip of her sherry.

Woodhouse stood up with the pogo stick. The drawing room was large and the ceiling was high. There was room for a little experimental pogoing, he felt.

On the TV, Audrey Hepburn strummed a guitar and started to sing *Moon River*.

'Dance with me, Lockhart,' commanded Mother, taking Father's hand. 'I love this song.'

Woodhouse stood the pogo stick on the floor in front of him. He had never been on one before but he had seen the adverts. It looked easy and really good fun. Holding the handles, he jumped up so his feet landed on the foot pegs. He felt the spring depress and:

BOING!

This is great!

BOING!

His parents stood up to dance. Audrey Hepburn's voice was breathy and fragile.

BOING!

Mother stumbled slightly and knocked a mince pie off the plate balanced on the arm of the settee. It fell to the floor and rolled.

BOING!

The ferrule of the pogo stick landed on the mince pie and slipped.

SPLOING!

Oh no!

Completely off-balance, the top of the pogoing boy's head caught his mother under the chin and propelled her over and into the tree, where a glass bauble shattered in her eye.

Woodhouse and his pogo stick slammed painfully into the bookcase, which rocked, causing the heavy marble bust of Lord Byron standing above to topple and fall on to Mother's knee eight feet below, smashing the bones to splinters. On the television, Audrey Hepburn finished singing and looked up through the fire escape to see George Peppard watching her adoringly from his window on the floor above. She smiled.

Lomax stands with his hands behind his back and surveys his kingdom through one of the rain-streaked windows of his living area. It is night and the lights of the city are blurred. He hears again the guitar chords and the voice of the American girl singing and he is satisfied that his message has been received and understood.

Hearing a noise behind him, he turns. It is the servant with the broken wrist bringing his coffee. He is a middle-aged man with thinning hair and he looks understandably nervous. The man is a fool and Lomax wonders why he continues to employ him.

Sitting down on a sofa, Lomax gestures imperiously for the man to put the cup on the coffee table. The servant's hand is shaking and the cup rattles in the saucer and a little of the coffee slops over. Hissing with annoyance, Lomax hands the man an empty brandy glass.

'Milk my snake,' he commands. The servant looks understandably horrified. Lomax points angrily at the tank containing the diamondback rattlesnake. 'Milk my snake, you cretin – I want the venom.'

Cautiously approaching the tank, the servant puts the brandy glass on an adjacent table and clumsily – he is nervous and his arm is in plaster – lifts off the lid and leans it against the wall. The snake stirs and gives a preparatory rattle. Tipping the coffee from the saucer back into the cup and taking a sip, Lomax settles back to enjoy the show.

The servant takes the long-handled hook from beside the tank and begins to manoeuvre it around the snake. He is trying to press the snake to the floor of the tank by applying pressure with the hook just behind the snake's head, to prevent the snake from striking while he picks it up with his other hand. But he is frightened. The hand holding the hook is shaking and the snake is getting angry. The rattling grows louder. Lomax wonders which of them has the bigger brain – the snake or the servant. His money would be on the snake.

Somehow the servant manages to get the snake pinned down with the hook. He reaches into the tank with his plastered right arm and nervously grasps the snake behind its head, removing the hook as he does so. Lomax chuckles and takes another sip of coffee.

'Careful, my friend,' he says spitefully.

Tongue protruding from the corner of his mouth in concentration, the servant slowly lifts the snake out of the tank. Light catches the rich pattern on its back and Lomax can see the membrane tissue over the fangs in its open mouth. The snake rattles and its tongue flickers. There are beads of sweat on the servant's forehead as he picks up the brandy glass with his other hand. The tension is palpable as he carefully brings the snake towards the glass. He looks fearfully at Lomax.

'Hook his teeth over the rim of the glass,' Lomax instructs.

Suddenly something goes wrong. Lomax can't see exactly what happens but one moment all is well and then there is a flurry of movement and the snake is hanging from the servant's wrist by its fangs. The brandy glass falls to the floor and bounces on the carpet. Lomax is annoyed.

'You are wasting the venom, you moron – I need it to make ink!'

'Oh God! Help me!' cries the man, falling to the floor and struggling with the snake. The glass breaks beneath him.

Lomax brightens again: this is fine entertainment. He picks up his cup and sits back to watch.

'Don't damage my snake,' he warns.

'Please, get it off me. It's killing me!'

'Ah, such melodrama!'

Lomax approaches the stricken servant and picks up the snake. He wraps it round his neck and sits down again. He knows the snake is harmless for the time being, having just struck, and in any case he has been self-immunising for some time.

'Get up immediately,' he says. 'I require more coffee – and a cigar, I think.'

The servant gets unsteadily to his feet. He does not look well. He is sweating profusely and his skin is blotchy. His eyes are half closed and his wrist is bleeding. He picks a shard of glass out of his back.

'Hurry up,' says Lomax. 'I am thirsty.'

'Sir – please! I must go to the hospital!'

'Go to the hospital in your free time if you wish. Now, fetch my coffee – unless you would like me to break your other arm.'

The servant leaves to fetch the coffee. On the way out he falls over twice. Lomax hisses to himself and pets the snake. It is annoying that the fool has wasted the venom (Lomax uses it to prevent the blood clotting when he mixes his ink) but it will be diverting to observe the man's suffering.

When the servant returns, he is gasping for breath and his face has gone a strange colour. His unplastered arm is already swelling. Again he slops coffee into the saucer, but Lomax is prepared to overlook it this time, given the circumstances.

'Where is my cigar?' he enquires, raising his eyebrows.

'I am sorry, sir. I will fetch it at once.'

'Be quick about it, you buffoon.'

The man is staggering like a drunk now and he misses the doorway and walks into the wall, clearly injuring himself. Lomax shouts with laughter – wonderful! The man is a genius of comedy!

While he is waiting for the servant to return with his cigar, Lomax puts the snake back into its tank then goes to the refrigerator and takes out a phial of anti-venom and a syringe. He had been intending to let the man die but has been quite won over by his performance. Shaking his head and smiling, Lomax fills the syringe and puts it on the table.

The servant returns carrying a cigar. He appears to be experiencing convulsions: every couple of seconds he is seized and strikes a dramatic pose. Lomax is delighted with this.

'Marvellous! Well done! What is your name, man? You must tell me your name.'

'M-my name is Maurice, sir.'

He hands Lomax the cigar and is struck by a convulsion so severe that he appears to leap over his own shoulder, landing on his head. Clearly this is the grand finale.

'Bravo, Maurice!' cries Lomax, clapping vigorously. 'Encore!'

But the performance is over. Maurice is twitching and being sick on the carpet. Lomax takes the syringe from the table, skilfully slides the needle into a vein on the back of the servant's hand and injects the anti-venom. It quietens him almost immediately.

Lomax removes the syringe and straightens up, looking down at the soiled figure. I shall keep him, he decides: I could never find another so talented.

When Woodhouse had finished telling Maryanne about that long-ago Christmas morning, they sat silently for what seemed like a long time. He regarded her dumbly from the armchair.

'Jesus Christ, Richie,' she said finally, 'this shit is fucked up!'

'I know,' he said miserably.

'You're saying this guy's got, like, powers or something?'

'It doesn't feel like a coincidence to me.'

'I guess not.'

They looked at each other. The cat looked tentatively round the doorframe at them.

'So,' she said, 'the Welrod guy was carrying this code as a personal message to you – some kind of wacked-out warning. That means the boss knew he wouldn't kill you and you'd find it.'

'And he made it easy enough to be sure that we'd solve it.'

'He's gone to a lot of trouble, Richie. He's pissed at you.'

She unwrapped a piece of gum and offered him the pack. He shook his head.

'How could he know, Maryanne? How could he possibly know? Maybe he could have found out about the accident, but nobody – I mean *nobody* – knows about the song. It's not possible.'

'What else does this guy know, Richie? It's scary.'

She leant forward and undid the ankle straps of her shoes. Slipping her feet out, she wriggled her toes and sighed. Her toenails were the same colour as her fingernails and her bubble-gum. Woodhouse was momentarily enthralled. The cat sidled in and rubbed his face on her feet, purring. She giggled.

'Sorry – his whiskers tickle!'

'What the fuck am I supposed to tell that bitch Taylor? Yes, ma'am, we deciphered the code but it doesn't really help us because the guy is just taunting me about something he couldn't possibly know about that happened thirty-odd years ago?'

'Do you still see your parents, Richie?' Her amber gaze was steady.

'Not for a while,' he admitted. 'It's difficult. They're a little, um, eccentric.'

'Eccentric.' She nodded. 'Sure.'

'Shall we have some tea?'

'Sure, why not.'

He walked through to the kitchen and she followed. The cat demanded milk, so Woodhouse poured some cat milk into the bowl and Walther lapped it loudly. Woodhouse filled the kettle and switched it on. He turned and Maryanne was there. He took a step forward and she looked up at him, her head slightly to one side. She took the gum out of her mouth, putting it in the sink, and he kissed her, handling her dangerous curves carefully. Her mouth tasted sweet. Gently she put her palms on his chest and pushed him away.

'It's not a good idea, Richie.'

'It seems like a pretty good idea to me.'

'We have to work together, honey. Let's not make it complicated.'

'It's already complicated.' He was trying not to sulk.

'I like you, Richie – you know I do – but it's not the time to be making out. We got work to do.'

'What about before,' he said peevishly, 'at the base?'

She smiled at him.

'I didn't know we'd be working together then, but it was real nice, Richie – real nice.'

He turned away and started banging the cups around on the counter. He felt her hand on his shoulder.

'There'll be another time, baby – a better time. When all this shit is over and the bad guy's dead or in jail. Then we can see what happens, if you still want to.'

He turned and gently put his hand to her face, stroking the curve of her cheekbone with his thumb. She looked so solemn that it made him smile.

'Okay,' he said. 'It's a deal. We'll defeat the bad man and then we'll see what happens.'

She smiled happily.

'We could take a vacation, maybe?' she suggested.

'A dirty weekend!'

She pouted.

'A weekend ain't long, Richie. I thought you liked me.'

'A dirty month, then?'

Her smile returned.

'Sure – a dirty month!' She pronounced it "doydy".

He held out his hand to seal the deal and she shook it, her expression serious again.

Craig pulled the car up outside the garage and they got out. He had been smoking cannabis all the way across town and consequently Cubby was feeling a bit strange. He was suffering the effects of second-hand toking. Unsteadily he followed Craig through the open doors of the garage. A battered radio was playing *Uptown Top Ranking* by Althea and Donna, and someone was tunelessly singing along from the inspection pit, beneath a dented Mondeo. Cubby could smell oil and other, less wholesome odours.

'Hello?' called Craig.

'Suffen, suffen, suffen, dah-dah-dah-dah-dah-dah, suffen, suffen worn leaf spring – ooh!' sang the cracked voice from the pit.

'Hello!'

'Suffen, suffen, sump's all cracked, I spuz I'll hafter TIG-weld that.'

'HELLO!' shouted Craig and Cubby together.

A face appeared in the pit, brown and furrowed as a walnut. A small man in oily blue overalls climbed out and wiped his hands on a rag.

'All right there, me ol' beauty?' he said to Craig.

'We need the address for the man on this paper,' said Craig, handing him the receipt.

'We found his wallet,' added Cubby, holding up his own wallet.

The mechanic looked at the paper.

'Oh ah,' he said. 'Rum un chap.' He put down his rag and consulted a ledger nearby, licking his filthy finger to turn the pages. 'I can't quite find the address where he live at, I can't.' He looked up and grinned, displaying a brown tooth or two. His eyes were cunning. Craig handed him a twenty-pound note which, for some reason, rolled itself up into a tube.

'Look a bit harder,' he said.

Cubby stood behind him trying not to laugh. He knew it was a serious business but he didn't feel serious at all. It must be something to do with the marijuana that Craig kept smoking in the car.

The mechanic unrolled the note and, after peering at it and folding it, put it in his pocket.

'He live on Farley Crescent, that bloke do. I can't quite see the number what his house is, mind.'

'I think you can,' said Craig, cracking his knuckles and taking a step closer.

'Oh ah, I see it now. He live at number twenty, that chap do. Rum un bloke he is – peculiar.'

'Number twenty, Farley Crescent,' said Craig, taking back the receipt. 'Let's go, brother.'

Cubby started to snigger; he couldn't help himself. As they walked out to the car the singing started again, accompanied now by metallic banging:

'I're now got oil all on my boots (BANG!). I're now got oil (BANG!) all on my boots.' (BANG-BANG!)

It was a touching domestic scene. Gruber sat at the dressing table, his laptop open in front of him, the Cat-Führer at his elbow, and Tallulah was tied to the bed. After his unfortunate experience in the sex shop Gruber had elected to order handcuffs and a ball-gag online, but for the time being the girl was tied.

'Can we watch TV or something, William?' asked Tallulah. 'I'm bored and my wrists hurt.'

Gruber completed his order and closed the laptop.

'You must promise to behave yourself, Tallulah. No fighting.' His black eye was painful and the scabs on his cheek itched.

'I don't want to fight with you. I want to be friends.'

'Careful, Gruber,' warned the Führer. 'She is good for the breeding, this one, but tricky.'

As he untied her, Gruber's heart was full of her beauty: perhaps he would just fall into her eyes and drown there again for a while.

'No, Gruber,' commanded the Führer. 'You are not Rudolph Valentino – have a care.'

Tallulah sat up and yawned.

'You know, William, you could just let me go. I would still come back and see you. I like being with you – you're interesting.'

'Straight to the police she will be going, Gruber, and it will be the prison for you.'

'I hope you can see it now, Tallulah – that we were made to be together.'

She looked up at him shyly.

'I don't know, William, it scares me a little.'

'There's nothing to be scared of. It will be the most wonderful thing in the world, to be together.'

The Führer snorted but made no comment.

'I've been hurt before, William. Perhaps in time I can learn to love again, but it is difficult – oh, so difficult.'

She leaned forward so her hair covered her face and she seemed to be crying. He sat down beside her and put his arm round her shoulders. She stiffened but did not pull away.

'Be brave, my darling,' he said. 'I will show you the way.'

She made a sound that might have been a sob and stood up.

'I can't talk about it anymore right now,' she said. 'Perhaps there will be an old film on TV we can watch together. It will help us get to know each other.'

The Führer muttered something that Gruber didn't catch.

'I like old films too,' said Gruber. 'We have so much in common.'

On the way over to Farley Crescent, Craig continued to smoke weed. He was working himself up into a fury, banging his palms on the steering wheel as he drove. He had reverted to youth-speak.

'Man t'ief away nudder man woman. Bring the beefs, cuz – fuckin' *bring* it!'

Cubby opened his window; he needed some air. Suddenly the situation seemed much less amusing than previously. The car slowed and Craig peered around.

'Farley fuckin' Crescent here somewhere, bruv.'

They both saw the sign at the same time and Craig pulled in and parked. He took something from under the seat and put it in the waistband of his trousers, at the back.

'Is that a gun, Craig?' Cubby was getting a bad feeling.

'Axe me no questions and I'll tell you no fuckin' lies, innit.'

They got out of the car. Farley Crescent was a long sweep of modern semi-detached houses with small squares of lawn in front. Some had cars parked outside and one had a small cabin cruiser on a trailer. It was quiet, although Cubby saw a curtain twitch across the way.

Number twenty had a neatly mown lawn with a bird table in the middle. There was no car on the drive. Craig walked briskly up and knocked loudly on the door. They waited.

Gruber and Tallulah were watching *The Seven Year Itch*. She was curled on her side with her head on the arm of the sofa and he sat nervously next to her, constantly listening for the voice of the Cat-Führer.

The film is about a married man who lusts after a beautiful upstairs neighbour while his wife is on vacation. The characters have just been to the cinema and, as they walk back, the girl – Marilyn Monroe – is standing on a subway grating when a train passes beneath. Her skirts blow up around her, revealing her legs as she stands innocently enjoying the breeze.

Tom Ewell's character makes a remark about the breeze cooling the girl's ankles, although his sidelong look at her legs hints at a less wholesome thought process.

'Dirty old man!' said Tallulah indignantly.

'He does look a bit old for her,' agreed Gruber.

'His poor wife! She seemed really nice – and they have a kid!'

On screen there is a kiss. The girl is ostensibly proving a point about the toothpaste she advertises.

'The tart!' exclaimed Gruber. 'She's leading him on!'

'She's single,' said Tallulah. 'She can do what she likes.'

'She's only after his air conditioning,' said Gruber disgustedly.

Tallulah sat up.

'She's been having trouble sleeping because of the heat,' she said angrily, 'and she wants to look her best for her TV appearance in the morning. What's wrong with that?'

'She's a prick teaser,' Gruber retorted. 'She should let him know where he stands. The poor guy thinks he's in with a chance now!'

'He should know better! He's old enough to be her father – and he's married, the pervert!'

'She's not as innocent as she makes out, standing there with her skirts up round her waist in the middle of the street!'

'She's *HOT!*' shouted Tallulah.

They looked at each other furiously. A loud knock came at the door.

When the Christmas holidays ended, Woodhouse was not sorry to go back to school. Since the accident, things had been difficult at home. Mother was still in hospital recovering from the removal of the remains of her eye and amputation of her leg, and Father had taken to wearing a flat cap around the house and talking in monosyllables, if at all. Woodhouse was traumatised and Christmas would be tainted forever. Father had dropped him at the end of the school drive and, with a curt 'Behave tha sen, our kid,' driven erratically away.

Things at school were difficult too. Since the confrontation in the woods, Jones and Bayliss had been making threats and aiming sly blows whenever they passed

Woodhouse. They were clearly biding their time until they could get him alone. They were tormenting Drinkley too but, unlike Woodhouse, he seemed to lack the instinct for self-preservation. He was always off on his own practising with the swazzle – he was obsessed with the thing. It was only a matter of time before the bullies caught up with him.

After lunch on Wednesday the headmaster made an announcement.

'ON SATURDAY AFTERNOON,' he roared, 'HARE AND HOUNDS WILL BE RUN. THE HARES WILL BE,' he consulted a list, 'RAFFERTY, DRINKLEY AND WOODFORDE.' Matron whispered something to him and he glared at her. 'WOODHOUSE.'

Woodhouse and Drinkley looked at each other over a huge bowl of mangled blancmange remains. Drinkley looked terrified. Rafferty seemed unconcerned as usual. The blancmange was petrified.

The headmaster sat down and angrily drained his water glass and gradually the volume in the dining hall increased as people started to relax.

'I'll never be able to run fast enough,' said Drinkley sadly. 'We'll get caught and beaten up.'

'They shouldn't make Drippy do it,' said Sketchley, agitating the blancmange with a ladle. 'They know he's a spastic with allergies and stuff.'

'Leave that blancmange alone, Sketchley,' called Carrigan from his place at the head of the table. 'It's suffered enough.'

'Not as much as I have,' muttered Sketchley. 'It's got skin like a rhino and it stinks of spew.'

'We'll look after you,' said Woodhouse to Drinkley. 'Won't we, Raffles?'

Rafferty was laughing at Sketchley's denigration of the blancmange.

'Yeah,' he said, wiping his eyes. 'We'll look after you, Drippy – we'll take our beating like men.'

Woodhouse felt eyes on him and looked up to see Jones and Bayliss watching him from across the room. Bayliss said something behind his hand and they laughed. Woodhouse looked away.

Lomax sits at the back of Notre-Dame-du-Travail. The church is hushed. A small bird is trapped inside. It darts through the latticed ironwork high above the nave and beats its wings against the glass. Lomax is filled with rage. Apparently there is a new priest here, the old one having disappeared in mysterious circumstances. Always there is another priest to leech on society and ensnare the vulnerable with children's stories and empty promises.

The bird flies down and perches on the end of a chair not far from Lomax. It looks around frantically for a way out. He sees the colours in its plumage: it is a starling.

Lomax bites down on his hatred and remembers…

It is a time of snow in the old country. Lomax is just a boy, twelve or thirteen, and he hurries through the darkness and the driving flakes, head down against the gusting wind. His coat is threadbare and he has no hat. The boy's father has been sick for a long time and now he is dying, calling desperately for the priest to administer the last rites. Lomax's father is a devout man. He believes, and therefore he must confess his sins and be absolved.

(In the empty church, Lomax's jaw tightens and he clenches his fists. He hears the eldritch shriek of the wind, borne skirling down the years and he grinds his teeth with fury and hisses, startling the starling into flight.)

Finally the church appears through the whirling snow and the boy hurries in, glad to be out of the wind. He knocks the snow from his boots and looks around. The small church is lit by candles while outside the wind cries like a soul in torment and batters at the windows.

'Father,' he calls. 'Father, are you there?'

There is no reply but the grieving of the wind. The boy genuflects to the altar, as he has been taught, and hurries up the aisle.

'Father,' he calls again, 'are you there?'

He passes the altar and opens the door to the sacristy. The priest is snoring there, on the floor, his vestments up around his fat belly. Trapped beneath his outstretched arm, its hand still clutching an empty wine bottle, is the idiot girl from the nearby farm. She is naked and her eyes are wide and fearful.

The boy stands frozen in horrified amazement for the longest moment. All these years later, sitting in the silent church where the trapped bird yearns for the sky, he sees it still and he can never forgive it.

'Father,' he says eventually. 'Father, you must wake up. My father is dying – he must have the last rites.'

The priest just grunts.

'He hurt me,' says the girl, her eyes filling with tears.

The boy shakes the priest's shoulder.

'Wake up, you swine, my father needs you. You must come now!'

The priest comes awake with a roar. He swings the bottle and it catches the boy on the side of the head, knocking him to the floor. The girl jumps up, grabbing her clothes, and runs from the room, dimpled buttocks wobbling. The priest throws the bottle after her and it smashes on the door as it closes behind her.

'You dare to wake me,' shouts the priest, advancing on the boy who lies stunned and disbelieving. 'I will give *you* the last rites, you scum!'

He leans down – breath reeking, eyes red and brutish – and grips the boy by the ears, lifting his head from the floor.

'The kingdom of Heaven is not for such as you and your shit of a father – dumb animals grubbing in the dirt. You know nothing of God. How could an animal like you possess a soul? The idea is laughable – that such as you should defile the sacred mysteries – *LAUGHABLE!*'

The boy is unable to speak, and he watches as the priest's face contorts with fury until with his right hand he tears the boy's left ear clean off his head, laughing delightedly as he does so.

(In Notre-Dame-du-Travail Lomax feels the nub of his missing ear grow hot beneath its ivory replacement. The calfskin straps burn at his face.)

When the boy regains consciousness, the priest is gone and the ear with him. The boy returns home, staggering, delirious, to find that his father has died unshriven, his face still twisted in terror of the damnation awaiting him.

Lomax was never able to find the priest, though he has combed the world over. Others must pay in his stead.

As he leaves the church, the starling swoops past him through the open door and away into the sky. Lomax is glad, though he knows there will be no such release for him. He takes out his mobile and keys in a number; there are arrangements to be made and certain events will come to pass. He turns his collar up against the wind and smiles as he prepares to further his instructions.

They waited outside the door of number twenty. Craig knocked again, even more loudly. The man who opened the door looked nervous.

'What do you want?' he asked querulously. 'I made an arrangement to pay in instalments.'

Craig pushed him into the house and Cubby followed, closing the door behind him.

'What have you done with her, you little cunt?' demanded Craig.

'I haven't done anything with her – she's gone shopping. Who are you?'

'We're your worst nightmare. Where is she?'

'She's gone to the Co-op. What's going on here?'

He was a small man with protruding front teeth and curly hair, wearing a flowery shirt and faded jeans. He looked a little like Fred West.

Craig produced the gun and cocked it with the slide. He put it to the man's jaw.

'You've got about five seconds to tell me where she is before I blow your fucking head off, bruv.'

'Craig, I'm not too sure—'

'Don't call man by his name, cuz – Jesus! Leave this piece-of-shit kidnapping scum to me. One!'

'I'm not a kidnapper – I work in Dixons. Don't shoot me, ah please God!'

The little man fell to his knees in the hallway and began to cry bitterly. Cubby felt extremely uncomfortable with the situation.

'I don't think this is right,' he said.

'He's lying. Where is she, you perv? Two!'

'Oh holy Jesus, Mary and baby Moses – don't shoot me. I haven't done anything!'

'Where's Tallulah? Three!'

'I don't know who that is, I swear! Sweet John the Baptist – don't kill me!'

'I really don't think this is right,' said Cubby.

Craig took the receipt from his back pocket and handed it to the frightened little man.

'This is you, right – your number plate?'

The little man unfolded it with shaking hands. Craig withdrew the gun slightly.

'It's my number plate,' said the little man, 'but I don't understand what I'm supposed to have done. Who's Tallulah?' He looked at the gun and began to shake. Tears rolled down his face and dripped on the cream-coloured carpet.

'You've grabbed her up in your car and molested her and that, you noncer! Where is she? Five!'

'Don't shoot!' screamed the little man, putting his hands over his ears. 'You missed out four! Please God Jesus – you missed out four!'

'Did I miss out four?' Craig asked Cubby. 'I'm pretty sure I said it.'

'I think maybe you did miss it out,' said Cubby. He leaned closer and whispered: 'I don't think it's him – maybe the receipt's got nothing to do with Tallulah.'

'I'll have to shoot him anyway cos he knows my name,' Craig whispered back. 'FOUR!' he shouted and pulled the trigger.

The report was deafening in the hallway. Cubby could hear a shrill sound in his ears which turned out to be the little man screaming. He seemed to be unscathed, however, other than having wet himself. Craig was laughing.

'Your face!' he shouted to Cubby. 'Classic! Blanks, innit! Let's go, fam – he won't say nothing, he's bricking it.'

'That's not funny, Craig,' said Cubby as they got into the car. 'Not funny at all.'

Gruber jumped up and put his hand over Tallulah's mouth.

'Keep quiet,' he warned.

The curtains were drawn so no one could see in. The knocking came again, louder. They waited. On television the ill-matched characters were sitting at a piano, playing chopsticks. Marilyn Monroe's character was singing along, 'Bah-bah-bah-bah-bah-bah.' There was a thump that shook the house and footsteps in the hall. Tallulah broke free and started to run to the door. Gruber jumped at her, grasping her jogging bottoms which slid down around her ankles. Falling to the floor, Tallulah kicked out at him and he clung on grimly to her bare legs. The sitting room door burst open and they both froze and looked up. A large woman stood in the doorway. She was panting and she looked furious.

'Now I see why you bolted the door,' she said, 'you nasty little sex maniac.'

'Florence!' gasped Gruber. 'It's not what it looks like!'

'It looks like what it looks like to me...'

'Help me!' cried Tallulah, trying to get up. 'He—'

'You dirty scrubber!' shouted Florence. 'I'll kill you! Leave my man alone!'

She advanced on them menacingly. Tallulah again tried to get up but Gruber clung on. They rolled on the floor.

'Stop trying to have sex!' roared Florence indignantly. 'You dirty bastards!'

She leant down and grasped Tallulah's hair with both hands. Tallulah gripped the front of her blouse and kicked out at Gruber and there was a tense moment as they all strained together. On the television, Tom Ewell's character lunged at the girl and they fell backwards off the piano stool.

Tallulah screamed and there was a tearing noise. Florence's blouse gave way, and her bra with it. Her breasts fell out – they were enormous! All three combatants were shocked by this development, particularly Tallulah: the gigantic bosoms were right in her face, quivering whitely.

Florence gasped and let go of Tallulah's hair to cover herself with her hands. She ran from the room sobbing and they heard the thump of her feet on the stairs.

'My wife,' explained Gruber unnecessarily.

Tallulah looked down at the torn blouse and bra she was holding. There didn't seem much to say.

'Nice knockers,' she said anyway, pulling up her trousers. 'Very large.'

The feet thumped down the stairs and the front door slammed in its frame. Florence was gone.

Woodhouse didn't like the look of the package from the off but he took it from the postman and scribbled on the screen of the proffered gizmo. The package was square and heavy, about the size of a couple of hardback books. It was wrapped in brown paper and parcel tape and postmarked

Paris. Woodhouse remembered that French cigarettes had been found on one of the assassins' corpses.

The package was addressed to Richard Abednego Woodhouse, c/o Universal Export and then his home address. Abednego – his hated middle name! Again someone was taunting him. Universal Export was significant too: it was the company name the service used as a cover in the Bond books. Simultaneously he was being informed that his occupation was known and that it wasn't taken very seriously. On balance he thought perhaps he would get someone else to open his present for him – possibly a bomb disposal robot. He carried the package carefully through into the living room and – oh, so gently – fitted it into the space between the sofa and the wall and slid it in as far as he could reach. If it went off, hopefully the sofa would soak up some of the blast. He left the room and closed the door behind him, not wanting Walther using up any of his lives in there.

In the kitchen he took the Taylor woman's card from the pinboard and keyed in the mobile number. Let's see if she's any good at her job, he thought as he waited for an answer.

'Taylor.'

'Woodhouse here. I have received a suspect package – could you send someone out to have a look at it?'

'I'm very busy, Woodhouse. Could you not have called this in at a lower level?'

'Yes, ma'am, but I thought you would want to know about it straight away. I think it's from the people who killed Greaves.'

'Ah yes, the stolen helicopter. I've been getting a good deal of pressure about this, Woodhouse, from the highest echelons. Last time we spoke I asked you to get on with it as a matter of some urgency, if I remember rightly. You were deciphering some plaintext, I think?'

Woodhouse held the phone to his ear with his shoulder so he had his hands free to roll a cigarette. The woman was stressing him out.

'Yes, ma'am. It seems to have been either a red herring or part of a more intricate code.'

There was a pause.

'Well,' she said curtly, 'what was it?'

'It was guitar tabulation, ma'am – the first four bars of *Moon River*.'

'Good God! Are you serious? What the hell am I supposed to do with that?'

'You could serenade someone.'

He smiled at her sharp intake of breath and lit his roll-up.

'You're verging on insubordination, Woodhouse.'

'Yes, ma'am.'

There was another pause. Woodhouse blew some smoke rings into the sunlight which was slanting through the kitchen window.

'Right,' she said, obviously struggling to contain her anger. 'I'll send some people over to sort out this package. You wait there while it's done and then come in and report to me in person, assuming you haven't been blown to bits. We need to have a little chat – about Mr Greaves's funeral, apart from anything else.'

'You'll be at the office, will you?'

'Yes, Woodhouse, the office – if you can remember where it is.'

He took great satisfaction in hanging up on her.

The tuck boxes were kept in a kind of oversized cloakroom adjacent to the main school building. Each boy had a peg and the boxes sat underneath on benches that ran the length of the room. At weekends the boys were allowed to visit the tuck shop, which sold cakes and sweets, and the more self-disciplined among them could keep the surplus in their boxes to eat during the week. The boxes were also used for storing toys, mementoes from home and all the little found objects that boys like to collect: stones, bones, feathers, leaves and the like. They were kept locked – some with keys, others with a combination – to deter the inevitable petty thievery.

It was often a quiet place and Woodhouse liked to go there to look through his Top Trumps cards, which were in vogue at the time, or handle his small collection of bird and rodent skulls. He never had any sweets because he would always eat them all immediately, no matter how sick it made him.

On the Thursday before they were due to be the prey in hare and hounds, he was in low spirits because he had been bollocked in Latin class again and threatened with a visit to the headmaster. He was a reasonably bright boy but there was something about Latin that his brain rebelled against. Just the word "Latin" made his head feel like it was full of porridge. A visit to the headmaster, however, was not a call that he was keen to pay. He would prefer that his bottom remain inviolate.

He came into the tuck room deep in a fantasy in which he heroically defeated the headmaster in single combat and snapped all his canes in half, subsequently becoming emperor of the school and being carried around in a sedan chair and worshipped by all.

He stood fumbling with his key while he ordered the beheadings of Jones and Bayliss and the flaying of Mr Beazley who took Latin.

'What does the "A" stand for?' said someone.

Woodhouse looked around, emerging from his daydream. Drinkley was sitting under his peg which was nearby.

'What?'

'On your box: "R. A. Woodhouse". What does the "A" stand for?'

'Oh, um, Andrew.'

'Oh. I thought it might be Algernon or Antonio or something.'

Christ, thought Woodhouse: if only you knew!

'No, nothing like that,' he said. 'Just Andrew. Do you want a game of Top Trumps?'

'Okay,' said Drinkley, getting up and coming over. 'Which ones have you got?'

Woodhouse finally succeeded in unlocking the box. He flicked open the twin catches and lifted the lid.

'Let's see,' he said, rummaging. 'Military planes, military vehicles – I did have the horror ones but they got confiscated.'

'Have you got any cars?' asked Drinkley. 'I like cars.'

'Yeah, these are pretty good.'

They sat down on the floor cross-legged and Woodhouse dealt the cards, half each. They began to play. Woodhouse had the advantage of knowing the cards and he won steadily but Drinkley had the Wolf Lamborghini, the strongest card in the pack, and Woodhouse was unable to finish him off. Three times Drinkley was down to his last two cards but always the Lamborghini won and Woodhouse lost the initiative.

'Engine, eight cylinders,' said Drinkley. 'Mercedes ABC exclusive.'

'Shit!' said Woodhouse bitterly. 'Nissan Lady Micra – four cylinders.' He handed it over.

'The Nissan Lady Micra's well rubbish.' Drinkley put the cards to the back of his sparse hand. 'I think the swazzle might be magic,' he said.

Woodhouse looked up.

'What are you talking about?'

'The swazzle – I think it might have special powers. When I was practising with it in the woods yesterday a deer came right up to me and sat down. It was listening.'

Woodhouse tried to think of something funny to say but he couldn't, so he said nothing.

'Speed, two hundred and fifty-eight kmh,' said Drinkley, after a moment. 'ISDERA Imperator.'

'Three hundred and five. Porsche 934.' Woodhouse took Drinkley's card. 'Cubic capacity, two thousand nine hundred and twenty-seven,' he said. 'Ferrari 308.'

Drinkley smiled.

'Cubic capacity five thousand. Wolf Lamborghini.' He took the Ferrari card. 'It sat there for ages, just looking at me and listening, and then the bell went for prep and I had to go in. It must be pretty old – the swazzle.' He took it out of his pocket and they both looked at it.

'Say something,' said Woodhouse.

Drinkley went to put it in his mouth then stopped.

'I better not,' he said. 'Someone might hear. I don't know what I'd do if it got confiscated.'

'Can you say much stuff with it?'

'It's pretty difficult but I'm getting better with it. Sometimes it says stuff on its own.'

'Shut up, Drinkley – no it doesn't!'

'It's true, I swear. Once it made me start talking in French.'

Woodhouse looked at him.

'I think you've gone a bit mental.' He thought about it. 'Can I borrow it for Latin?'

Drinkley laughed.

'I don't think it does Latin. Doors, four. Pfeba Renault 21.' He put the swazzle away.

Woodhouse looked at him for a long moment and then back at his top card.

'Doors two,' he said. 'Porsche 911 Turbo.'

Lomax's limo pulls up at the farm. The Stealth Hawk is being kept in an open-ended barn so she can roll in one end, fuel up rotors-running, and out the other. The South African crew are throwing a rugby ball about – four big freckly men in shorts and vest tops.

Lomax gets out and rolls his shoulders, stiff from travel. The crew gather round expectantly.

'Howzit, boss,' says one.

Lomax looks at them.

'How is the machine? She is ready?'

'She's smoking, boss – it'll be carrots for that old fudge-nudger!'

'Quarter of a million euros each,' says Lomax. 'This is a great deal of money, yes? There must be no mistakes.'

'The old guy is biltong, bra – believe it.'

'You are ready – you have everything you need?'

The crew look at each other and grin.

'Ja, we're jacked, boss. Everything's lekker, just waiting for the word from you.'

Lomax nods.

'Good, good. Soon we will make them all sit up and take notice, yes?'

He walks into the barn and looks lovingly at the Stealth Hawk. It is a vision of the Apocalypse, angular and blackly menacing, ready to bound into the air and rain down destruction on the evildoers. No external weapons mar its sleek lines, the missiles being housed in retractable bays so as not to compromise the radar signature.

It is cool in the barn, out of the sunshine, and the fifty calibre door gun feels cold to Lomax's touch. He smiles, remembering how it had felt to shoot the old man on the golf course. It was glorious – lumps of him were flying everywhere! Soon it will be time to go to war for real and cut off the head of the snake; time to poke a big stick into the hornets' nest and crush the insects.

Outside the crew are scuffling over the ball. There is banter.

'Are you tuning me kak?' demands someone. 'I'll ding your pip, bru!'

A strange language that they speak, muses Lomax, but they are hard men and good at their work. They will fight for their money, and – very possibly – they will die.

Lomax runs his hand along the fuselage of the Stealth Hawk. He can hear the explosions, the screams and the rattle of the guns, the hydraulic whine, and the soft "whop-whop" of the rotors. He hears voices too, of course: the man as a child, an adolescent, becoming a threat; the past, the present and glimpses of things to come. A word, a whisper, a cry. There will be pain; there will be death; there will be heartbreak. All along the watchtower he can hear the call to arms.

Lomax hisses and adjusts the straps that hold his ear. He hears some of it but not enough; the outcome is uncertain, but this is the fun of the thing; this is the game that they play for the highest stakes of all. The blood courses through his veins like vintage port and he walks back into the sunshine, putting on his sunglasses and hissing to himself a little. He is satisfied.

The crew stop their game and look at him as he emerges.

'Soon, my good boys,' he says. 'Soon it will be time for death or glory.'

Cubby stood in his workshop, surrounded by his creations. His mind was filled with Tallulah: her eyes, her face, her hair, her smile. He took a mould from the shelf and began to remove the strips of inner tube stretched around it that he used to bind the pieces of the mould together and keep it tight while the liquid clay set.

He couldn't believe they had gone to the wrong person's house. They had been so sure that the MOT receipt belonged to Tallulah's kidnapper. Maybe she had just gone off somewhere, thrown the apron down in disgust and got on a bus or a train? And Craig was a ruddy madman, smoking drugs and waving guns about – that poor little man! What if he called the police? Carefully Cubby removed the two pieces that made up the top half of the mould. A cat skulked damply within. Cubby regarded it with disdain.

The shop doorbell rang and Cubby went through, wiping his hands on his apron. A woman waited there, dressed in a suit and carrying a briefcase.

'Mr Arbuthnot?'

'Yes, good morning.'

'Good morning. My name is Susan Carlisle and I represent Winter and Vaughan. I'm here to make the usual checks.'

'About my grandfather's will? What's happened to the other chap? Mr—?'

'Gruber? He's not with us anymore, I'm afraid.' The look on her face spoke volumes; clearly the parting had not been amicable.

As he showed her round the workshop and answered her questions, Cubby was wondering. He remembered the way Gruber had been looking at the cat with the unfortunate resemblance to Hitler. And now that cat was gone. Cubby had assumed that it had been broken when the shelves had tipped over but, now that he thought about it, it hadn't been on those ones at all – it had been on the other side of the room.

He shook hands with the woman from the lawyers and saw her to the door. On the way back through the shop he stopped and looked at the shelves. No – it must have been on that side and got broken when that damn cat pulled the thing over. It wasn't likely that someone would steal such a hideous object. He shook his head in irritation and went back to work. He had more important things to think about than some Hitler-cat, because Tallulah was missing. Cubby's cats looked at him with boss-eyed resignation: he was a fool.

Tallulah was giving Gruber a makeover. He sat at the dressing table dressed in his wife's clothes while Tallulah applied foundation to his face.

'Gruber, this is not usual,' warned the Führer.

Gruber didn't care. He was beautiful; Tallulah had told him so.

'Look up, William,' she said, 'while I do some concealer here.' She dabbed around his eyes with a dainty finger. 'You're going to look amazing. Does your wife have any wigs?'

'She does wear wigs sometimes – her hair's a bit thin on top.'

'Oh, I didn't notice,' lied Tallulah. 'Do you know where they might be?'

'I think in the spare room, maybe.'

Gruber was putty in her hands. Her proximity was so intoxicating to him that he would have let her do anything to him.

'Perhaps we could have a drink,' she suggested. 'Some wine, if you have it?'

'There's some Liebfraumilch in the fridge – Florence likes it. I'll go and get it.'

Gruber got up and went downstairs in his stockinged feet. His wife's clothes were a bit big for him. They had had to pin the waist of the skirt, and the sleeves of the blouse half covered his hands. He opened the wine and took some glasses from the cupboard. On the way back he checked the lock on the front door. He had done a good job of repairing it and it was secure. In the spare room he found two wigs, a long ash-blonde one and a luxuriant red Pre-Raphaelite number.

'Wow!' exclaimed Tallulah. 'They're awesome!'

He put the wigs on the bed and poured the wine. They touched glasses.

'Cheers,' he said.

'To us,' said Tallulah, without even a hint of sarcasm.

They drank. Gruber sat back down at the dressing table and Tallulah began to apply his eyeshadow.

'This is not pleasant, Gruber,' complained the Führer, 'or entirely normal. To dress as a woman is disturbing, I think.'

'I want to look nice for the party,' retorted Gruber.

'Are we having a party?' asked Tallulah.

'Yes,' said Gruber, glaring at the Führer, 'we're going to have a lovely party.'

'Hooray!' cried Tallulah, putting down the make-up brush to clap her hands excitedly. 'I love parties!'

The Führer was silent. Gruber took a swig of his wine. It was horrible but he liked it. He closed his eyes again so Tallulah could finish the eyeshadow. The brush tickled pleasantly. He wanted to reach for her but was afraid of breaking the spell.

'I am reluctant to hurt you, Gruber,' said the Führer, 'but this wearing of the women's clothes and painting of the face is offending to me. It is not seemly.'

'I don't care!' shouted Gruber. 'I want to be beautiful!'

'And so you shall, William,' said Tallulah, soothingly. 'It's healthy for a man to want to be in touch with his feminine side.'

'You should be shot, Gruber. You are a degenerate!'

'It's not true – I'm normal!'

'Calm down, William – it's perfectly normal; we're just playing a game.'

'Normal!' sneered the Führer. 'This Lili Marlene scarecrow is *normal?* Up against the wall you should go, Gruber, and BANG! BANG! No more pervert Gruber!'

'I don't care,' said Gruber. 'I'm not listening anymore – I like it.'

'Okay, then. Let's do some mascara, shall we?'

Shockingly, the cat began to sing in German. His voice was terrible: like a drunk who has found a violin. Gruber ignored him as best he could. Disturbingly, Tallulah started humming the tune too.

'Dum-de-dum-de-dum-dum, dum-de-dum-de-dee – now a little blusher, I think, William. Dum-de-dum-de-dee-dum, de-deedle-deedle-dee. Do you know what this tune is called?'

'I think it's called Lili Marlene,' said Gruber, as the echoes of the Führer's singing died hard in his brain. 'It's an old German song.'

'It's pretty,' said Tallulah. 'I wonder why I started singing that.' She cocked her head to one side and considered her handiwork. 'Some lipstick now, and then we can try the wigs. Shall we have some more wine?'

'Definitely,' Gruber said. 'Perhaps I should use a straw so I don't spoil my lipstick? And I would like to have a bow in my hair,' he pouted at the Führer, 'since we are having a party.'

'You swine, Gruber! You wretched depraved swine!'

Woodhouse had never been visited by a robot before. It had a squat body on treads, with a long questing arm culminating in a camera and pincers. It looked as though it had been designed for goosing girls at geeky office parties.

'Come in,' said Woodhouse.

The robot was having trouble with the doorstep so one of its handlers gave it a judicious shove with his Kevlar-clad foot. The two humans were a bit odd looking too. They wore thick olive-green coats with high collars, not unlike duffle coats, and helmets with visors. They were how you might imagine a space beatnik would look.

'Wotcher, mate,' said one of them, raising his visor. 'Where's this package, then?'

'It's in there,' said Woodhouse, motioning. 'Behind the sofa.'

'Very prudent, very prudent indeed,' the man said approvingly.

His colleague applied himself to the remote control device he carried and the robot lurched towards the living room door with much whining of machinery. Woodhouse leaned to open the door for it.

'No, no,' admonished the admirer of prudence. 'Let him do it himself.'

The robot fumbled with the door handle for what seemed like a long time and there were muttered curses from the man with the controls. Finally it got the door open and went in. They closed the door behind it and watched its progress on the monitor.

It looked round the room and then trundled towards the sofa. The screen showed the robot's point of view, with the pincers in the foreground. It stopped at the gap between the sofa and the wall.

'I just slid it in there a couple of feet,' said Woodhouse.

A light came on and shone into the gap. They could see the box. The robot reached its long arm over to the far side of the box and then began to reverse, dragging the box out. They could see a dusty beer can and something that might once have been a slice of pizza. Woodhouse cleared his throat.

The robot pulled the box clear and sat back to examine it by X-ray. The technicians moved jealously in on the monitor, crowding Woodhouse out. They were communicating via their headsets. Woodhouse shrugged and went to put the kettle on. After a while one of the technicians came in and removed his helmet. He was surprisingly young.

'There's definitely a trigger mechanism in there,' he said, 'and a charge of some kind. Also something that looks like a small grenade and another object of some sort. We're hopeful that we can render it safe so we'll give you a call when you can come and take a look.'

He put his helmet on again and went out. Woodhouse waited for the explosion. The technician returned some time later, again removing his helmet.

'It was quite a small device,' he said, sounding disappointed. 'If you had opened it you would have lost maybe a few fingers. The contents are quite unusual, if you want to come and have a look.'

They went through to the living room. Bits of the package were scattered about on the floor and the robot seemed to be looking out of the window. Perhaps they've had a row, thought Woodhouse. The other technician raised his visor.

'This is what we thought was a grenade,' he said, handing Woodhouse a golf ball.

Woodhouse looked at it.

'You bastard!' he said with feeling.

'What?'

'Not you.'

This must be Greaves's golf ball – he had never thought to ask if they had found it on the course. It hadn't seemed important at the time. The fucker was taunting him – *again!*

'There was this as well.'

The technician handed Woodhouse something like a bead necklace. There was a small crucifix on it.

'It's a rosary,' said the technician.

They sat on the bench seats in the changing room, dressed in white shirts and shorts, cutting up paper from a stack of A4 and putting it into bags. The mood was sombre.

'I'll never be able to run fast enough,' said Drinkley, not for the first time. 'You'll have to leave me behind.'

'Nah, we'll be all right,' said Rafferty, patting him on the back. 'Maybe we could leave a false trail and double back on ourselves.'

'It'll be fun,' Woodhouse said unconvincingly. 'You did all right last time, Drippy. Have you got your inhaler?'

Drinkley checked his pocket.

'Yep, and the swazzle for luck.'

Rafferty shook his head.

'You're obsessed with that manky old thing.'

'It's not manky!' Drinkley said fiercely. 'It's a power object.'

'Well, I "object" to it on the grounds that it's manky. What's so powerful about it – the smell? It must taste like shit!'

'Your mum tastes like shit!'

'Girls, girls,' Woodhouse said soothingly, 'save your energy for running. Shake hands.'

They shook hands grudgingly then Rafferty smiled.

'You don't even know my mum. She's a lovely woman.'

'Sorry, Raffles, I'm just nervous.'

'We'll be all right, and at least it's not raining. We'll get off to a quick start and I'll double back a couple of times and lose them in the woods, no trouble.'

'Yeah, don't sweat it, Drippy,' put in Woodhouse. 'Raffles knows the woods – we'll be fine; they'll never catch us.'

Mr Sidebottom came in wearing his tracksuit, his whistle round his neck.

'Have you not done that yet? Get your finger out, the lot of you. The hounds will be here soon.' He looked at them angrily. 'I want a good run out of you lot – no prancing along like a bunch of fairies and getting caught before you get half a mile. And you, Drinkley – I know you can run if you want to. You're just bloody lazy! I'm sick and tired of you going off crying to Matron every five minutes because you can't be bothered to make the effort. You'll grow up to be a ruddy nancy boy if you're not careful. Do you hear?'

'Yes, sir,' said Drinkley, eyes downcast.

'I want a good quick run and no gaps in the trail. I'll be checking as I go, and woe betide you three jessies if I see any gaps in the paper – you'll be for the high jump! I want it spread nice and even as you go and make sure you don't run out. So, you'd better cut it a damn sight quicker, hadn't you?'

'Yes, sir,' they all mumbled, snipping away at the paper.

With a sniff and a 'Huh!' he stalked away and gradually boys started arriving and getting changed.

Drinkley was muttering under his breath:

'Oh Christ! Shit! Bloody hell! Bollocks!'

Carrigan came past and tousled his hair.

'Good luck, lads. When I catch you I'm going to kick you right up the arse, Rafferty.'

'You'll never catch us, Carrie – you're much too fat!'

Carrigan, an athletic youth and a fine runner, looked horrified.

'I'm not fat… am I?' He walked away with his shirt pulled up, looking worriedly at his stomach.

As the changing room filled up, the volume increased and there was banter and good-natured threats. They finished cutting up the paper and looked at each other nervously. Woodhouse felt someone tread heavily on his foot and continue to stand there. Jones smiled down at him and winked.

'Good luck out there in the woods,' he said conspiratorially.

Bayliss was standing next to him and he smiled and started stretching his legs, limbering up meaningfully. They moved away and Woodhouse looked to see whether Drinkley had seen them. Luckily he hadn't. He was nervous enough without any added stress. Woodhouse knew that Jones and Bayliss were both handy runners but hopefully they would be too lazy to catch up. The trouble was how to manage with Drinkley… Woodhouse sighed. It was simple: he would run and scatter paper and hope for the best.

The whistle sounded and they went outside. The afternoon sun was shining fitfully and the ground was firm. They made their way to the front of the crowd, being jostled all the way, and waited. Woodhouse looked at the track stretching away up towards the distant trees and cleared his mind: just run and scatter paper; it's simple. He adjusted the strap of his paper bag and licked his lips.

Above the fields a murmuration of starlings wheeled and turned in the breeze, the sun flashing on their iridescent plumage as they described patterns in the sky, sweeping and falling, stalling and climbing, their aerobatic arabesques orchestrated by some mysterious collective instinct. Woodhouse heard the whistle and he ran. The starlings scattered like leaves.

Cubby was trying to relax but it was no use. The ottoman felt lumpy and uncomfortable and Charlotte Brontë's prose seemed convoluted to the point of being impenetrable. Half of it was in French, for heaven's sake, necessitating continual reference to the notes at the end. Rebelliously, he threw down the dog-eared copy of *Shirley*. He was a modern man with no time for such outmoded and sedentary pursuits, he determined.

Balls to the Brontës and *arse* to Austen! he shocked himself by inwardly declaring. He would renounce the quasi-religious romantic ramblings of sexually repressed spinsters dreaming on the shelf (Charlotte married eventually but Cubby either didn't know this or regarded it as the exception that somehow proved his rule) and become, henceforth, a man of literary action. He would read Steinbeck and Hemingway: colonial heavyweights mercilessly crushing sentences like so many empty beer cans, a loaded pistol by the typewriter and a still-dripping marlin on the balcony. He would take the world by the horns and wrestle it mooing into submission! Hell, yes!

He loved his grandmother still, but she had been an old woman and he was a young man, full of urine and vinegar – what need had he of the outdated witterings of repressed plain Janes driven to distraction by unrequited love and (with the exception of Miss Austen who inhabited a less restrictive era) overly-tight corsets? He leapt from the ottoman and began to pace the room. Taking Grandfather's fencing foil from its brackets above the fireplace he lunged at the standard lamp. Have at you! Ah, you would, would you, you villain? En garde! Where is she, you dog? Action: he must have action! He was the Hero and he must rescue the Distressed Damsel at once. He must find his Tallulah and to hell with that crazy lunatic Craig and anyone else who stood in the way of true love.

Cubby slew the lamp and flung away the foil. He had no need to burn his brassiere for he was a man and he had no bra (though, in truth, he could have done with one – he had lost a lot of weight but they were still a bit saggy). He tore off his shirt and threw it away and kicked his way angrily out of his trousers. He removed his pants and held them aloft, standing proudly in his socks. I love you, Grandmother, but I am a man now and I must put away womanly things and fight to fulfil my destiny. He marched to the kitchen, stuff all a-dangle, and lit the stove.

'I am Pendleton Chuzzlewit Arbuthnot,' he roared, as the flame licked at the pants, 'and I am a man of action!'

He jumped back as the nylon caught furiously alight and then went to the sink to fill a saucepan. He would clean the stove and then he would consult the phone book and find out where this Gruber fellow lived, just to make sure. And if he was keeping Tallulah there, well – Cubby smiled grimly – there would be trouble! He let out a shriek as the molten pants spat a lump of burning nylon onto his naked buttock. It burns! Oh, how it burns!

Gruber adjusted the red wig and pouted. They regarded his reflection in the dressing table mirror. It has to be said that he looked good. He was fine-boned anyway, with small, feminine features, and the make-up and lipstick suited him well. He was not an attractive man but he made a great woman, despite his swollen eye and clawed cheek.

'You look amazing,' said Tallulah.

'You are sickening to me, Gruber,' complained the Führer.

'I mus' get some more wine,' insisted Gruber, 'and a straw so's I don' smudge my lipstick.'

Getting up, he stumbled across the room. Why should he care what the cat said? He felt free for the first time in ages. He turned and smiled at Tallulah, getting lipstick on his teeth in the process.

'Don' go 'way,' he warned, wagging a finger and arching a pencilled eyebrow coquettishly. 'I wanna talk to you inna minute, gorgeous.'

'My God, Gruber – you are drunk! This is disgraceful, you weak-minded fool. You should be whipped soundly and then shot, you animal!'

Tallulah was feeling a bit tiddly herself but her plan was progressing nicely. Perhaps just a couple more drinks, though, and maybe a spliff.

When Gruber returned with the wine he was giggling.

'I got my tights all tangled up in the toilet,' he explained. 'I'm not used to being a girl.'

Tallulah was doing something complicated with cigarette papers.

'I'm making a joint,' she said, in answer to his puzzled look. 'I've got some weed. I thought we could have a smoke together – it'll be nice.'

'I'm not that kind of girl,' protested Gruber, tittering and tottering about.

'It'll make a real woman of you,' Tallulah promised.

'Gruber, I order you to stop this at once,' said the Führer coldly. 'To dress in the clothes like a woman, this is disgusting, but to dress in the clothes like a woman and smoking then drugs? This is the behaviour of a gypsy or a prostitute. I forbid it, Gruber – absolutely it is verboten!'

Gruber leant over to the cat on the dressing table.

'You're not the boss of me,' he whispered. 'I'm gonna smoke some pot with a pretty girl cos I'm a pretty girl too, and then –' he put his finger to his lips and shushed himself before leaning even closer and dropping his voice still lower – 'then I'm gonna kiss her!' He stood back, nodding and working his eyebrows suggestively at the cat. 'Whaddya think of that, eh?'

'Come and pour me a drink, William,' said Tallulah sweetly, 'and then we'll sit on the bed together and have a little smoke.'

Gruber flounced drunkenly over to her and sat down on the bed, winking suggestively at the Führer.

'You are a swine, Gruber,' the Führer said weakly. 'An absolute swine!'

'I regret that I lack my predecessor's flair for the dramatic,' said Taylor, 'but I always feel that these meetings are best conducted in the office, where all the relevant information is readily to hand.'

Woodhouse approached her desk. Through the window behind her he could see a police launch passing under Vauxhall Bridge. The sun picked out the ripples on the Thames and gilded the fairground red and yellow of the bridge, which a double decker bus was cumbersomely negotiating. Taylor regarded him with no hint of a smile. He took the golf ball and the rosary from his pocket and handed them to her, watching as she examined them. Her hands were strong looking, he noted, the nails cut short and unvarnished.

'A rosary?' she wondered.

'Catholic worry beads,' explained Woodhouse, sitting down opposite her unbidden.

'I know what a rosary is, Woodhouse!' she snapped. 'I attended a convent school. I was wondering why someone sent it to you.' She put on her glasses to scrutinise it more closely. 'It's Italian, by the look of it.'

'Perhaps he was suggesting that I should say my prayers – or pray for Greaves, maybe.'

She took off the glasses and looked across at him. Her eyes were black, like a snake's.

'I had a talk with Interpol in Lyon. It seems they're aware of a man in Paris who may be of interest to us. It's all frustratingly nebulous – they're certain he's involved in organised crime and various other nefarious activities but they can't pin anything on him and nobody will talk about him.' She paused. 'Apparently he has an ivory ear, so he shouldn't be hard to spot.'

Woodhouse couldn't help smiling, although he also felt a chill run through him. *He sees with his ear*, the Welrod guy had said…

'An ivory ear? He certainly sounds like a character,' he heard himself saying.

'From the little I know, he sounds like a deeply unpleasant character… Here's what we're going to do,

Woodhouse – Greaves's funeral is on Monday afternoon at a place called Warpingham, in Norfolk. We will have an armed presence there and if anyone unusual is in attendance or hanging around I want them taken down hard and we'll ask questions later. On Wednesday morning you will report to the airbase where you will be flown to Paris by helicopter. They're detailing another Black Hawk to search for the stealth version they so carelessly mislaid – presumably adhering to the principle that if you lose an arrow, you loose another one after it and watch more carefully the second time.'

'I know Warpingham,' said Woodhouse. 'I was brought up out that way.'

'You won't get lost, then. Whatever's going on here, we need to up our game. I want this man stopped and I want that stolen helicopter destroyed or recovered. God only knows what they're planning to use it for. It's time to get proactive, Woodhouse.'

'Absolutely, ma'am, so I'm to fly to Paris and search for a man who has an ivory ear and a stealth helicopter.'

'Essentially yes, only you're not just to search for him – you're to find him. This whole business is becoming extremely embarrassing. I want you to stop fannying about, Woodhouse, and do your damn job.'

Woodhouse fought to control his temper.

'Mr Greaves was a man I thought very highly of, ma'am, and I fully intend to avenge him. I'll take these with me, if you don't mind.' He reached over and took the golf ball and the rosary.

Taylor stood up.

'Good luck,' she said without smiling and held out her hand.

After a moment's hesitation Woodhouse reciprocated and they shook hands. She exerted so much force that he had to stop himself grimacing. Instead, he looked her calmly in the face.

'Thank you, ma'am.'

Outside, he shook the kinks out of his hand. Christ! She must be a bodybuilder or something!

They went up the farm track fast. The ground was much firmer, apart from the odd sticky patch that they hurdled or ran around, and they were able to make good time. Fear was obviously lending wings to Drinkley's feet, although whether it would also provide iron for his lungs remained to be seen. They soon fell into a rhythm, taking it in turns to scatter a handful of paper scraps from their shoulder bags every few paces.

'Piece of cake!' panted Drinkley, as they reached the top of the track.

They stopped for a second to look back before turning the corner. They could see the crowd in the distance milling about, waiting for the whistle. Drinkley took a hit on his inhaler.

'Come on,' said Rafferty. 'No stopping.'

They ran along the level ground beside the woods, their footsteps synchronised for a while then ragged again as someone stumbled. They heard the knocking of a woodpecker and the harsh cackle of a jay. The breeze brought salt from the sea to mingle with the smell of the earth and then, faintly, a whistle and a muted roar.

'Oh God!' gasped Drinkley, speeding up. 'They're coming!'

Woodhouse matched his speed and scattered some more paper.

'Don't worry, they're miles away.'

'But they're quicker than us!'

'Save your breath for running,' said Rafferty. 'We need to keep enough of a lead to give me time to double back.'

They were silent then and just ran, falling into single file as the track narrowed into a path and veered down into the woods. It was dark in there and they had to concentrate so as not to trip over exposed tree roots. Several times the path divided and Rafferty hesitated before choosing a direction.

Finally they came to another fork and he stopped. The path split into two, the larger going downhill and to the right, the smaller and less clearly-defined scrambling up to the left through saplings and partial undergrowth.

'This is the one,' said Rafferty. 'You two go up there. Don't drop any paper for twenty or thirty yards, so there's a gap in the trail, and then just keep going straight. I'll trail some paper down here for a while to lead them away and then double back and cut through. I'll catch you up in a bit, by the cliffs.'

'Are you sure this'll work?' asked Woodhouse.

Rafferty grinned.

'What's the worst that can happen? Go!'

He went off at speed, scattering paper lavishly and disappearing down into the darkness. Woodhouse and Drinkley clambered up the steep rise, using the trunks of the saplings to pull themselves up.

'Try not to leave any footmarks,' said Woodhouse.

At the top they looked down. The trail of paper led past their vantage point and away down the other fork. They had made a couple of scuffs in the soft earth climbing up, but nothing too noticeable. They could hear running feet and the occasional excited shout echoing through the tree trunks.

'They're catching up,' said Drinkley, fumbling for his inhaler. 'Let's go.'

The path was tortuous and they had to duck and twist through undergrowth and overhanging branches.

'I don't know where we're going,' said Drinkley, dropping a few bits of paper to one side of the path for form's sake. 'I hope we don't get lost.'

'We'll be alright,' Woodhouse replied, with more confidence than he felt. 'Raffles'll find us. We'll just follow the path and wait for him to catch up. He knows what he's doing.'

Drinkley was tiring and their pace was slackening. The light grew dimmer and the wind began to wail and whip the top branches of the trees above them. They pressed on grimly, two small boys running in the woods.

'Hold it in for as long as you can,' advised Tallulah, 'and then let it come out slowly.'

She was talking about the smoke; they were sitting on the bed smoking cannabis. Gruber kept the smoke in his lungs until it began to escape through his nose. He coughed and spluttered. Tallulah laughed and patted him on the back. Gruber passed her the joint. There were tears in his eyes but he wasn't sad.

'Don't wipe your eyes,' Tallulah said, divining his intention. 'You'll ruin your make-up.'

He dabbed at them instead and peered at himself in the mirror.

'I forgot I was so beautiful,' he said. He looked at her woozily. 'You're beautiful too.'

Tallulah was made-up too, flawless as a geisha, because she was planning to escape.

'Why, thank you, William. Shall we have some more wine?'

He topped up their glasses. His hands felt big and clumsy and yet small and far away. He was drunk and also stoned, he realised. He giggled.

'I can't believe I thought that cat was talking to me,' he said. 'Love can do strange things to a person.'

This struck Tallulah as funny for several reasons and she burst out laughing and lay back on the bed, spilling wine on herself in the process. She drew on the joint, held the smoke for a few moments and began to exhale.

'It's just one of Cubby's cats,' she said hoarsely. 'He's too nice to make anything evil – he's a woolly lambkins!'

She started laughing again at this and Gruber shrugged and joined in. He was so mashed he was borderline retarded – it was great! He was suddenly serious.

'I'm sorry I put you in the boot of the car and tied you up and stuff, Lulah. I s'pose sometimes a person can do the wrong thing for the right reasons?'

Tallulah sat up. She felt like punching him but managed to refrain.

'Are you trying to tell me that you kidnapped me for love?'

Gruber shook his head sadly.

'What else is there? What else could there ever be?' He started to snivel. From outside they heard a scream.

'What the hell was that?' Tallulah asked uneasily. 'I keep hearing it and I don't like it at all.'

'It's peacocks in the wood – it's mating season. The farmer breeds them.'

'It's fucking creepy!'

Tallulah got up and went unsteadily to the window. She looked through the gap in the curtains. Gruber's back garden was unkempt and surrounded by trees. It was sunny outside. It's only afternoon, she realised.

'Where the hell are we anyway?'

'We're safe. Come away from the window. Someone might see you.'

'Who's gonna see me? You've got me out in the arse-end of nowhere here, mate.'

Gruber's consciousness underwent a seismic shift and he was suddenly beset by doubts and fears. Paranoia had been lurking beneath a cloak of drunkenness and now it burst out at him, grinning.

'Oh Christ,' he said miserably. 'They're going to put me in prison, aren't they? That cat told me to do bad things and now I'm going to go to prison. I need a drink!'

The wine glass rattled against his teeth.

'You'll be all right. I'll tell them you didn't mean it – they'll help you, William.'

'Ja, Wilhelm, they will help you to some beatings – and some rapings too, I am thinking, in the prison. This one – this girl – she will tell her stories and it will be black for you, Gruber, oh so black!'

'No, go away – leave me alone!'

'It'll be fine, William. You've not been very well, that's all.'

'Stones they will throw at the prison van, Gruber, when they are taking you away. She will tell her so-sad stories and all the fools on the jury, they will to crying! Yes, and giving to you the life sentence! The knife, little Gruber – take the knife and lay her down softly then with a necklace of rubies. So beautiful, like a princess she will be in the woods, and her tongue then it will be silent and the earth and the leaves and the stars will garland her golden hair, and the birds a cloak of silver will weave her with their song. Like the magical fairy tale, Gruber, she will be beautiful forever when you with the knife enchant her.'

Very slowly Gruber got up and put his glass down on the dressing table. He reached for the knife.

Tallulah's plan had been simple: dress him up as a woman, ply him with drink and drugs and then run. She reasoned that, hindered by women's clothes, he would be unable to catch her since she was wearing jogging trousers and trainers.

Now she saw the look in his eye and she was up and off in an instant, halfway down the stairs before he had finished picking up the knife. She had earlier undone the bolts at the top and bottom of the french windows so they were only locked with the key – and now there was no time for hesitation. As she heard him thumping down the stairs she ran through the sitting room, turning her shoulder and ducking her head, and simply burst through the doors, glass shattering around her.

Woodhouse parked in the pay and display in the town centre. He looked at his watch and found he was early. Realising that he was hungry and remembering that there was a bakery on the high street, he walked there, noticing how much – and at the same time how little – the place had changed.

The bakery was closed and there was a poster in the window with a blurred picture of a missing girl. She was blonde and probably pretty and Woodhouse hoped she was all right, though he had his doubts. Lamenting the inhumanity of man he crossed the road to The Crown and went in, conspicuous in his black suit.

It was much as he remembered it, dark and smelling of stale beer, a long room with the bar at its centre, the jukebox and pool table at one end. A young couple were playing pool and Woodhouse didn't recognise the song on the jukebox. He bought a Guinness and a cheese and onion roll from the world-weary barmaid and went and sat at the table most distant from the pool table. He looked blankly at the lights on the fruit machine as he bit into the roll. He grimaced – too much margarine – but he was hungry so he finished it and washed it down with Guinness.

A big skinhead came in, arms sleeved with tattoos, and sat at the bar, giving Woodhouse a long look. Woodhouse made himself a roll-up and put it behind his ear. He glanced up in time to see the skinhead looking again. Picking up his pint Woodhouse went out to the smoking shelter. If the guy wanted to fight he could follow and there would be no witnesses out here. Woodhouse didn't give a shit – he had bigger fish to fry.

He lit his roll-up in the ramshackle smoking shelter and considered the beer garden as he smoked. He had misspent some of his youth in this pub and there had been a tearful farewell with a girl in this garden many years ago. He felt an echo of the pain.

The skinhead came out with a cigarette in his mouth which he lit with a Clipper. He looked at Woodhouse.

'I thought it was you, Woody,' he said, smiling.

Woodhouse looked at him, half-angrily at first and then – as the years and tattoos dropped away and the smiling ginger-haired boy was revealed – with amazement.

'Raffles!'

'It is I.'

'I haven't seen you in – what? – twenty years? Christ!'

'More than that, probably.'

They grinned at each other and shook hands. It didn't seem enough so they embraced, banging each other on the back and laughing delightedly. They sat down together at the stained and wobbly table.

'Where the hell have you been?' asked Rafferty. 'You just disappeared.'

'I went off to London. I was in the army for a while and got posted here and there – you know… How about you?'

'I had a few problems with drink and drugs,' Rafferty said soberly, 'but I'm all good now. I've got the tattooist's on White Lion Street.'

'That's cool; maybe I'll come and get something done when I've got more time. I'm just in town for a funeral.'

They looked at each other, remembering things.

'I hate funerals,' said Rafferty. There was a pause. 'What happened to that girl – the one you were seeing back then? What was her name?'

'Grace. Her name was Grace. Her parents sent her away somewhere. That was partly why I left – I was heartbroken at the time.'

'Yeah, shit! Of course – Grace. She was crazy, man!'

Woodhouse laughed.

'Yeah, she was crazy all right.'

'But fun.'

'Definitely fun. I loved that girl, brother.'

They sipped their drinks and Woodhouse began to roll another cigarette.

'They never found him, you know,' said Rafferty quietly.

Woodhouse shook his head sadly. He hadn't thought about it for a long time but now it all came flooding back, shockingly vivid and raw.

They had to stop so Drinkley could use his inhaler. He was gasping with every step. They heard a long low grumble of thunder, like a bowling ball rolling down an alley.

'You all right?' asked Woodhouse.

'Yeah, I'm okay. Let's keep going.'

They ran on, the wind whipping in and whisking the paper away as soon as they dropped it. It was getting very dark and the bowling ball rolled closer. The woods thinned out and suddenly they were on the cliffs. The sea below was wild: white horses rearing and breakers booming. As they looked there was a great flash of sheet lightning that brought everything into stark relief and then a peal of thunder so loud that it shook the ground and they could feel it through their feet. The ball had struck the pins. They stood still for a moment, dazzled and deafened.

'Come on,' said Woodhouse.

Drinkley just stood there. He was terrified. Woodhouse took his arm and dragged him along until he started to run. They followed the rough path between the cliff edge and the woods. It ran closer to the woods than the cliffs but near enough to the cliffs for them to hear the angry smash and roar of the waves below. The sky lit up again, so bright that they could almost see each other's skeletons running along, and the thunder clapped instantaneously. There was a pause, as though for dramatic effect, and then the rain fell like a guillotine blade, so heavy that it drove them to take cover in the woods.

They wove their way through the trees until they found a big fir that kept most of the rain off and sat down under it. It was so dark that they could hardly see. Their teeth were chattering uncontrollably and it might have been funny if they hadn't been so miserable.

'Well, well, well,' said an unpleasantly familiar voice above the rain, 'it seems we have caught some hares.'

The lightning and thunder came again, directly overhead, and there was a crash from nearby. The momentary light was enough to see Jones and Bayliss sitting virtually next to them, sheltering under the same tree. They were smiling. Woodhouse found that his teeth had stopped chattering.

'Why don't you just leave us alone,' he suggested.

'That would be the Christian thing to do, wouldn't it,' agreed (by the sound of it) Bayliss, 'but the thing is, you see, we're heathens and, besides, Jones has a new toy that he's just *dying* to show you.'

Woodhouse felt Drinkley's hand on his arm; his friend was shaking. There was movement in the gloom, rain spattered around them and branches thrashed and groaned. Woodhouse's eyes had adjusted enough to see Jones standing over him.

'My father sent it to me,' explained Jones. 'I've been wanting to try it out on something bigger.'

The lightning flashed and, frozen like a photograph, Woodhouse saw the knife in his hand and the look on his face. He heard Drinkley cry out and saw that Bayliss had hold of him.

'It's a Swiss Army,' elaborated Jones proudly. 'It has all kinds of different blades – this one's a corkscrew.'

He took Woodhouse by the shirt and lifted him to his feet, pushing the point of the corkscrew into his stomach and beginning to turn it. Woodhouse felt it break the skin and the blood was momentarily warm as it ran down. He looked up at Jones as the lightning flashed again and saw that his face was blank and cold as a mask. Jones tore the corkscrew out of Woodhouse's flesh and handed the knife to Bayliss.

'Try the one for taking stones out of a horse's hoof,' he suggested.

'Let me see,' said Bayliss. 'No, that's the scissors… Ah – here we are.'

Woodhouse heard Drinkley's scream, and the lightning revealed the scene for him. *Here is a photograph for you to keep always*, it promised. It was an arty black and white shot taken in profile, the faces close together in sharp focus. Bayliss held the knife to the soft skin under Drinkley's chin with a look on his face that was almost loving. Drinkley's head was back and his mouth was open, as though he were crying out to heaven. Tears and rain streaked his cheeks and his eyes were wide. The flash ended and the darkness returned. They were in a pocket in time and the seconds beat down mercilessly with the rain.

'Let him go!' shouted Woodhouse. 'Let him go, you bastard!'

'I can recommend the scissors,' said Bayliss, passing the knife to Jones. 'Nice and sharp.'

'I think perhaps the knife-blade would be best. Perhaps I will cut out his eye.'

The scene lit up again and the thunder split the air. There was an almighty crack from above and sounds of a falling branch. They all instinctively ducked.

'Run!' screamed Woodhouse, breaking free. 'Run!' And he ran into the woods, ducking and weaving through the trees and the rain and slipping in the mud.

After a time he looked round for Drinkley but he wasn't there. They never saw each other again.

Later when they combed the woods for him they found his inhaler by the cliffs. It was eventually decided that he must have fallen and been washed out to sea. The body was not recovered.

'I left him,' said Woodhouse. 'I ran away and I left him to die.'

Even after all this time he still felt like weeping. He saw the lightning photograph of Drinkley crying out to heaven. How could he not when it was imprinted on his brain forever? Rafferty sipped his drink, a lime and soda, and put it carefully down on the table, fitting it neatly onto the wet ring it had left previously. His hand shook slightly.

'It wasn't your fault,' he said. 'I should have been there instead of getting lost. It wouldn't have happened if there'd been three of us.'

'I'd like to meet those two again, now that I'm not a little kid anymore.'

'Nobody knows what happened to them after they got expelled. I've looked for them online but had no luck.'

Woodhouse looked at his watch.

'Shit. I've got to go. Give me your number and I'll give you a call later if you're about.'

'I'll be about,' said Rafferty, getting out his phone.

They exchanged numbers and Woodhouse stood up. They shook hands again.

'It's good to see you, mate,' said Woodhouse.

'You too. I hope it's no one close – the funeral, I mean.'

'It's to do with work. My old boss. He was a good old boy so I need to pay my respects. I never even knew he was from out this way.'

'Small world.'

They smiled at each other.

'Small world,' agreed Woodhouse. 'I'll call you later.'

Tallulah raced down the garden like a tipsy gazelle. The grass felt springy beneath her feet; she was free! She leapt at the fence and pulled herself over, into the woods. As she disappeared into the pine trees she heard Gruber clambering over the fence behind her. He had stopped to put his shoes on but he was over the fence fast, knife clamped between his teeth. He laddered his tights but he didn't care. She must not escape; the Führer had spoken.

Tallulah had no idea where she was or where she was going, she just ran. A beautiful dryad in tracksuit trousers flitting through the trees, breasts and buttocks jiggling gloriously, small chin set determinedly, her golden tresses streaming behind her. The peacock seemed suddenly dowdy as she ran by, this sylvan vision of womanhood, magnificent in motion.

Gruber, on the other hand, was a less attractive proposition. His skirt was torn, his tights laddered, his lipstick smeared and the pine needles had dragged at his wig until it stood up around him like a ragged red flag. He grasped the hunting knife in his hand and his face was twisted as he tried to focus without his glasses. Small wonder then that the peacock was startled. It simply wanted to go about its pavonine business, to find a peahen and do things to her with its pea-penis, but here was a threatening apparition indeed, with what appeared to be some kind of fan displayed around its head. The peacock stepped in front of Gruber and screamed. Proudly, it displayed its own fan. Gruber screamed back. He was having some kind of psychotic episode as it was and now he was confronted with an array of shimmering iridescent eyes, all shivering as the peacock rustled its tail feathers. Tallulah heard the screams and crept back a little way to watch. This was too good to miss.

Gruber feinted at the peacock with the knife. It stepped around neatly as a matador, drew closed its tail and then fanned it again, crying out triumphantly. The shivering eyes gazed into Gruber's soul without pity. He cried out himself, in horror, and backed away. The peacock followed. Tallulah watched through the trees.

The peacock pretended to lose interest, turning away and dragging its tail along like a train. It turned and fixed Gruber with a beady glare. He licked his lips nervously and tightened his grip on the knife. The peacock proceeded towards him, stately as a bride. It threw back its head and shrieked defiance and then charged, hurling itself at Gruber's groin in a great flapping, pecking, feathery bundle.

Tallulah jumped up and down and clapped her hands with glee as Gruber fell screaming to the ground and dropped the knife. He covered his eyes with his hands and rolled into the foetal position, the peacock standing on top of him with its fan displayed as it pecked at his face.

'Goodbye, William,' called Tallulah. 'Good luck in prison!'

Gruber reacted badly to this possibly well-meant message of support.

'You *bitch!*' she heard him say.

Gruber reached for the knife and plunged it into the peacock, which gave a gurgling cry and emitted a fine spray of pulsing blood, like a lawn sprinkler.

'*Bitch! Bitch! Bitch!*' chanted Gruber, driving the knife repeatedly into the dying bird. Blood sprayed onto the peacock's tail and ran down the eyes, which vibrated in its death throes.

Horrified, and realising that her gloating might have been premature, Tallulah turned and ran. Gruber threw the limp body of the peacock to one side, where it landed with a rustle, and followed. If he hadn't been mad before, he certainly was now.

Lomax sits at the kitchen table of the farmhouse, waiting for word from his contacts. Maurice is in attendance, mostly recovered from his ordeal at the fangs of the snake. He stands at Lomax's elbow as he pores over an unusual looking map. Lomax leans back and rubs his eyes; he is tired.

'Ah, Maurice, my friend – my dear, dear friend. It is a fine thing that we do, is it not?'

'A fine thing, sir,' agrees the servant.

'And necessary.'

'Very necessary, sir.'

'I expect you are looking forward to it greatly, are you not?'

'Sir?' Maurice is confused.

'To our trip, old friend. You surely did not imagine that I would leave you behind, after all the good times we have shared.'

'I am not really much of a man of action, sir,' Maurice says carefully.

Lomax stands up and looks down at him, frowning. He places a huge scarred hand paternally on the servant's shoulder.

'Nonsense,' he says. 'Remember when you were playing with the snake?' He chuckles at the recollection. 'You are a very fine acrobat indeed, Maurice. Of course I will not leave you behind. Perhaps you will fight some snakes, yes? Like Indiana Jones in the movies!'

Lomax roars with laughter and bangs Maurice on the back so hard that he almost knocks him over. Angry shouts come from outside so Lomax goes to investigate and, after a moment's hesitation, Maurice follows.

Outside in the yard, the South Africans have been fighting. Two of them are facing each other angrily, dusty and dishevelled. The other two look on.

'What is this commotion that you make?' asks Lomax mildly. 'You wish, perhaps, to alert the police to our presence here?'

'This dickhead was checking me skeef,' says one of them.

'Fuck you, pricklicker,' says the other, and they are fighting again, rolling on the floor.

Lomax walks over to them and picks them up, one with each hand, separating them in the process. They are big men and half his age yet he lifts them both at once with no visible effort. It is comical but no one feels like laughing. The two protagonists are still and silent as Lomax holds them by their shirt fronts. He lifts them again and smashes their skulls together then drops them back on to the ground, where they lie stunned.

'This behaviour is not good,' he says. 'We have important work to complete. I cannot tolerate this insurrection – it shall be reflected in your wages. Do you understand?'

'Ja.'

'Yes, boss.'

'Go and run your checks on the helicopter.'

'We checked it already, boss.'

It is obvious that the man on the ground regrets saying this as soon as it leaves his mouth. There is a collective intake of breath. Lomax seems to swell. His face grows red and seems set to burst the calfskin straps. He leans down to the man on the ground so their faces are almost touching.

'Check it again,' he whispers. 'Check it again.'

Attendance at the funeral was sparse. There were perhaps twenty-five people, including several burly men with earpieces who muttered occasionally into handsets. Taylor was there; she turned and gave Woodhouse a curt nod when he entered the church. He nodded back in kind. There were one or two other people he recognised from work scattered about but no obvious family apart from a very old woman wearing a hat with a veil and sitting at the front – Greaves's mother, presumably.

Woodhouse took a seat in a central pew and remembered to turn off his phone. An unseen organist began to play a piece Woodhouse thought might be by J. S. Bach (it was Pachelbel's Canon in D, in fact) and they stood as the coffin was carried in by stern-faced men, again sporting earpieces. They placed it on trestles in front of the altar, and coloured sunshine fell from the stained-glass window on to the lilies that covered the lid.

As the vicar began to speak, Woodhouse looked at the picture of Greaves on a pamphlet he found there, younger than when Woodhouse had known him but still with the ubiquitous pipe. Woodhouse tried to imagine him in the box but couldn't. The organist started to play a hymn. Woodhouse looked at the words printed in the pamphlet and moved his lips numbly but made no sound. He didn't much care for funerals.

The service passed by in a blur. Woodhouse listened without emotion as the vicar intoned platitudes about a man he had clearly never met and they all stood as the coffin was carried out into the graveyard. The old lady followed shakily and the rest of them filed out after her, Woodhouse folding the pamphlet and putting it in the inside pocket of his suit jacket. His hand brushed the grip of the Walther in its holster and the touch brought comfort. The afternoon sun was bright and he loosened his tie and put on his sunglasses as they made their way to the graveside. Taylor fell into step beside him.

'I need to see you after,' she said quietly. 'There have been some developments.'

The men with headsets took up positions at vantage points around the graveyard as the coffin was lowered. All was quiet save for the distant cry of a peacock. Woodhouse looked down at the coffin and remembered how in awe he had been of Greaves when he'd first joined the service. He smiled. Greaves had been straight out of John le Carré: a gentle English eccentric with a core of steel.

There was movement in the woods to the side of the graveyard and the men with headsets all reached inside their jackets. Woodhouse did the same, fingers curling round the grip of his pistol. A girl emerged from the woods beside the church, running smoothly, blonde and pretty. She seemed to hesitate when she saw them and then ran on through the gravestones, looking back once towards the woods. She looked not unlike the girl Woodhouse had seen in the missing poster. No one else came from the woods and, as she disappeared out of the lych-gate, hands were removed from jackets and reassurances muttered into transmitters. If it was the missing girl she was safe now.

The vicar finished what he had been saying and bowed his head. The old lady threw the first handful of dirt onto the coffin and those who were so inclined followed suit. Woodhouse in turn reached into the soil at the graveside. It was rich and dark, slightly damp to the touch despite the sun. He tossed it gently down into the space beside the coffin, not wanting to disturb the flowers. I will get him, sir. Have no doubt of that.

Gradually the focus shifted away from the grave and people started to gather outside the doors of the church to offer condolences. Taylor motioned Woodhouse to follow her and led him round the side of the church.

'Look at this,' she said, producing her phone.

On the screen was a photograph of a section of the Eiffel Tower's ironwork with a crescent moon behind it. It was a beautiful shot. Taylor pointed to something.

'Zoom in here,' she said.

Woodhouse could see it now but he zoomed in anyway. The silhouetted shape was unmistakeable, framed by girders as it passed in front of the lower horn of the moon. The modified tail boom and rear rotor housing, the general stripped-down shape of the thing.

'Holy Christ! That's our missing Stealth Hawk.'

'So it would seem, Woodhouse, but there is still no need for blasphemy, particularly on this day and in this place.'

'Where did this picture come from?'

'Can you believe someone posted it online? It's dated three days ago. Our people had a look at it and estimated its projected course and we've been examining satellite pictures from along that approximate line, more in hope than expectation it must be admitted.'

She swept the screen with her finger to reveal a grainy shot of some kind of altercation in a picturesque farmyard. There was really nothing there of particular interest but Woodhouse knew – he just *knew*. He could feel the bad vibes coming out of the screen. It was him. One of the ill-defined figures was Lomax.

'Where is this place?'

'It's a farm near Chasteuil, in Provence. There's been some unusual activity there and the old chap who owns the place hasn't been seen for some time.'

'Never mind Paris, then, I want to go directly there.' He looked at the picture again. 'Do you think there's a stolen helicopter in that barn?'

'Could be. What do you suppose they're doing there?'

'Unless he just likes joyriding in the thing I'd say they're fuelling up and preparing to do whatever it is he's been planning.' Woodhouse thought for a moment. 'If I might make a suggestion, ma'am?'

'Of course.'

'We need to work up a list of possible targets within their combat radius, and we need to do it fast. Have you got someone on the ground watching them?'

She bristled.

'Not yet, Woodhouse. We don't actually know that it's them for certain. We've got them under satellite surveillance – we'll know if they lift off.'

'With respect, it'll be too late by then.'

'You mentioned combat radius; do we know what theirs is?'

Woodhouse smiled. His homework was about to bear fruit.

'Combat radius assumes that they intend to fly to their target, do whatever they have planned and then return. If it's a suicide mission the radius doubles.'

'For the moment, let's assume they intend to survive.'

'Off the top of my head, ma'am, the combat radius of a Black Hawk is around three hundred and fifty miles unless they have extra fuel on the stub wings. Since this is a stealth machine it doesn't use external stores because they would compromise the radar signature so, unless there's some experimental business that we don't know about on board, we're looking at three hundred and fifty miles, or seven hundred if they're planning to go out in a blaze of glory.'

Taylor nodded.

'I'm impressed,' she admitted. 'We'd better look at what's inside both circles, I think.'

'I agree, ma'am. Obviously their range is partly defined by how much weight they're carrying, which we have no way of knowing, but three-fifty and seven hundred seem like sensible figures to work with.'

'I'll get on to the base and let them know what we're thinking. Also, I'll check the fuel capabilities. We need to get on with this, so I would like you to make your way there tonight rather than Wednesday as originally planned. You'll leave at oh two hundred hours.'

'No problem, ma'am.'

They shook hands; she was gentler this time.

'I'll be in touch when we've worked up the lists. Good luck, Woodhouse.'

'Thank you.'

As Woodhouse walked towards the lych-gate, Greaves's mother was being helped into a long black Daimler. He would have liked to have paid his respects but there really wasn't time. In the car he sat for a moment looking at the rosary hanging from the rear-view mirror, and then he drove away.

Gruber was relieved. Although he knew it boded ill for him, he was glad Tallulah was gone. He looked at the bloodstained knife in his hand and shuddered. Passing the corpse of the peacock, just a forlorn heap of feathers now, he retraced his steps and climbed over the fence, laddering his tights again. He threw the knife over first this time, not wanting to put it in his mouth.

Back in the house he stripped off, put the bloodied clothes and wig in the washing machine and set it running. He washed the knife and left it on the draining board. In the bedroom the Führer was mercifully silent. Gruber showered and washed off the make-up and then, towel around his waist, sat down at the dressing table to think. His eye looked less swollen now and he had sobered up.

'What to do, eh, Gruber?' said the Führer at length. 'Straight to the police she will go, of course.'

Gruber nodded thoughtfully and began to apply foundation to his face, paying particular attention to his bruised eye.

'Ach, what is this? You have now a taste for this depravity, I think. This is not healthy, Gruber.'

Gruber started to pencil in his eyebrows, which were sparse and blond by nature. He had watched Tallulah closely, smitten as he was, and was confident he could replicate her work.

'Gruber! I am speaking to you! Answer to me immediately!'

Gruber applied eyeliner, wincing as he worked on the injured eye.

'You wanted me to kill her,' he said.

'She is a Delilah, Gruber – a Jezebel. She is dangerous to us.'

'She's just a young girl. I am not a murderer of young girls.'

The Führer laughed.

'No, Gruber, you are the murderer of the peacock, I think. And the dresser in the clothes of the woman. You are not a man at all, you are a floozy!'

'Perhaps I will smash you,' suggested Gruber, closing an eye as he shaded the lid. 'Then you would be quiet.'

There was a pause while the Führer digested this.

'I have told you, Gruber,' it said silkily. 'If I break, you break too. I do not think you will put this to the test.'

Gruber winced as he shaded the other lid. He picked up the Führer and looked at it.

'Are you sure about that?'

The cat smiled and seemed to give a little wriggle in Gruber's hand.

'Ah, Wilhelm, this is good. A little of the English spunk, yes? Bravo, my pretty friend!'

Gruber smiled back and returned the Führer gently to the dressing table.

'We understand each other then,' he said and went to find some clothes.

He returned wearing ladies' slacks, and a bra which he was engaged in stuffing with toilet paper.

'Oh, Gruber,' sighed the Führer. 'This I can never understand.'

'I'm not enjoying it,' claimed Gruber. 'It's necessary.'

The Führer kept silent but the air was heavy with disapproval. Gruber applied blusher, mascara and lipstick and put on a blouse and Florence's watch, which was slightly too big for him. There was a knock at the door. Gruber looked out of the front window and saw Cubby.

'It's that idiot Arbuthnot.'

'You must to get rid of him, Gruber. Use the wily ways of the woman, yes?'

Gruber nodded and started to go downstairs.

'The wig, you oaf – you must to wearing the wig!'

Gruber put on the ash-blonde wig and straightened it in the mirror. He looked good. The knocking came again, louder.

'Just coming,' he called, trying to keep his voice light.

Cubby looked surprised to see him.

'I'm sorry,' he said. 'I was looking for Mr Gruber.'

'I'm afraid he's not here,' said Gruber, dropping his gaze demurely.

'Could you tell me when he'll be back?'

'He won't be *coming* back!' vowed Gruber fiercely, warming to his role.

He raised his head defiantly and looked at Cubby, turning his head slightly so the light would fall on his injured eye. Cubby took half a step back.

'Oh, I—' he stammered, 'I'm terribly sorry. I had no idea.'

'It's quite all right, dear,' said Gruber, modulating his tone carefully and trying a sad yet brave, and possibly even slightly flirtatious, smile. 'You weren't to know.'

'I'm very sorry to have disturbed you.'

Cubby was blushing and backing away.

'It's perfectly all right, darling.'

Gruber pursed his lips and tried a sultry look through his eyelashes but he didn't really know what he was doing and he could feel that it wasn't successful. Arbuthnot had turned and was actually running away down the path.

'Bye-bye, darling,' called Gruber after him.

'Goodbye,' responded Cubby tremulously, over his shoulder.

PART FOUR

THROUGH
THE BLADES

Woodhouse parked on White Lion Street. Making sure nobody was watching, he took off his jacket and removed the harness and shoulder holster that held his Walther. Sliding the bundle under the seat he got out of the car. Rafferty's shop was called The Illuminated Hide and the sign depicted a grinning monk with the sleeve of his robe pushed up to display a muscular arm covered in colourful tattoos. Woodhouse smiled at this, put his jacket back on and went in.

The shop was small but bright and clean, and racks containing flash cards of tattoo designs covered the walls. The glass-topped counter displayed piercing accoutrements: studs, plugs, rings and the like. Behind it stood a girl with wild, partially shaved blonde hair and a ring through her lip. The buzz of the tattoo gun sounded through a doorway behind her.

'Sorry, we're just about to close,' she said, making a comically sad face to soften the blow. Woodhouse liked her for it.

'That's all right, I just came in to see—'

What the fuck was his first name? Woodhouse realised he had no idea. He gestured lamely towards the noise of the gun.

'Sean,' she supplied.

'Sean,' Woodhouse agreed.

'He shouldn't be long. I'll tell him you're here.'

'Thanks. It's Woodhouse – Richard.'

She flashed him a smile and went through. Woodhouse checked out some tattoo designs. There were dragons, tigers, panthers and peacocks; skulls, bones and butterflies; pin-up girls, geisha girls and sailor girls; ships and sharks and swallows; intricate knotwork patterns, Art Nouveau influenced work; Betty Boop, Bettie Page, Jesus Christ, Salvador Dali, Bugs Bunny... All tastes were provided for.

'You must be Richard,' said Rafferty behind him.

'And you must be Sean. I'm impressed with your shop.'

'Be careful with it,' Rafferty called to a young man who was leaving, his forearm bound up in cling film. 'It's a masterpiece!' He turned back to Woodhouse. 'Shall we go for a drink? Molly can lock up.'

Woodhouse left his car where it was and they walked to The Crown. It was muggy and he took his jacket off, thankful that he had left the gun behind. During the short walk Rafferty told Woodhouse a little about his tattooing business. Woodhouse's phone rang. With an apologetic look at Rafferty, he answered it.

'Hey, Richie,' she said. 'I hear you're going on vacation.'

'Hello there, young woman. Yeah, a short trip to Provence.'

'I was worried about Walther – did you get someone to feed him?'

'No, I had him put down. It seemed like too much trouble having to organise someone to look after him.'

There was a short silence. Rafferty was clearly trying not to listen.

'Are you shitting me, Richie? You know that I would kick your ass if any harm befell that cat.' She was laughing.

'The old girl across the road feeds him when I go away. If he gets hungry he just goes round her house and miaows, Maryanne – don't worry.'

'I was kinda worried about you too, but not as much as Walther.'

'As long as I know where I stand.'

'Be careful, Richie.'

'I will, honey, I promise.'

'Call me when you get back and we'll take a vacation of our own, maybe.'

'Maybe so.'

She blew him a kiss and disconnected.

Woodhouse and Rafferty went into the pub. The atmosphere was rowdy, people at the bar were doing rounds of shots and Thin Lizzy's *The Boys are Back in Town* was on the jukebox. Woodhouse and Rafferty grinned at each other. The song had been part of both their lives for a long time.

They took their drinks outside and sat at a table in the garden where Woodhouse's heart had once been broken. It was warm in the sun and he took off his tie and put it in his pocket.

'I was wondering if you fancied a drive out to the old school,' he said after a while. 'I've been wanting to have a look at the place.'

'Get some closure,' suggested Rafferty.

'Yeah, something like that.'

'Yeah, I'm up for that. I heard it's closed. It was a rehab for a while, you know.' Rafferty took a sip of his orange juice.

'I didn't know that. Drugs?'

'No thanks, I'm trying to give them up.' They laughed. 'Yeah, drugs and alcohol. The government moved the goalposts about funding so it had to close. It's been shut three or four years now – I've been meaning to have a look at it myself.'

There was a silence. *Valley of the Dolls* by Generation X was coming from the pub and a passenger jet crossed the sky in the east, sun glinting on its fuselage. Woodhouse lit a roll-up.

'Have you got any ink?' asked Rafferty.

'Just the one,' said Woodhouse. 'On my back.'

'Can I have a look? Professional curiosity.'

Woodhouse looked around. The garden was deserted. Turning away from Rafferty, he pulled his shirt up to his shoulders to reveal the artwork on his back. Rafferty leaned forward to see better. The tattoo was immense. At the base of Woodhouse's spine sat an oriental figure smoking a long pipe. The detail in his baggy clothes was intricate and the shading delicate. His face was blissful, his eyes were closed and he seemed unaware of the pipe smoke weaving up in interlacing tendrils until it massed and became the tail of the huge dragon that occupied most of Woodhouse's muscular back. Its wings were curved ready to envelope the seated figure, and its mouth was open exposing savage rows of teeth. The talons on its powerful feet were poised to either side of the oblivious smoker's head, seemingly preparing to seize him. The piece was rendered in black and shades of grey, like an old sumi-e brush and ink illustration.

'That is truly amazing,' said Rafferty after a time. 'Where did you get it done?'

'I had it done in Hong Kong a few years ago. I'll tell you about it sometime – there's a story attached to it.'

Woodhouse sat back down, adjusting his shirt. He took a swig of his drink and regarded Rafferty seriously.

'I can't believe they never found the body,' he said.

'I know. It's fucked up… He was a good kid, clever.'

'Brave too. You really think he fell into the sea?'

'He must have done or they'd have found the body, I suppose.'

Woodhouse drained his pint.

'Let's go back to school, shall we?'

As Cubby walked back up the hill to town he was troubled. Mrs Gruber had been an unsettling woman; there was something about her but he couldn't quite put his finger on it. Her husband had clearly been beating her, the swine, yet she had been flirting shamelessly. Cubby shook his head; he was no nearer to finding Tallulah. He had been sure she would be at Gruber's house and had been looking forward to rescuing her and earning her eternal gratitude. As he was trudging past the police station, hands in pockets and deep in thought, Tallulah came out, beautiful as ever, and banished his gloom with a dazzling smile. He stood stunned, as she walked over, stood on tiptoes and kissed him on the cheek.

'Hello, Cubby,' she said. 'I missed you.'

'Tallulah! You're safe! Where have you been?'

'A lunatic had one of your cats in the boot of his car. He's been holding me at the gamekeeper's cottage down the hill there.' She gestured in the direction Cubby had come from.

'Gruber! I knew it! I've just been down there – his wife said he'd left her.'

'His wife?' Tallulah frowned. 'What did she look like? Was she a big woman with enormous breasts?'

Cubby flushed.

'I didn't look at her breasts but she seemed quite a delicate sort of woman. She had blonde hair and a black eye. She was quite friendly.'

'That was him! He must have cleaned himself up and changed wigs. They're going to go down and pick him up in a minute.'

Even as she said this, there was sudden activity as four uniformed officers came out of the station, distributed themselves between two marked cars and set off towards Gruber's house. As they passed, the passenger in the leading car nodded to Cubby and Tallulah.

'Did he hurt you?' Cubby asked.

She smiled.

'Not as much as I hurt him. Where do you think he got the black eye?'

'But you're okay? Really okay?'

'I'm fine, Cubby, honestly.'

'Me and Craig went looking for you yesterday but we went to the wrong house. There was a bit of a mix-up, to be honest.'

'I'd forgotten about Craig. I'll have to have a talk with him.'

'He says you're his girlfriend.'

She raised her eyebrows.

'Does he now? We'll have to see about that, won't we?'

She looked down, suddenly shy, and scuffed at the pavement with her trainers. Cubby wanted to kiss her of course. He always wanted to kiss her; but he was shy as well. They were shy together for a few moments and Cubby admired all the different colours the sun revealed in her hair. White-blonde and ash-blonde, wheaten and gold, rose-gold and copper: all the delicate filaments in the hair of the girl that he loved. She looked up.

'I'm going to go and stay with my parents for a couple of days. Maybe we could meet up after that, if you'd like to?'

'I'd like that very much.'

'Give me your number and I'll call you.'

'I don't have a phone,' Cubby admitted.

'You must have a landline at your shop or the house.'

'It got cut off because I forgot to pay the bill. I'm not very good at things like that.'

Tallulah sighed.

'You exasperating man! I shall have to drag you into the twenty-first century, shan't I?'

'You won't have to drag me. I'll follow gladly anywhere you lead.'

'That's sweet, Cubby.'

To his very great delight she stood on tiptoes again and kissed him softly on the mouth. As she pulled away there was a tiny crackle and a bead of static electricity passed between their lips.

'Wow!' exclaimed Cubby. 'Did you feel that?'

Tallulah nodded. Her eyes were sparkling. She grinned.

'I felt it. It promises great things for the future.'

'How do you mean? Oh, I see…!'

Cubby blushed. She meant *sex!* What unimaginable luxury it would be to lie naked with this wonderful vibrant girl, to see the soft light fall on her skin, to taste the smooth curves at her throat. How exotic to caress the sweetness of her… His imagination spiralled away from him and he stood gaping like a halfwit. And here she was in front of him! He pulled himself together. She was laughing at him, but not unkindly. A small car with a glamorous older woman inside pulled up.

'That's my mum,' Tallulah said. 'Give me a couple of days, Cubby, and I'll come and find you at your shop.'

'Promise?'

'I promise.'

They smiled at each other then she turned and ran to the car. Tallulah's mother gave Cubby a rather disdainful look as they drove away but he didn't care – he was on a promise! He just hoped Tallulah would have forgotten that he was not necessarily tremendously kind to animals, particularly cats.

'Nice car,' said Rafferty as they got in. 'I see you've had some work done on it.' He was looking at the weapons control panel. 'What is it exactly that you do, mate?'

'I'm just a civil servant,' said Woodhouse.

Rafferty smiled but said nothing.

It was a pleasant drive out to the coast with the windows down but the mood was sombre. They were both thinking about the boy who had disappeared all those years ago. The tune of *Moon River* cycled round Woodhouse's head, with its accompanying traumas.

As they approached their old school, the air seemed to

become thick and difficult to breathe, like the atmosphere before a storm, although the evening sky was blue. They parked by the church and stood looking down at the sea. It was calm and the blades of the distant offshore wind turbines were still.

'Shall we walk up to where they found his inhaler?' asked Rafferty.

Woodhouse nodded. He felt too choked to speak. They walked along the cliffs with the sea to their left, reversing the hare and hounds route. They could see the roof of the school away down among the trees on the right and they heard the cawing of distant rooks in the treetops there. As they got closer to the woods it became easier to breathe and Woodhouse felt better.

'They found it round here somewhere,' said Rafferty, stopping.

Woodhouse looked around. He couldn't tell exactly where he and Drinkley had taken shelter; they had been just stumbling blindly through the downpour. Gingerly, he approached the cliff edge and craned his neck to look over. Eighty or a hundred feet below, the sea sucked curiously at the rocks and then rolled back with a disappointed sigh.

'Christ!' said Woodhouse.

'Doesn't bear thinking about, does it? Did you want to look in the woods?'

Images from the night of the storm flicked through Woodhouse's mind like a slideshow, *Moon River* echoing distantly in the background.

'No,' he said. 'Let's have a look at the school.'

They walked back towards the church and Woodhouse went to the car and removed a crowbar and a torch from the boot.

'Just in case,' he said.

They cut across the playing fields, now overgrown, and came at the school obliquely, through the trees, the same way Woodhouse had once walked with his tooth in his hand.

As they came closer they could see that the main building had fallen into disrepair. The lead flashing was gone from the roof and, here and there, slates were missing or broken. The once-white paintwork was dirty and peeling and most of the windows were broken or boarded up. It had a raffish, menacing air, like a Georgian gentleman of good family, perhaps, who has fallen among bad company and taken to drink and vicious amusement. Fences encircled it and there were security signs warning of guard dogs. Rooks cawed and circled above. The place looked deserted.

Woodhouse stepped out of the trees, picked up a flint and pitched it through one of the dining hall windows, breaking the glass. They took cover and waited to see if anyone would come. Nobody did.

'Shall we?' he asked.

Rafferty nodded. They scaled the chain-link fence and walked round the side to the kitchen door. Woodhouse jemmied the padlock and hasp and they went in.

The kitchen was dusty and empty, the soft light from the setting sun tranquil. They walked through into the main entrance hall and looked around. It was darker in there but still light enough to see. The floor and stairs had been cheaply carpeted and the walls inexpertly painted a nasty mushroom colour. Woodhouse made a face.

'Dirty rehab,' said Rafferty.

They sat down on the stairs.

'What if he didn't fall into the sea?' wondered Woodhouse.

'He died in the woods, then.'

'They would have found him in the woods… Suppose he was trying to get back to school, to get another inhaler. He had a spare, didn't he?'

They looked at each other.

'He lost his spare one,' said Rafferty slowly. 'I remember now – he dropped it when we were in the attic.'

'He would have gone to Matron for another one, wouldn't he? Anyway, someone would have seen him if he got back to school that day.'

'What if it was late?' asked Rafferty. 'What if it took him a long time to get back to school because he was sick and those bastards had been torturing him? What if everyone was asleep and he was too scared to wake Matron because he'd been getting in trouble for pestering her?'

'He would have needed a torch,' objected Woodhouse.

'He might have had one in his tuck box. He could have picked it up on his way through the school.'

'No. He must have fallen over the cliff.'

'We've got to look,' said Rafferty.

Woodhouse sighed.

'I know.'

They got up and climbed the stairs.

Upstairs, Woodhouse saw that the panelled doors he remembered had been replaced with fire doors and the unpleasant colour scheme continued. There was a musty, oppressive odour. They came to the cupboard door through which they had accessed the attic. It looked even smaller than Woodhouse remembered and had been painted shut.

'We'd never fit through that way anyhow,' Rafferty said. 'I know where the main hatch is.'

He led the way to what had been the sanatorium. The sign on the fire door said *Detox Wing*. They came out on to a landing and Rafferty pointed up to a large loft hatch. Woodhouse reached up, hooked the claw of the crowbar through the ring on the door and pulled. With a groan the hatch opened, revealing sliding wooden loft ladders. Rafferty slid them down until they locked into place.

'You don't really think he's up there, do you?' he said.

They looked up at the darkness.

'I don't know,' said Woodhouse, 'but we've got to find out.'

He took a deep breath and climbed the ladder. Rafferty followed. The attic was empty. Woodhouse shone the torch on dust and bare rafters.

'Where did it all go?' wondered Rafferty.

'Maybe it was never here – maybe we dreamed it all… It doesn't look like he's up here anyway.'

As he said this Woodhouse remembered the gold coin he had taken from the chest all those years ago. It must be still in his tuck box in the attic at his parents' house. They looked around. There was nothing apart from a roll of carpet in a corner and a large block and tackle hanging above the hatch.

'Let's go,' said Rafferty. 'There's nothing here.'

'Wait a minute.'

Woodhouse hunted about, trying to get his bearings; it had all been such a long time ago. Round the side of some brick chimney breasts he found the small door. It was stuck fast. He wedged the tip of the crowbar into the jamb and forced it until it opened with a splintering crack, releasing the descendant of a bad smell. Woodhouse hung his suit jacket on a rusty nail and followed the torch beam in, crawling awkwardly, only just able to fit. He tried to ignore the sense of rising panic.

'Can you see anything?' called Rafferty behind him.

'No,' he called back.

He reached the vertical shaft they had climbed and shone the torch down. He could see ends of bricks extending here and there for foot and handholds; it was probably a chimney that had been built in the wrong place and left uncompleted, he surmised. There was no way he could fit down there anyway. He started to back his way out, sweating.

'Let's go, mate,' said Rafferty as Woodhouse stood up and dusted himself off. 'This place is giving me the creeps.'

They went back down, not bothering to close the hatch behind them, and retraced their steps until they were at the cupboard door again.

'Let's just make absolutely sure,' said Woodhouse, prying it open. Some old vacuum cleaners were inside. He pulled them out, squeezed through the low door and brushed the disused cleaning products off the shelves. The gap at the top, through which they had climbed as boys, had since been plaster-boarded but the crowbar made short work of it and Woodhouse was able to intrude his head and the hand holding the torch.

A long-dead hand holding another torch was less than three feet away from his own.

'Oh Jesus!' he said, seeing what remained of Drinkley's face. 'He's here.'

He cleared some more of the plasterboard so Rafferty could look as well.

'He was on his way back,' said Rafferty. 'He couldn't find it. Shit! I don't need to see that…'

He went away but Woodhouse continued to look. Drinkley's skin and clothes were all but gone and his bones were surrounded by dust and dead insect casings. His face was turned towards Woodhouse and his yellowed teeth were still recognisable. Drinkley had had slightly prominent front teeth as a result of sucking his thumb. His lower jaw had dropped as the muscle decayed, and something was wedged there. Woodhouse put the torch in the dust and gingerly reached out his hand. Gently he removed the swazzle from Drinkley's mouth.

'I'm sorry, mate,' he whispered to the bones. 'I'm so sorry.'

As they walked back to the car Woodhouse made an anonymous call to the local police station. There didn't seem much to say during the drive back to town. Woodhouse dropped Rafferty off at his shop and promised to call him. Rafferty gave him a weak smile and walked away.

Woodhouse got to the base just after one and showed his ID to the yawning guard at the main gate. He was trying not to remember how much he hated and feared helicopters. He parked and sat in the car for a few minutes thinking. He took the Walther and its holster from under the seat and, on a whim, removed the rosary from the rear-view mirror and put it in his pocket with Drinkley's swazzle. He needed all the talismanic help he could get.

There was a knock on the driver's side window and he looked up, startled, to see Maryanne. She was wearing black combat gear and smiling.

'Hey, Richie – you made it!'

He got out of the car.

'Yeah, the world won't save itself. You come to see me off?'

'I'm coming with you, honey. I ain't about to let the bad man spoil our vacation.'

Woodhouse was horrified.

'This is no mission for a girl. This guy is seriously crazy!'

His world tilted suddenly and he discovered he was lying on his back in the car park with Maryanne's boot on his throat. She regarded him seriously down the barrel of a Glock, star-spangled sky framing her silhouette.

'I told you I was tough,' she said softly.

She helped him up and put the gun away. He was shame-faced so she kissed him on the cheek. She smelt good.

'Come on,' she said as he dusted off his suit. 'Let's go find the crew.'

He got the kitbag containing his combat gear from the boot of the car and she led him inside. As he watched her bottom wiggle he was reminded of their first meeting; she was continually surprising him, this girl, and he liked it. If all bottoms looked this enticing in combat trousers, he mused, battlefields would become orgies, the gunfire and cries of the wounded replaced by slapping flesh and squeals of ecstasy. His mind wandered happily away with its hands in its pockets.

The crew of five were waiting for them in a briefing room, capable looking men dressed in desert camouflage. Woodhouse recognised them as rangers. They carried sidearms and wore bulky black vests. Helmets were dotted around on the tables. Maryanne introduced Woodhouse and the rangers nodded coolly, looking at his soiled suit.

'I need to get changed,' he said to Maryanne.

'There's a locker room across the way, hun.'

He hung his suit and holster in a vacant locker and put on the combat gear he always kept in the car. It was faded to various shades of grey, comfortable and comforting. He transferred the Walther to a holster strapped to his right thigh, just in front of his Bowie knife in its sheath, then put the rosary and the swazzle in his map pocket and tied his bootlaces. He was nervous and felt slightly foolish.

When he returned to the briefing room Taylor was there along with a US army bigwig in dress uniform.

'Ah, there you are, Woodhouse. This is General O'Keefe.'

Woodhouse sat down next to Maryanne. Her hair was in a ponytail and her freckles were charmingly in evidence.

'We've had a look at the combat radius,' continued Taylor, 'and if the stolen helicopter is indeed where we suspect then they're poised to attack any number of population centres and installations. Rather than speculate fruitlessly, we think the best course of action is to get you out there as quickly as possible so you're ready to react as soon as they move. In an ideal world General O'Keefe would like his helicopter back in one piece but of course we realise that it might be impractical.'

There was a ripple of laughter from the rangers. Taylor sat down, flushing slightly, and O'Keefe looked round the room, hands on hips. He was a big man with a craggy determined face.

'Gentlemen,' he said, 'and lady – there are a lot of red faces about this whole business and we're hoping you people can get us out of a considerable hole here. Thus far we've managed to keep the press in the dark and that's the way we would like it to stay. We're seriously reluctant to scramble a whole bunch of aircraft and make a big noise, because the world will be watching and the American military can do without another public relations disaster. Having said that, we'll be monitoring the situation carefully and readying ourselves for various worst-case scenarios. This isn't just a missing helicopter, people, this is an unfolding calamity. Quite apart from the damage the thing can do, it's chock-full of innovative modifications that absolutely *must* not fall into the wrong hands. If you can't recover it then I want it completely destroyed. Is that clear?'

He looked around the room at them and they nodded.

'You should be there by first light. We've arranged a rotors-running refuel at Grenoble so you'll have plenty of gas left in case of a chase situation. You outgun them and you're better at your jobs. If you can get in on the ground and clear the whole thing up quietly then so much the better, but if you have to blow them out of the sky then you have my blessing. HOO-AH!'

'HOO-AH!' roared the rangers, standing up. Woodhouse and Maryanne smiled at each other. Taylor looked faintly disgusted.

They sit round the table in the farmhouse and Maurice pours the brandy. Lomax looks round at the South Africans.

'One drink for luck, my boys, and then to sleep. We must leave early tomorrow. The old man likes to walk in his garden in the morning and we will visit him. Like an avenging angel we shall descend from the sky and wipe him from the face of the earth.' He grins, the straps distorting his face. 'It will be your finest hour, eh, Maurice?'

The South Africans laugh at the servant's obvious fear.

'Yes, sir,' he says miserably.

Lomax raises his glass and the others follow suit.

'To death,' he says, 'and to everlasting glory.'

They drink. Maurice slurps his and the South Africans laugh again. He hangs his head.

In the cabin of the Black Hawk, Woodhouse felt suddenly calm. It was too late for fear or regret. The die had been cast and the endgame was beginning. The rotors were running as the pilot and co-pilot performed their pre-flight checks. Woodhouse and Maryanne were strapped in alongside the other three rangers, each helmeted and vested and holding an M16 assault rifle. The cabin doors were open and Woodhouse looked out past the starboard door gun, past the rocket pod and chain gun on the stub wing, to the waxing crescent moon and its attendant stars. It was a beautiful night. He grinned at the others.

'Fuck yeah!' he said, as they lifted off into the night. 'Fuck yeah!'

They grinned back.

'Fuck yeah!' they agreed.

Once they were under way they slid the doors shut to keep the wind out and the rangers handed sandwiches around. Woodhouse wasn't hungry but knew he needed to eat. His sandwich was some kind of smoky cheese in sweet white bread and it tasted good. They washed the food down with water from their canteens and settled back to doze in the darkened cabin. The vibrations through the airframe were soothing and Woodhouse felt his eyes beginning to close. Maryanne took her helmet off and rested her head on his shoulder, the rangers concealing their smiles. With the now familiar scent of her hair in his nostrils Woodhouse slept with a faint smile on his face.

He was awoken by the Black Hawk touching down at Grenoble. As they trooped across the hardstanding to use a nearby toilet, the sky was beginning to lighten in the east and a sleepy blackbird gave tremulous voice from the perimeter fence. Woodhouse smoked a cigarette as they refuelled and then they were up again, doors open now as they neared their destination. The sun was beginning to rise as they approached Chasteuil and they flew lower, following the nap of the mountains.

'What's the pilot's name?' Woodhouse asked one of the rangers.

'His name's Rufus, bud, Rufus Cornwell.'

'Hey, Rufus,' said Woodhouse into his headset. 'Don't get too close – we don't want them to know we're here.'

'Sure thing,' said Rufus. 'I'll circle around real low and sneaky till we find somewhere to set down and keep watch on these here individuals.'

'That'd be great.'

They were flying so low now that the rotor wash was disturbing the tops of the pine trees and startling the wildlife. In a clearing, a deer looked up at them mournfully as they passed.

'It reminds me of home,' said Maryanne wistfully.

'Where d'you hail from, darlin'?' asked a ranger through a mouthful of chewing tobacco.

'Virginia originally,' she said.

'Shoot! A lil ole farm girl, huh? All growed up!'

The other two rangers in the cabin were smiling at this. Woodhouse couldn't help but feel protective, although he knew only too well that she could look after herself.

'They call me Dixie,' bragged the ranger, banging his fist on his vest for emphasis. 'I hail from Texas and there ain't no creature on God's green earth I cain't rope, rassle and ride, little missy. Yee-haw!'

'I had a friend called Dixie in high school,' Maryanne told him. 'She's got a couple of kids now, I think. Nice girl; we were on the cheerleading squad together.'

The crestfallen Texan gave the appearance of being a sadder and wiser man, while Maryanne smiled pensively as though still reminiscing about her old friend. The other rangers were enjoying Dixie's discomfort and Woodhouse shook his head admiringly – what a girl! She was spectacular!

The chopper banked left and then straightened.

'I see the farm,' said Rufus through the comms. 'I'm gonna put her down.'

He dropped the aircraft gently, rear wheels first, into a meadow filled with wild flowers, and they all got out and stretched. The long grass was dewy and the morning light soft. When the rotors stopped there was silence for a few moments and then, one by one, shyly at first, the birds began to sing.

'They're in a valley just to our south,' said Rufus to Woodhouse as they removed their helmets. 'Reckon we should be able to see them from over this-a-way.'

They waded through the damp grass and cuckoo spit until they reached a fence. The ground sloped away downhill and, nestled in the distance by a twisting stream, they could see a cluster of farm buildings, still in the shadow of the mountains. A wisp of smoke drifted from the chimney of the farmhouse. It was an idyllic scene.

'You're sure this is the right place?' Woodhouse asked.

Rufus shrugged.

'We're at the coordinates I was given, buddy.'

He handed Woodhouse some binoculars. Woodhouse focussed and the scene sprang into sharp relief. There was no sign of any vehicles and no movement. He sighed and handed the binoculars back.

'Okay, listen,' he said to Rufus as they walked to the Black Hawk. 'I'm going to take a team down and have a look. You and your mate better stay here and keep watch. If you see them lift off then pick the rest of us up quick. We'll get out into the open as soon as we see them move. If you see us go into the farm, get airborne and be ready to come if I signal. There may be casualties.'

Rufus nodded.

'Sure, no problem,' he said.

Maryanne and the rangers were sitting in the cabin doorways smoking and performing weapons checks. Seeing him approach, she winked at him and blew a bubble with her gum.

'Let's get down there,' said Woodhouse, shouldering his rifle. 'Before they wake up.'

Woodhouse, Maryanne and three of the five rangers moved off in the direction of the farm. Dixie spat a stream of tobacco juice at an awakening butterfly as it perched on a poppy to dry in the sun. It tumbled to the ground to die instead. Maryanne glared at him.

Lomax hears them coming, of course. He has heard many things: the screams of the dying peacock; Woodhouse whispering to the bones; Generation X on the jukebox. Now he hears his enemies pushing through the wet grass in the field above the farm and he hears the old man stir and mumble in his sleep. It is time to go.

'Come, my friends,' he says. 'To the sky.'

The South Africans are ready. Their combat gear is motley, patched together from various different uniforms, and they look like the mercenaries they are. They are equipped with Heckler & Koch assault rifles – part of a stolen shipment – as well as sidearms. Lomax has a pump action shotgun that looks like a toy in his great scarred hands and bandoliers full of shells cross his barrel chest. Maurice is trying to edge behind the door. Perhaps the boss was just joking; surely he will not really make him go with them. He is just a servant, not a man of violence.

'Ah, Maurice,' says Lomax, seeing him there. 'The man of the hour!' He puts a vast tattooed arm around him and hugs him so tight that his bones crack audibly. The South Africans are grinning. 'You must have a weapon, my friend. Take my pistol.' He hands him a .44 Magnum in a tooled leather holster and smiles fondly at his obvious discomfort. 'Now, we go.'

From the field above, Woodhouse saw them cross the farmyard, bristling with weapons. He dropped to one knee, thumbing his rifle off safe, and took aim. As he was adjusting his rear sight, the largest of the men in the farmyard five hundred metres away turned and looked straight at him. Woodhouse froze, shocked.

'Shoot, Richie,' whispered Maryanne fervently. 'Shoot that motherfucker.'

The figures in the farmyard went into the barn, all except Lomax. He turned to face Woodhouse and his companions and spread his arms wide, daring them to fire. The sun caught the barrel of the weapon in his hand and he seemed to be smiling. Woodhouse fired. The shot felt true but Lomax bowed extravagantly and blew them a kiss as he went into the barn.

They heard the sound of rotors behind them and the Black Hawk appeared overhead and lowered itself politely so they could clamber in, battered by the downwash. As they took their seats, the machine seemed to catch a scent and swept enthusiastically down towards the barn, and they saw the sinister shape of the stealth helicopter emerge from the other end of it and take flight, banking right and curving away towards the mountains.

There was a roar of exultation from the rangers as their gunship accelerated and imitated the turn, gathering speed as it settled into pursuit. They watched the streamlined black shape ahead as it skimmed the mountaintops, drawing ever so slightly away from them, it seemed, as it headed towards the coast.

'This guy can fly,' said Rufus in Woodhouse's headset, 'and their machine's quick. Do I fire on them?'

'Wait a bit,' said Woodhouse. 'There's civilians underneath us. Can you make radio contact?'

His headset went quiet while Rufus tried it.

'They don't respond,' he said after a while. 'Looks like they're headed towards Nice – any idea what they're doing?'

'None,' said Woodhouse. 'If they carry on out to sea we'll take a shot at them.'

They hung on grimly in pursuit, every now and then seeming to gain a little and then falling further back again, their machine clearly straining every mechanical sinew. They flew with the cabin doors closed to minimise wind resistance but their prey was lighter and sleeker without the stub wings and their clumsy armaments, and the pilot knew his work.

They flew low over the suburbs of Nice, over the town and the harbour and out above the blue water as the sun cleared the horizon. The stealth helicopter banked right again and settled into its path.

'Looks like they're heading for Italy,' said Rufus.

Woodhouse took the Italian rosary from his pocket and looked at it.

'Oh Christ!' he said, half to himself. He put the rosary around his neck and tucked it away inside his shirt. 'Can't hurt,' he said in response to Maryanne's quizzical look.

'Turn around,' says Lomax into his headset, 'and shoot them down.'

'We don't need to turn around, boss,' replies the pilot. 'We can outrun them and we have countermeasures for their missiles.'

'Turn around,' says Lomax, 'or I will come up there and knock out every tooth from your disobedient head.'

'Yes, boss.'

The pilot banks hard left and goes into a hammerhead manoeuvre, dropping the nose of the Stealth Hawk so it almost touches the water. He pulls up hard towards the pursuing craft, which is just starting to turn, and unleashes a missile. The Hellfire flips out of the starboard missile bay on its rail and sets off smartly towards the approaching Black Hawk, which straightens and pulls up to starboard, releasing flares to draw the missile away from its heat signature. It is a near thing.

'You missed, you clown!' roars Lomax, sliding open the cabin door and manning the Browning. 'Bring me close to them and I will show you how we wage war!' He grins at Maurice, who is white and shaking. 'Take heart, old friend – we are quite certain to prevail.'

The two helicopters manoeuvre and counter-manoeuvre for a time, each striving for an advantageous position. Lomax sees that the cabin doors on the other machine are also open and he grins in anticipation of a gun battle.

The stealth machine pulls up and away from the water, seeking more room for a turn, and easily evades a brace of stinger missiles which veer away harmlessly as it releases flares and gives an arrogant shimmy, like a showboating quarterback. The helicopters bank away in opposite directions and then turn and approach each other along parallel lines, Rufus firing the chain guns. They pass so close that Woodhouse and Lomax, each manning the port-side door gun, can see one another's eyes as they each rake the other's machine with heavy fire, shell casings jingling and spinning in the morning sunlight.

Rounds clatter along the fuselage of the Black Hawk and whip through the cabin. One of the rangers is hit. The shell enters his mouth and exits through the back of his neck, scattering blood, teeth and bits of spine. His head lolls and he flops over.

'Bobby!' cried Dixie. 'Bobby's hit! The goddamn sons of bitches kilt Bobby!'

Woodhouse had a bad taste in his mouth and he spat out of the door and turned to check on Maryanne. She smiled at him nervously, M16 at the ready, and blew a pink bubble.

One of the South Africans is also hit, in the thigh. A bright gout of blood squirts into Maurice's face and he screams like a startled schoolgirl.

'For fuck's sake, bru,' says the man who has been hit. 'Stop making that fucking noise, hey.'

'Be quiet, Maurice,' says Lomax, slapping him affectionately and chipping one of his teeth. 'You are too excitable.'

The helicopters turn again and the stealth chopper fires a Sidewinder. In the Black Hawk, Rufus releases flares and attempts a spiral descent but the missile explodes just above them, triggered by its proximity fuse and, although most of the expanding rod-blast passes over them, they are hit in the tail by two rods. One punches through the boom and the other glances off the tail rotor. The machine wobbles as Rufus attempts to pull up.

'Again,' demands Lomax. 'Finish them.'

Nothing happens.

'Shut the cabin doors,' shouts the pilot. 'It's stuck on the fucking rail. Shut the doors quick, bro!'

They slide the doors closed just as the Hellfire explodes on the rail. They are enveloped in a ball of flame.

'Holy fuck!' said Rufus reverently. 'Would you look at this shit!'

The fireball was heading straight for them as he struggled to control the damaged Black Hawk. Alarms sounded in the cockpit.

'Rufus,' said Woodhouse, 'can you get us out of the way of that please?'

Rufus banked gingerly away to the right and they watched as the flames blew out and the Stealth Hawk flew by, smoking.

Lomax is gasping for breath and laughing as he opens the cabin door, burning his fingers in the process.

'They have not yet perfected this aircraft, eh, boys?'

The others laugh too, apart from Maurice who is dry-heaving and the mercenary with the wounded thigh who, despite having been tourniqueted, has lost a lot of blood.

'We've got some damage along the port side, boss,' says the pilot. 'Not sure how extensive yet.'

'Just get us to Rome,' says Lomax. 'We have an urgent appointment with God's earthly representative and I would hate that we should miss him.'

The smouldering aircraft turns towards the Holy City and the wobbly one follows it.

'Get it while it's hot!' shouted Woodhouse. 'Hit the fuckers while they're hot, Rufus.'

Twin stingers left the port and starboard rocket pods simultaneously and converged on the smoking Stealth Hawk's heat signature. Realising the danger belatedly, it released flares and started to turn. One missile veered away, distracted by a flare, but the other struck the main rotor housing and exploded. The Stealth Hawk's starboard door gun returned fire and the pursuing Black Hawk took hits to its nose and cockpit.

'Oh fuck!' cried Rufus. 'I'm hit! I can't fucking see for shit! Take over, Danny.'

Woodhouse looked into the cockpit. Danny wasn't about to do any flying unless it was to heaven; he was dead and most of his face was gone. Wind was howling in through holes in the cockpit screen and alarms were sounding. Woodhouse undid Danny's seatbelt and dragged him through into the cabin, accidentally depressing buttons on the lower console as he did so.

'Keep it steady, Rufus,' he said. 'I'll come and help you.'

'Okay,' said Rufus, taking deep breaths. 'We can do this, no problem.'

Woodhouse climbed into the co-pilot's seat and looked around helplessly at the overwhelming array of dials and buttons. Rufus was covered in blood and his eyes were wide.

'Are you there, buddy?' he asked. 'I need you to look at this here panel,' he pointed to a panel on the lower console, 'and tell me if the failure advisory lights are showing.'

'No, it looks good.'

'And this one here?' He pointed to part of the main instrument panel.

'It says "*Master Caution, press to reset*".'

'Okay,' said Rufus, pressing it. 'That's not so bad. The automatic flight control system seems to be working and the engines are all right. Are we still over Corsica?'

Woodhouse had a look: blue water broken only by a solitary yacht in the distance.

'We're over the sea again.'

'And we're not upside down or anything?' Rufus was grinning under the blood.

'No, we're all good. We're a little bit higher than them – they've been losing altitude since they took that hit.'

Rufus eased them down carefully.

'How's that?'

'That's good.'

Maryanne appeared behind them and leant through.

'How's it going, boys?'

'We're managing just fine,' said Rufus. 'We'll get her down somehow.'

In the Stealth Hawk the pilot is struggling.

'We're losing revs on the rotor, boss,' he says. 'It's not looking good.'

'Can you get us there?' asks Lomax.

'I don't know – I doubt it.'

Up ahead a coastline is appearing. The machine is shaking and straining and all is clearly not well with it. Maurice's lips are moving, presumably in prayer, as he tries to wipe the blood from his face with the sleeve of his shirt.

'My friend,' says Lomax to the pilot, 'make for me the flare angel in order that we may send a message to God and also, perhaps, to the Devil – in the event that either of them should actually exist.'

The pilot shrugs and dumps all his remaining flares.

In the juddering Black Hawk they watched as the multiple phosphorus flares suddenly radiated from the Stealth Hawk to port and starboard, the trails of smoke shaping the wings of an angel against the tender dawn sky and then falling gently away.

The old man shuffles slowly through the parterre garden, the two security officers keeping a respectful distance behind him. Age weighs heavily on him these days but he is mindful of his responsibilities. The day ahead will be long and sometimes confusing but the early morning sun is warm and the song of the birds breeds contentment.

'They're going down,' said Woodhouse as the stealth craft flew lower and more erratically over the outskirts of Rome. 'He's losing control.'

The familiar outline of the Colosseum appeared in the distance, lit up by the sun, and the stealth helicopter crash-landed clumsily in a park.

'Brace yourselves, boys,' warns the pilot. 'She won't flare – I can't get the nose up.'

The stealth machine gives up the ghost and hurls itself nose first into the rose beds. It jounces on its suspension and rolls half onto its side in a flurry of petals, rotor blades scything into the adjacent turf and shearing off one by one. In the cabin they watch groggily as the Black Hawk executes a near-faultless landing nearby.

Suddenly Maurice pulls out the .44 Magnum and shoots off the head of the man next to him; the man with the wounded thigh. Everybody is shocked, especially Maurice.

'I was aiming for them,' he explains weakly, gesturing at the other helicopter.

The surviving South Africans do not look amused. Lomax, however, begins to laugh.

'Ah, Maurice,' he says, wiping away a tear. 'Always you know how to cheer me up, old friend, with your tricks. Come, perhaps I will let you play this same joke on the Holy Father, eh?'

He throws a grenade towards the enemy – to give them something to think about – and climbs out of the cabin door and makes off across the park. Those who still have heads follow.

The air of relief when they touched down safely was rudely dispelled by a grenade going off underneath them. Luckily they were protected by the Kevlar floor panels.

'Maryanne, you'd better stay here with Rufus and keep people away from these machines,' said Woodhouse.

'Fuck you, Richie. I'm coming wit' you, ya Limey asshole!'

Woodhouse sighed, knowing better than to argue, particularly when she was in Brooklyn mode.

'Fine. You, then,' he pointed at one of the remaining rangers, 'you stay here and call base. Tell them there's a maniac loose in Rome, and you – Roy Rogers – you come with us.'

Woodhouse, Maryanne and Dixie, all carrying their rifles, set off after Lomax and his unhappy little band, the pigeons in the park scattering into the sky as they passed.

In the gardens of the Vatican, the old man kneels at the ivy-covered shrine. The security men retire discreetly and leave him in peace. He prays silently and the Latin phrases are worn and smooth to his mind. He forgets many things but never these; they are as much a part of him as his rheumatic old fingers or his purblind eyes. Perhaps more so, for fingers and eyes will soon be just so much dust but the words will endure and their power will grow. His eyes may be dim but he sees his way clearly; his fingers may be weak but he holds fast to his faith. The old man prays and the pain in his knees is as pure as the song of the blackbird.

The Eternal City is busy although it is still early. Cars stuck in traffic sound their horns as scooters weave carelessly around them. Lomax knocks a dapper young man to the ground and mounts his Lambretta.

'Come, Maurice,' he says, throwing him the shotgun. 'No time to lose.'

Maurice climbs awkwardly on and they set off. Two of the South Africans borrow a Vespa from a handsome young couple and follow, rifles on their backs. The young couple are unsure what to do, but they are very much in love so they kiss and blood rushes to their private parts. The third South African is knocked down by a tram and dragged along being horribly mangled.

'Ah, shit!' he cries as onlookers scream in disgust.

Woodhouse waves down a man in full leathers on a Ducati.

'Scuzi,' he says as he motions with his M16 for the man to dismount. 'Prego,' he adds as he hands the M16 to Maryanne and gets on, although he is not certain what it means. This is pretty much the extent of his Italian, apart from foodstuffs and wine. Rifle on her back, Maryanne climbs on and puts her arms around him and they are off through the traffic, Woodhouse pulling an exuberant wheelie for good measure. Dixie follows more sedately on an electric bicycle.

'If our enemies approach,' Lomax shouts over his shoulder to Maurice, 'you must shoot them with the shotgun. But you must not shoot off my head, eh, Maurice? I know you and your tricks!'

Lomax knows exactly where he is going: plan A may have failed but he has a plan B and a plan C. He is a sociopath and he is thorough.

As they pass the Forum, Maryanne draws Woodhouse's Walther and tries for a clear shot at the South Africans but finds she daren't fire for fear of hitting a civilian. Maurice, however, has no such concerns and he has discovered an unexpected taste for gunplay. He turns and glimpses Woodhouse and Maryanne on the Ducati and fires the shotgun without hesitation, the barrel resting on his plaster cast, just as the scooter goes over a drain cover. The blast decimates a low-flying pigeon and the pieces rain down like grisly confetti on to an ageing Lothario in an open-topped Bugatti. Lomax sees it in some of the several mirrors on the Lambretta.

'Bravo, Maurice!' he shouts above the noise of the traffic. 'A pièce de résistance! Again you astound me!'

Lomax takes to the pavement, scattering a small group of nuns, who cross themselves frantically, and the South Africans follow on their Vespa, catching an elderly nun a glancing blow. She spins round like a teetotum and emits a sound like a whistling kettle: 'Eeee!'

Maurice takes another shot at Woodhouse and Maryanne. He is more accurate this time but still misses and instead hits the tailgate of a flatbed truck as it passes in the other direction. The tailgate opens and a lawnmower rolls off the truck and into the road. An old man driving a small Fiat swerves to avoid it and knocks Dixie off his electric bicycle. Lomax sees it in his mirrors and shakes his head admiringly.

Dixie seems to be unharmed but the electric bicycle is ruined, so he commandeers a rickety old moped from an enormously fat woman in a headscarf. She screams furious abuse and runs down the road after him, shaking her fist. The rest of her shakes of its own accord.

Woodhouse is unable to make the superior speed of the Ducati count in the congestion, since the scooters are more nimble and their riders less careful of pedestrians. A motorcycle carabiniere joins the chase, lights and siren going, and Maurice fires at him, falling off the back of the Lambretta as he does so. He flips over as he falls and shoots the carabiniere's BMW in its front wheel as it approaches. The policeman sails over the handlebars, and while he is in the air Maurice lands in the road and the shotgun goes off again, hitting the airborne officer as he passes overhead. Lomax, who has stopped to wait for Maurice, is open mouthed with awe.

'This defies belief, Maurice,' he says as the servant climbs back on to the Lambretta. 'You can work miracles with the firearms, I think!'

Maryanne takes careful aim with Woodhouse's Walther and shoots the South African who is riding pillion, hitting him in the shoulder.

'Ag, I'm hit, bru!' he says indignantly.

'That's swak, bra,' says his compatriot sympathetically. 'Hang in there, bro.'

Dixie is having trouble with the moped. It keeps coughing and spluttering and he is finding it difficult to keep in touch with the chase. He throws it down in disgust and looks around for a more suitable conveyance. Suddenly his collar is gripped by an enormous hand. He smells sweat and petunias, and a terrible feeling of déjà vu and impending doom envelopes him. He is a big man but the fat woman in the headscarf is enormously strong. She gives vent to her feelings loudly in Italian and accompanies her words with stinging slaps. Dixie's M16 clatters to the ground. He is as helpless as a child, frozen in horror as the fat woman's beady eyes bore into him.

The stricken carabiniere has landed in the open-topped Bugatti. It is not the ageing Lothario's day: his upholstery is ruined and the lemon-yellow sweater draped around his shoulders is mottled with blood. Also, his girlfriend is younger than his daughter and he is finding it difficult to satisfy her sexually. And his wife is a very vengeful woman, he is discovering.

'I will take you to the hospital,' he says to the policeman.

Lomax veers into an alley and the others follow, apart from the captured Dixie. Woodhouse and Maryanne are some way behind, and they park the Ducati by the discarded scooters which lie beneath a rusty fire escape. An open door nearby leads into a busy kitchen, full of steam and clashing pans and crockery.

Taking back the rifle, Woodhouse looks along the alley, up at the fire escape and through the open door to the kitchen. Maryanne's eyes are big but she is smiling. She is enjoying herself. Woodhouse grins at her.

'In here, I reckon,' he says and they enter the kitchen.

'Where did they go?' he asks a swarthy man who is washing pots. The man shrugs.

Maryanne points to something on the floor: a drop of blood. Woodhouse puts the mouth of the M16's barrel into the flesh behind the man's ear and says again:

'Where did they go?'

The man takes his hands out of the sink and dries them on his apron, raises them and walks through the kitchen. He is surprisingly graceful – perhaps he moonlights as a dancer. The chefs working on the line are careful not to notice the group as they pass.

The washer-up, who may also be a dancer, stops and indicates a closed door, which Woodhouse gestures with the rifle for him to open. He does so, revealing stairs leading down. Woodhouse is suspicious, so he gestures again and the graceful man descends, Woodhouse and Maryanne following. The steps are rickety and they creak and groan.

The wine cellar was old: cool and vaulted. At the far end a door, heavy-timbered and arched like a church door, stood open. Woodhouse and Maryanne left the man – who probably wasn't a dancer after all – standing among the barrels and bottles and hurried through it. They descended another flight of steps, these ones cut into rock. A passage stretched ahead, dusty and musty with time, ancient light bulbs dangling here and there, humming and flickering in accordance with some unsteady power source. Their eerie glow revealed recesses in the walls housing human bones, reminding Woodhouse poignantly of Drinkley. He put his hand in his pocket and felt the swazzle there.

'Kinda creepy, huh, Richie?' said Maryanne nervously.

'We're in the catacombs,' he explained unnecessarily.

'We don't got this shit in the Apple. Where the hell are these guys going?'

'He's going to the Vatican, I'm sure of it. He's one of your religious-type nutcases, I reckon.'

'You think he wants to whack the Pope, hun?'

'He ain't gonna kiss his ring, that's for sure!'

They laughed at this feeble joke but it wasn't particularly happy laughter. The passage opened out into a chamber festooned with skulls, and the wounded South African fired on them from a niche at the far end, striking chips and sparks from the stone by Woodhouse's head.

'Fuck,' said Woodhouse. 'We don't have time for this guy's shit.'

They took cover either side of the doorway and returned fire. The gunfire was loud in the confined space, and a row of skulls decorating the edge of the South African's niche shattered with a flourish, like morbid castanets.

Knowing he would have to take a risk, Woodhouse darted through the doorway and performed a flawless tactical roll through the ambusher's arc of fire, managing in the process to get off a short burst with the M16, one round of which fortuitously hit the South African in the throat. Regaining his feet, Woodhouse dodged back to the dying man's niche, snatched his rifle away and threw it across the room.

'Let's go,' he called to Maryanne.

'Fok jou, trilkop!' croaked the South African to Woodhouse as they passed.

In the Papal sacristy, a great walk-in wardrobe panelled with mahogany, the old man stands in front of a full-length mirror, wearing a white watered-silk cassock. He is surrounded by splendour: bejewelled crowns, chalices and rings in glass cases; lavish robes, mitres and pectoral crosses; the ceremonial crozier surmounted by an emaciated Christ on the cross. The old man places a lace rochet around his shoulders and then dons the red satin Papal mozzetta. His fingers tremble as he fastens the buttons on the front, and for a moment he is bewildered by his reflection. He breathes deeply and the feeling passes so he puts the zucchetto on his head and then clasps his hands and bows his head. He is ready.

Lomax hears the old man's prayers through the ether and he quickens his step; they are getting close now.

'What is your name?' he asks the surviving South African as they hurry through a chamber crammed with hidebound books and old manuscripts, a skeleton in a cassock appearing to have died while standing guard.

'Markus, boss.'

'You wish to avenge your friends, Markus?'

'Ja, boss.' His face is grim and his knuckles white on the Heckler & Koch.

'And you, Maurice, you are ready to display some tricks with the pistol, eh? Like Wild Bill Hickok!'

'I will do my best, sir.'

Lomax has reclaimed the shotgun and he loads it as they pass through a circular room containing astrolabes and planetary models as well as medieval instruments of torture. Manacles hang from the walls and an iron maiden stands open with a mummified corpse twisted inside. It barely merits a glance. Death is all around down here and the ghastly has become commonplace.

'If my calculations are correct,' says Lomax, 'we are now underneath the Vatican, and I begin to tire of being pursued. I have important business to conduct upstairs and I do not wish to be interrupted. Perhaps, Markus, you could hold them at bay, or better still kill them. I am sure Maurice would like to help you, with his big gun like Clint Eastwood.'

Lomax's gold tooth glints in the gloom as he grins at them.

'I can manage on my own, boss,' insists Markus, directing a poisonous glance at Maurice, who he has plainly not forgiven for the decapitation of his comrade. He mutters something in Afrikaans.

'Very well,' says Lomax. 'My stuntman shall stay with me – I may need his special talents. Perhaps this would be a good place for you to lie in wait, Markus.'

Barely visible in the wall of the passageway is a doorway, half covered by hanging cobwebs and dust. Markus squeezes inside, careful not to disturb the webs.

'Good luck, my friend,' calls Lomax to him. Markus says nothing.

A dim light filters from some unknown light source above and Markus can see that he is in some kind of long-forgotten shrine. An altar is hewn from the stone, and niches above it house obscure relics of some sort. He readies himself and listens for the footsteps.

Woodhouse saw the muzzle flash a split second before he heard the reports. The rounds tore through the dusty curtain and struck Maryanne, picking her up and throwing her against the passage wall. Woodhouse returned fire immediately, killing the South African and riddling clangorously a dirty old goblet in a niche above.

Maryanne was trying to speak but no words were coming out. Woodhouse knelt down beside her and hoped that her vest might have borne the brunt of it. She looked up at him, her eyes appearing black in the ill-lit passageway.

'Maryanne, are you okay?' he asked. 'Speak to me, please.'

Her lips moved and she tried to smile. She took a long shuddering breath.

'I'm okay,' she said at last. 'It knocked the air out of me.'

'Thank Christ for that!' He helped her up.

'I'm tough, Richie. You remember.' She smiled at him.

'Yeah, I remember.'

The passage began to incline upwards and wind between squat columns of masonry. Leering skeletons were crammed into every available space. Maryanne was limping a little so Woodhouse put his arm around her waist and kissed her on the cheek. She shrugged him away but the colour had returned to her face and she was smiling.

'Keep your hands to yourself, bud,' she said. 'I ain't no piece a meat!'

'Absolutely not,' he agreed.

There was a subdued crackle of electricity and the lights grew brighter and then went out. Woodhouse switched on the torch on his rifle.

'So, now, dear friend,' says Lomax, hearing the gunfire behind them, 'I suspect that it is just the two of us. You know, Maurice, that Vatica was the Etruscan goddess of the underworld? Apt, is it not, considering my own small efforts in that direction.'

They enter a circular chamber with a dusty mosaic floor. Several passageways lead off it and Lomax considers for a moment.

'This one, I think.'

As they go into the darkened passage, the lights behind them are extinguished and Lomax takes a torch from his pocket and switches it on.

'How is it, sir, that you know the way?' asks Maurice.

'Ah, I am glad that you have asked me this,' says Lomax. 'It is interesting, provided you do not object to a short lesson of history?'

Unsurprisingly, Maurice does not object.

'As you know,' begins Lomax, 'for reasons of my own I am a keen student of religion in general and of Catholicism in particular and for some years have been an avid collector of unusual artefacts and so on. I am not boring you, Maurice?'

'Not at all, sir.'

'So. Many years ago, the Basilica of Saint Peter was built on top of the old Roman necropolis – the city of the dead, Maurice!' Lomax laughs hoarsely and a passing rat squeaks with fear. 'Where the apostle Peter was buried after his inverted crucifixion by the crazy emperor Nero. Over the years the various palaces were added by subsequent popes, some of whom required secret passageways to be included. You have heard of the Borgias, have you not, Maurice?'

'I have, sir, yes.'

They ascend a flight of narrow stone steps.

'Machiavellian, Maurice, in the extreme. In any case – if you are absolutely certain that my discourse is not tiring for you? Good, so – in the early part of the nineteenth century Napoleon had a disagreement with the Pope, eventually causing him to be arrested and having him removed to France, where he languished for some years. The Vatican archives were also taken and, when the Pope was reinstated after Napoleon's eventual defeat – if this isn't all just too terribly tedious for you, Maurice? Very well, then – it was deemed too expensive to return the huge number of documents and so on to Rome, and many of them were distributed around Paris – used by the baker to wrap the baguette, perhaps, or the mother to swaddle the infant. It matters not.'

They were clearly in the walls of some great building now and Lomax was able to put the torch away as natural light filtered in through windows and arrow slits cunningly concealed behind mouldings or statues on the outside of the building. On the inside walls peepholes and slim doors gave in to various rooms, but there was no time to stop and look. They hurried onwards and always upwards, via steps, stairs and, once, a ladder.

'So, my friend,' continued Lomax, lowering his voice to a whisper, 'over the years I accumulated many of these lost archives. I have many friends in France, eh, Maurice! Among these papers I discovered architects' drawings, Maurice, intricate plans of the secret passageways built by the Borgias – among others – for their intrigues and, perhaps, their escapes. The vengeance is now at hand, my friend, because I have watched and I have waited, I have studied and I have remembered and I would not be diverted from my purpose.'

Lomax stops by some wooden panelling and hands the shotgun to Maurice.

'And now my studies and my patience come finally to fruition, I think.'

He takes a silenced pistol from its holster and an intricate looking key from his pocket. He turns to Maurice and grins.

'*Con clave*, Maurice – with a key!'

Lomax fits the key gently into a carved escutcheon in the panelling and turns it softly. There is an almost inaudible click. He slides the section of panelling carefully along its runners, raises the pistol and steps through the opening into the light, into the sacristy. Maurice follows with the shotgun.

They were running now but when they came to the circular chamber with the mosaic floor they stopped, confused by the choice of passageways.

'Which way, Richie?' asked Maryanne.

He inclined the barrel of the M16 down, and in the torchlight they clearly saw the footprints in the dust.

'We need to hurry,' he said, and they started to run again.

They look around for a moment, dazzled by the sudden light and the opulence of their surroundings. Lomax gives a hiss and shakes his head, disgusted by it all. The room is empty. Through the open door they hear an Italian voice coming from a nearby television. Lomax leads the way and, silent on rubber soles, they move towards the sound.

Two security officers in black suits are standing silently in the long hallway. Lomax shoots them expertly with the silenced pistol – *Phut! Phut!* – before they have a chance to react. They crumple to the marble floor and one of them hits his head with a soggy crack. Lomax and Maurice wait for a moment to see if anyone else will come but all is quiet apart from the television. Blood begins to pool around the corpses as they pass.

Lomax follows the cylindrical silencer of the pistol round the doorframe of the living room and shoots the waiting security man; he is making it look easy. He sees that the Pope is sitting in a green velvet armchair watching the news, dressed in the familiar red and white robes, his right hand, the one on which he wears the fisherman's ring, holding an espresso cup. Seeing the security man fall, the old man stands up slowly, as Lomax and Maurice enter, and puts down his cup.

Lomax crosses the room and picks up the remote control, muting the volume on the television. There is a heavy silence while the old man and the two assassins size each other up, the old man looking with particular interest at Lomax's ivory ear.

'So, Holy Father,' says Lomax at length, his tone bitter, 'you enjoy watching television while your subjects starve and murders and atrocities are committed in your name.'

'Ah,' says the old man, smiling, 'a theological discussion with my unexpected guests. Yes, I like to keep abreast of current events, dispiriting though they often are. I also enjoy the football, although I sometimes fall asleep. Are you a follower of the Azzuri, my friend?'

'I prefer Les Bleus,' growls Lomax.

'It is the same thing, perhaps. You are French, then, monsieur – I thought your accent was not English.'

'It is not about me that I have come to talk. I am just a man – you lay claim to something greater.'

'I make no such claim – I merely perform my humble duty as I see fit, my son.'

Lomax is becoming enraged by the old man's grace under pressure.

'I am not your son,' he says fiercely, raising the pistol with a scarred and steady hand. 'I had a father once – he suffers torment now since one of your parasitic ilk denied him grace. You will meet him soon enough, old man, when you fall from your palace into the flames.'

The old man removes the zucchetto from his head, looking suddenly frail. He mops his brow with it and puts it on the table.

'It is true,' he says, 'that I have sinned. Which of us can truthfully say otherwise? I have sinned and I have agonised and I have prayed and made my peace. You are troubled, my child – let us pray together and find solace.'

He kneels down and assumes the position of prayer. Lomax looks at him for a moment.

'What do you think, Maurice – should I make prayer with the Pope?'

Maurice looks uncomfortable.

'It is not for me to know this, sir,' he says.

Lomax nods thoughtfully and adjusts the straps of his ear.

'Very well,' he says. 'I will pray with you, old man, if you will answer me one question.' The old man bows his head in assent. 'What,' asks Lomax, 'do you think your Messiah, should he return, would do with this place – this Vatican?'

The old man looks up and smiles.

'The answer is simple, my friend – he would chase the moneylenders from the temple and sell it to feed the hungry and, if he would permit me, I would serve him.'

'A good answer,' admits Lomax grudgingly. He kneels opposite the old man and puts down the pistol. 'Bless me, Father.'

The old man hesitates and then gives the Papal blessing, making the sign of the cross in the air with his hand. Lomax calmly picks up the pistol and shoots him in the forehead. The old man folds to the floor and lies still. Blood gradually darkens the red satin of the mozzetta around his shoulders and they hear the sound of running feet approaching.

Woodhouse appears in the doorway with Maryanne at his shoulder. They duck as Maurice fires the shotgun. Splinters fly from the doorframe and a painting of the Madonna and Child on the wall behind them is peppered with pellets.

Lomax roars and charges at them, hitting Woodhouse with his shoulder and causing him to fire into the ceiling and ruin a chandelier. They fall backwards into the corridor, taking Maryanne down with them, and they roll around, wrestling. Maurice dare not fire for fear of hitting his boss.

Maryanne is getting in Lomax's way; he knocks her aside with a backhanded blow and she lies still. Woodhouse is fighting for his life, his M16 out of reach and no chance of drawing his Walther or his knife. Lomax is twenty years older but he is still immensely strong and this kind of fighting is child's play to him. He is hitting Woodhouse with heavy blows to the head, hardly any of which he is able to block, despite his martial arts training.

Lomax pauses, knowing he has the best of it. He looks down at Woodhouse, who is half unconscious underneath him, and leans towards him, smiling.

'You left your friend to die,' he says mockingly. 'In the storm I heard him call your name.'

Woodhouse's eyes open wide.

'That's not possible!'

Lomax nods. He is enjoying himself.

'I hear many things. *Moon River*, for example – you like this song, I think?'

Woodhouse manages to get a hand free and reaches up and takes hold of Lomax's ivory ear. Lomax's hands automatically follow and with his other hand Woodhouse goes for the Walther but, for some reason, he finds himself holding the swazzle instead. He pushes it hard into Lomax's open mouth and forces his jaws closed with the heel of his hand. Lomax freezes for a moment in shock and then starts to choke and scream through the swazzle. He breaks free of Woodhouse and gets to his feet, doubled over, holding his head and making terrible sounds. He tears at the straps holding his ear and hurls it to the ground but does not seem to be able to dislodge the swazzle that is causing him so much pain.

Everyone is too horror-struck to react for a moment and then they all react at once. Maryanne has awoken and is raising her Glock, Woodhouse has drawn the Walther and Maurice now has a clear shot with the shotgun. There are shouts and running feet, as well as Lomax's tortured screams, and they all fire at once.

Maurice is hit by both Maryanne and Woodhouse but he manages to fire again as he falls. Lomax is pierced through the neck by a thrown halberd and then hit by three more, as well as sub-machine gun fire, as the Swiss Guard, the gendarmerie and security arrive at the scene. Lomax falls to his knees and the hafts of the halberds rattle on the marble floor. There is silence for a moment and then he looks up, first at Woodhouse and then at Maryanne. He begins to laugh through the swazzle and everyone is frozen by the hideous, inhuman sound. The laughter turns to coughing and the swazzle flies from his mouth, propelled by a jet of bright blood. He rolls onto his side and finally lies still. He dies then, and perhaps finds peace, and the swazzle spins lazily in the blood that pools the marble.

The echoes of the gunfire died away and then there was a boom as the fallen Maurice got off a shot with the Magnum and then lay still. A security man went over and shot him twice in the head to make sure.

Woodhouse watched the Swiss Guard surrounding the body of the pontiff and then turned to Maryanne, who was standing by the wall. She smiled at him.

'Hey, Richie,' she said. 'Who'd a thought it?'

He shook his head.

'What a fuck-up!'

Maryanne looked down. Something was dripping from the tips of her fingers and on to the floor. It was blood. She looked up at Woodhouse and her eyes were big. She slid down the wall and the marks she left behind her were red.

'Oh no,' he said. 'Oh please, God, no.'

He went over and knelt beside her and she looked at him. She was beautiful. He cradled her head.

'I guess I may have to take a rain check on our vacation, Richie,' she said, and the Brooklyn accent was gone.

'Don't you fucking dare, Maryanne. Don't you fucking *dare* die.'

She smiled at him and her smile was wistful.

'It's okay, honey,' she said. 'Happy endings are for other people, Richie, you know that. For people like us a little happiness along the way should be enough. Don't be greedy, Richie.'

He couldn't speak, he just held her, and as the light died from her eyes he seemed to see something imprisoned there, in the amber. It wasn't until much later that he realised it was his heart.

Cubby was sitting at the workbench with a sponge in his hand, half-heartedly dabbing paint on to a small ceramic cat, when he heard the shop bell go. He got up and went through, wiping his hands on his apron. It was Tallulah and she gave him a hug.

'How are you?' he asked, letting go of her reluctantly.

'I'm fine,' she said. 'My mum's been making a fuss of me.'

'Did they catch him? I haven't heard anything. Please – come through.'

'They called me yesterday,' she said, as they went through to the workshop. 'Apparently when they got to the house he was gone. They found his car near the railway station.'

They sat down and he saw her looking at the cat they had been making that day. He had biscuit-fired it but it was still waiting to be finished.

'They'll catch him,' he said. 'I'm glad he didn't hurt you, Tallulah.'

She smiled.

'I'm glad too. That Hitler-cat of yours was making him seriously crazy, poor man.'

'They make me a bit crazy too,' admitted Cubby.

'You're not crazy, Cubby – you're sweet.'

He blushed, making her laugh.

'I was wondering,' she said, 'if you would come and hold my hand while I get a tattoo?'

'A tattoo?' He frowned, unable to hide his disapproval.

'I'm having a Māori design done on one side of my face – you know, like Mike Tyson?'

He grinned, fairly certain she was having him on.

'I found a peacock design that I want to get done,' she explained, 'because the peacock died saving me and I want to commemorate it.'

'Goodness, I think I need to hear about this!'

'I'll tell you about it, then,' she said.

They had to drag him away from Maryanne's body. They took him to the nearby barracks and made him drink sweet tea. He was numb. He just sat through the flight back to England, disconnected, disbelieving.

At the base they let him sleep for a time and then Taylor de-briefed him. And no, I don't mean she took his pants off – you have such a dirty mind! She explained that they had contacted the Vatican after hearing from Rufus, and security had been stepped up, but there had been no way to predict that Lomax would appear right inside the Papal apartments. As a precaution, however, the Pope had been moved – via an escape route in a viaduct – to Castel Sant'Angelo and his place taken by a double: a de-frocked priest. This priest had been disgraced after having been discovered indulging certain proclivities, Taylor continued, turning her mouth down in disgust, and the Vatican kept him around in case of situations like this as he was considered expendable and was apparently content to accept the risk as part of what he regarded as his penance. Woodhouse could barely muster the energy to shrug, so he didn't bother.

The helicopters, Taylor went on, were being brought back by road and sea and the crash explained as a malfunction during a training exercise. Woodhouse rolled his eyes.

Rufus was expected to regain his sight but, oddly, one of the rangers was still unaccounted for. Did Woodhouse know anything about this? He shook his head. The ivory ear was also missing; presumably someone had taken it for a souvenir. Woodhouse experienced a flash of déjà vu as Taylor said this, and also a presentiment of future, of future – but the feeling was gone, engulfed by his grief.

Courts martial were expected to take place for those accountable for the original loss of the helicopter but there was talk of medals for Woodhouse and Miss Carter. Miss

Carter's, of course, to be awarded posthumously. Woodhouse was almost grateful to feel a genuine flash of anger at this.

'You can stick your medal up your arse, Taylor,' he said, getting up to leave. 'She was worth a thousand of you.'

In The Illuminated Hide, Cubby stood transfixed by the colours. Some of the designs were amazing; maybe he would get a tattoo. Grandmother would not have approved, but he had burnt his pants now – he was a liberated man!

Tallulah was beside him, looking a little nervous and – daringly – he put his arm round her. She didn't object, seeming to nestle a little, even. He was delighted and amazed.

The tattooist came through from the back room and the punky blonde girl behind the counter gave a little squeal as he passed. They were obviously on friendly terms.

'You can come through now,' he said to Tallulah.

'Do you mind if my friend comes too?' she asked.

Rafferty smiled reassuringly.

'That's fine,' he said.

They went through and Rafferty sat Tallulah down as she took off her cardigan. Cubby parked himself as unobtrusively as possible in the small room and watched with interest.

'You said you wanted it on your shoulder,' said Rafferty.

'On my left shoulder,' confirmed Tallulah, moving the strap of her bra to around her bicep and making Cubby gulp.

'I drew it up last night,' said Rafferty. 'Very cool design – it'll look great.'

'Will it hurt?' she asked as he prepared her skin and gently applied the transfer.

Rafferty laughed, but not unkindly.

'It's not so bad. If you need to take a break just ask me. The main thing is to keep still, obviously. What do you think?'

She checked the positioning of the transfer in the mirror he was holding.

'Looks good to me. What do you think, Cubby?'

'Looks good to me too,' said Cubby. He approved of the design: the peacock was viewed from behind, eye-feathers spread but not raised and head turned in profile. The lines were intricate without being fussy.

'Okay, then,' Rafferty said, 'let's get started. I'll line it all in first and then we'll get to some colour.'

He started the gun, dipped it in the ink and leaned in. Tallulah made a slight moue of discomfort but then smiled at Cubby, her eyes bright with excitement. There was silence apart from the buzz of the gun for a while as Rafferty worked, making a line, wiping away the blood and excess ink with the other hand and leaning back to consider. Now and again he looked at Cubby.

'You look very familiar to me,' he said eventually. 'Maybe I know your parents or something?'

'I wouldn't have thought so,' said Cubby. 'I never knew my father, and my mother died when I was little.'

'I'm sorry. Was she a local girl?'

'She was, yes. Her name was Grace.'

Rafferty switched off the gun.

'Grace Arbuthnot?'

'That's right – did you know her?'

'I did know her,' said Rafferty thoughtfully. 'I see something of her in you, but also…'

'What?'

Rafferty rubbed his chin, thinking.

'Listen – Cubby, is it?' Cubby nodded. 'How old are you?'

'I'm twenty-two.'

Rafferty looked at him, reckoning it up, wondering.

'Do you know if your father's name's on your birth certificate?'

'You know who he is, don't you?' broke in Tallulah excitedly, unable to help herself. 'It's not you, is it?'

'Hold on,' said Rafferty to her, and to Cubby, laughing: 'Don't worry, it's not me!'

'I don't think there's a father's name on my birth certificate,' said Cubby sadly.

'That doesn't matter. Jesus Christ, you look so much like him and it would explain a lot!' He thought for a moment. 'Give me your number and let me speak to him, and I'll get in touch.'

'I don't have a phone.'

'You can take my number,' said Tallulah. 'We'll be seeing a lot of each other, won't we, Cubby?'

'I hope so,' he said, smiling happily.

Rafferty started the gun and bent to his work again, and every now and then he looked up at Cubby and shook his head, smiling, marvelling. The peacock took shape, blood mingling with the colours on its tail once again, and the world continued to turn in its usual, unusual way.

Woodhouse sat in his flat alone, trying not to think of Maryanne, trying not to remember because the loss was just too great. Walther miaowed hopefully but Woodhouse was oblivious. He stared blankly at the television: one of the *Rocky* films was on. Rocky was covered in blood and sweat, mumbling about something and crying. Woodhouse was crying too but he didn't know it. In the background his phone was ringing and, as the end credits rolled, the answer machine cut in and he was dimly aware of Rafferty's voice but the words made no sense to him. He was lost in grief, encased in amber.

In Perthshire a bespectacled young woman held up a garage at knifepoint, escaping with several hundred pounds. Unusually, during the robbery (the Asian proprietor insisted) she appeared to be listening intently to something that was concealed inside her handbag, although the proprietor could hear nothing.

Florence Gruber received a weighty package addressed to her absent husband. She was surprised and perturbed to discover that it contained four pairs of handcuffs and a ball-gag.

Far away, in a shabby room in the outskirts of Rome, a young American man and a large Italian woman are making love, or an approximation of it. The air is heavy with sweat and the essence of petunias. The large Italian woman sits astride the young American and the springs of the bed complain loudly as she grinds on him. Dixie has finally found something he is unable to ride. He is screwed.

The man in the wheelchair put down the phone and smiled: he felt lucky. Not many people could have survived such a mauling. The tram had severed both his legs below the knee, as well as smashing most of his ribs, his jaw and left arm. But he had survived and, he had just discovered, been paid for his part in the attempt on the Vatican. Quarter of a million euros, less twenty thousand – deducted for his part in the farmyard brawl, he supposed. He mourned the loss of his friends but fuck it! He was a lonely cripple, but he was a *rich* lonely cripple. Lekker!